The Walls of Woodmyst

THE WOODMYST CHRONICLES BOOK I

Robert E Kreig

WHITEKEEP BOOKS

THE WALLS OF WOODMYST

For Dad and Mum.

First Printing, 2021

The Realm

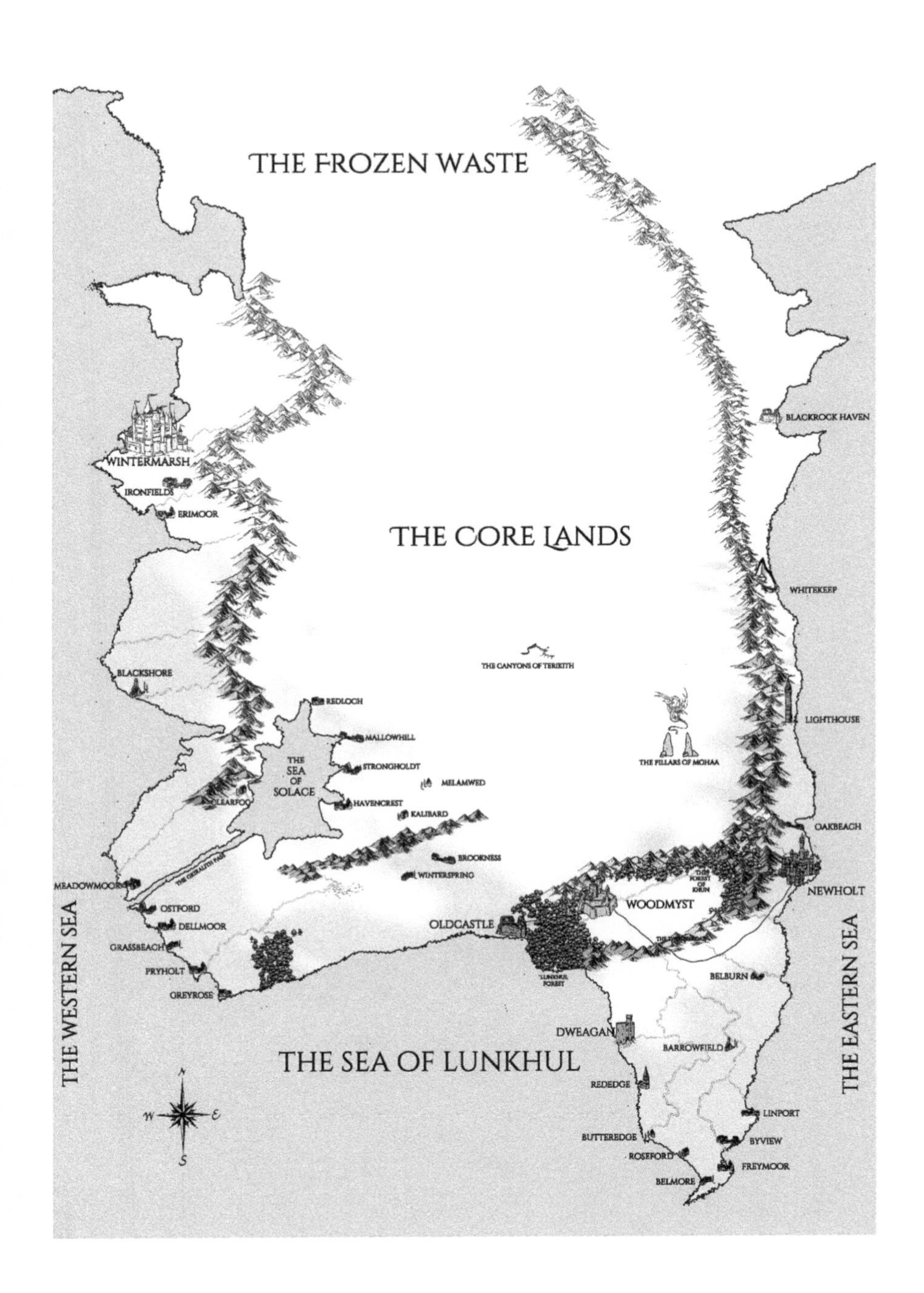

THE FROZEN WASTE
BLACKROCK HAVEN
WINTERMARSH
IRONFIELDS
ERIMOOR
THE CORE LANDS
WHITEKEEP
THE CANYONS OF TERIKITH
BLACKSHORE
REDLOCH
LIGHTHOUSE
MALLOWHILL
THE SEA OF SOLACE
STRONGHOLDT
THE PILLARS OF MOHAA
MELAMWED
HAVENCREST
KALIBARD
OAKBEACH
BROOKNESS
WINTERSPRING
MEADOWMOOR
NEWHOLT
THE FOREST OF KHUN
OSTFORD
WOODMYST
DELLMOOR
OLDCASTLE
THE WESTERN SEA
THE EASTERN SEA
GRASSBEACH
PRYHOLT
LUNKHUL FOREST
BELBURN
GREYROSE
DWEAGAN
BARROWFIELD
THE SEA OF LUNKHUL
N
W
E
S
REDEDGE
LINPORT
BUTTEREDGE
BYVIEW
ROSEFORD
FREYMOOR
BELMORE

Prologue

From the shadows they watched.

Hidden in the cover of trees and darkness, they studied the comings and goings of men and women passing through the gates.

They examined the actions of the men upon the grasslands outside the walls.

The high walls of the village obscured their view of the streets within. But this mattered not.

They had a strategy.

They had the resources.

Biding their time, they watched.

Waited.

Organised.

Soon, they would act.

Their timing needed to be perfect.

The result had to be exact.

For so long, they had been planning.

For so long, they had waited.

Soon.

Soon their patience would be rewarded.

Soon.

Soon.

One

The hunting party moved swiftly through the undergrowth. They held their spears low as they raced after the dogs that tracked their quarry. Growling and barking, the canines were excited.

They were close.

Their breath wafted in the cold air as they kicked and crunched through the small patches of frost and snow that collected overnight. Winter had been long and the warmer season approached slowly.

The men paused as the hounds split into two groups. Four raced to the left while three veered to the right.

Peter signalled to his friend to go right. Alan nodded and turned to the other men. He pointed randomly to two of them and chased the three dogs that ran up a slight embankment. The other three men went after the four hounds that sped into a gully.

The vegetation was thick here. Moving at significant speed, the three men ducked under low branches and vines, leapt over fallen logs and clambered over large rocks as they pursued the sound of the barking dogs ahead of them. Attempts to dodge thistles and thorns proved vain as more than one found bare flesh, leaving several small stinging scratches on their hands and faces.

Peter soon realised, from the noise that the dogs made, that their gully wound around the embankment the other group had ascended and made its way towards their companions. The two groups were about to meet up.

This could mean only one of two things.

The dogs had either trapped their prey or the game had got away.

Peter and his men burst through the thick undergrowth into an open clearing. Tall trees and thick bushes surrounded the field like an audience. The dogs had reunited and surrounded the beast in the middle of the grassy arena. There was no means of escape.

Alan entered the open ground from the right and came to a halt. He raised his spear and readied himself for the attack. The dogs instinctively moved to block the creature's getaway.

It squawked menacingly at the little creatures that snapped and barked around its feet. Stomping its two giant, black, scaly legs, it attempted to attack the dogs but was quickly moved back into place.

It opened its curved beak wide and squawked defiantly as it brought a sharp claw down upon one canine, crushing it into the ground.

The dog gave a small yelp as its rib cage collapsed and bones crunched from the weight of the monster.

Flapping its tiny wings, the beast snapped its head around on its long neck, looking for a way out. It ruffled its dark plumage and lifted its head high, exposing a red stripe that extended from the base of its beak to the tip of its breast.

The men moved in closer, tightening the circle with the dogs.

Alan lined up his aim and hurled his spear.

The long rod flew, straight and true. Its iron tip pierced the creature's eye and buried itself deep into the head.

The creature fell to the ground, lifeless.

One dog raced in for a late attack and gripped a mouthful of feathers at the tip of the wing.

"Argh!" Alan rebuked the dog as he approached the fallen beast. "Get out of it, you bitch!"

"Give her the wing," Peter laughed. "We can feed all the dogs in the village tonight on just that piece alone."

"We need to carve it up first," Alan replied. "I don't want dog slobber all over this thing before we have time to take the best pieces."

"Might I suggest we get the horses?" called a man in Peter's group. "We could drag the bird out of here and carve it up back at the village."

"Then why don't you go all the way back and get the horses, Michael?" Peter smiled.

"Fine," Michael said. He gave a sharp whistle as he turned. One dog ran to his master's side.

"Wait, Michael," Peter called. "I'll come with you." He too gave a quick whistle, and another dog left the kill.

"Damned thing killed my dog," said another man who had been gawking silently at the scene before him. He was a tall man with a red beard that draped down to his chest. "How will I explain this to my children?"

"Lawrence," Alan began, "you will simply tell them the truth. You will say that... What was the dog's name?"

"Sugar," Lawrence replied.

The remaining men laughed wildly.

"My daughter named him," the man spat.

"Sure, she did," one of the other men chuckled.

"Eat sheep dung," Lawrence snapped.

"All right." Alan stifled his laughter. "All right. Tell your daughter that poor Sugar died a hero today. I'm sure that will suffice."

"When she's ready," one of the other men said sympathetically, "come and see me. She can have one pup from my bitch."

"Thank you, Hugh."

"We should make a stretcher," the last man suggested.

"For the dog?" Lawrence queried.

"For the fowl."

"That's going to be a rather big stretcher," said Alan. "But it would mean less damage to the bird when we try to drag it home.

It's a good idea, Richard. That's why we bring you along on these hunts. You're the thinker in this group."

Richard smiled to himself.

"We need to find vines and long pieces of timber," Alan called out.

The men dispersed into the tree line.

After several hours of trudging through thick forest, directing six horses tethered to a wooden stretcher carrying the slain beast, the hunting party finally made it to the open fields that overlooked their home.

The men paused for breath as they soaked in the view before them. Nestled neatly in the fold where three hills met sat the large village of Woodmyst. A gentle river ran through its middle, from east to west. Three stone bridges, wide enough to allow horses and carriages to pass one another, linked the two sides of the community.

Tiny boats dotted the waterway as men fished for their supper. Storekeepers and peddlers lined the main road that stretched from the south and ran through the centre from south to north, crossing the centre bridge and continuing to the steps of a large wooden building known as the Great Hall.

A wooden wall surrounded the village. Three great towers stood along each edge, the larger at each corner, with a raised walkway linking them along the top of the wall.

Further out from the town and dotting the hillsides all around were small farms with freshly ploughed ground, ready for the coming season. In places, flocks of sheep gathered where the grass was tall.

Beyond the hills to the east and north were rugged, snow-capped mountains. To the west were the forests and the direction of the river's run. The river eventually opened into a lake. Good folk lived there. Civilised people who dealt in trade and property. Frugal people who discussed commerce and wealth. Things that the inhabitants of Woodmyst didn't have need of.

In Woodmyst, cares were few, and material goods were shared. Food and clothing, health and wellbeing were the responsibility of the neighbour. If the neighbour could not fulfil the responsibility, the next neighbour would step up to offer help.

It was a simple life with simple principles, and it worked.

Peter looked at the sky. The sun was still high, but it was moving towards its resting place.

"We have about four hours of day left," he announced. "We should get moving."

The grand fireplace in the centre of the room blazed with light and heat as portions of the bird continued cooking above the flames. The meat was skewered onto long metal rods that rested upon iron stands as high as a man's shoulder. The metal rods had handles attached at one end to allow the Serves to turn the meat occasionally.

The smell of roasting fowl wafted through the Great Hall, out through the large oak doors, and into the streets beyond. Many village folk were gathering for the feast, which would celebrate the beginning of the new harvest season.

The Great Hall stood taller than any other building in Woodmyst. Decorated with adornments of wooden dragons that twisted around giant beams, it acted as the meeting place for the village, and offered protection during extreme weather or from the threat of invaders. It was also the home of the village Chief whose living quarters were in the upper level.

The lower level comprised of one room; the auditorium, a vast expanse that stretched from the doors to an elevated platform at the rear where a long table sat. At the centre of the table stood a large throne upon which the Chief sat during village meetings and festivities. On either side of the throne were smaller chairs for the Chief's wife, council members, and their spouses.

Behind the platform, stairs led to the upper level. They were wide at the base and narrowed fractionally as they climbed to a levelled area against the wall. A large tapestry hung above the staircase; a splendid display of different shades of green with silver dragons dancing across its expanse and gold edges. Two sets of stairs then ascended the rest of the way to the living quarters, one on the left and another on the right. The staircases disappeared into the ceiling, out of the view of anyone inhabiting the Great Hall.

Banners decorated the hall, echoing the design of the great tapestry above. Many long tables and benches lined the room from front to back. A large green rug with golden flowers woven throughout filled the area between the fireplace and the platform.

Two sets of oak columns, nine on each side, stood sentry between the fireplace and walls. Adorned in carved scales that twisted from floor to ceiling, where they formed into the heads of snarling dragons that overlooked the tables below them.

Torches were lit upon four sides of each of the columns and along the walls of the Great Hall. Adornments of crystal, dangling from long chains attached to the ceiling beams halfway between the dragon's heads and the walls, captured the light from the fire and the torches and reflected it throughout the room.

Alan Warde sat in his seat at the Chief's table. He was admiring the craftsmanship of the columns and did not see the serve approach.

"Ale, sire?" the serve asked. He was around thirteen and held a mug in one hand and a pitcher in the other.

"Thank you," Alan replied, "but not at the moment."

The boy nodded and moved on to Alan's wife. "For the lady?"

"I will," she answered.

The serve poured a mug and placed it before her and moved on.

"What's the matter, Warde?" called a burly man sitting on the throne at the middle of the table. "Not drinking?"

"I plan to enjoy the feast first," Alan smiled. "Besides, the first ale of the night causes me to fart."

The man burst out laughing as he raised his mug. His enormous belly jiggled about and his drink splashed into his beard.

"I have the same problem," he admitted.

"We know, old friend. Believe me, we know," Alan replied.

He burst out laughing again and rose to his feet.

"Good folk of Woodmyst," he bellowed, stifling his laughter as he addressed the crowd sitting at the tables before him. "The new harvest season is upon us. Sowing the fields begins tomorrow. Lambing will follow as is the way every year. Let us hope for a season of new life, plentiful crops and long warmth. May the gods look well upon Woodmyst."

"May the gods look well upon Woodmyst," the villagers chorused.

"For Woodmyst," he called.

"For Woodmyst," they repeated.

"Now, bring on the feast before I'm too drunk to eat."

The hall erupted in cheering and laughter as the serves carved meat from the roasting bird and delivered plates of meat and bread to each table.

Twelve minstrels gathered to one side of the elevated platform and played a soft rhythm upon stringed instruments, flutes, and small drums. As they played, the fire roared and the men and women of Woodmyst feasted and drank, laughed and told stories into the night.

As the night developed, the burly man on the throne moved his gaze along his table, reflecting upon his most trusted men who shared the place of honour. Those he considered his council.

Beside him on his left sat his wife, Sybil; a vision of beauty. Her golden hair draped down to her shoulder blades, where it rested upon a red shawl. Beneath this, she wore an orange dress as bright as the sun.

Their two daughters sat at a table to the side of the room, where many of the children sat together. They both took after their mother in the way of appearance. He was thankful to the gods for that.

Isabel, at nine, was the elder of the two. She displayed her childishness still as she prepared a fork full of meat to fling at her sister sitting across from her. In the last moment, she caught her father's eye and lowered the fork with a sheepish smile.

The sudden change in temperament caused her younger sister to turn in his direction. Alanna, seven, smiled a wide, tooth-filled grin and waved to her father. He smiled and waved back.

There were no sons to carry on his name. Once, he had thought it was a curse. Perhaps something he had done to anger the gods. But then, as his daughters grew, he realised how blessed he had been. He would give them the world if he could.

"What's wrong, Barnard?" his wife asked, leaning in close to him.

"Nothing, my love," he answered. "Nothing at all."

He looked past his wife to his friend Alan Warde. In the Chief's mind, there was none more upstanding in Woodmyst than Alan. This was a man who always put others above himself, especially his wife and children. Catherine Warde placed her hand on Alan's as he rested it on the table. He leant into her and kissed her gently on the cheek.

Alan moved his gaze across the room to his Chief. He smiled and raised his mug. Barnard returned the gesture. "Finally drinking, my friend?"

"I've finished my meat," Alan returned. "Now I'm thirsty."

"Me too," called Peter from beside Catherine. "But I think my Martha has downed more mugs than I can ever drink. And you know what that does to her. It may be a long night for me."

"Peter Fysher," she snapped back, smacking him on the arm as she blushed.

"See," Peter called along the table. "She's already started. She likes it rough."

"Stop it, you dirty cretin," she chuckled, hitting him in the same place again and again.

"Yes! Yes!" he cried, closing his eyes and rolling his head back in mock ecstasy.

They all laughed loudly.

Lawrence Verney sat beside them at the far end of the table with his wife Elara. She stroked his long red beard as they both watched the children dotingly.

The Chief turned to the other end of the table where three men sat. These men were younger than the other three. Some dwellers in Woodmyst could not understand why the Chief had included them on the council. He didn't need to explain himself to the villagers, but he had told them the three were loyal to him.

It was a part truth.

They were, in fact, loyal to Alan Warde.

Alan had stuck his neck out for many folks in Woodmyst and had never sought recognition for anything he had done. These three men, however, pledged their friendship after he assisted them through a tough time. Simple gestures like some food when their stores were low in winter or a place to stay when the snow had caused the roof to collapse in their dwelling, or spending six nights in the sleet and rain to track down a missing sheep or two had worked their magic. All Alan asked was that they should follow his example, and help all others before helping themselves.

They were honourable to their word. Their vow had seen them fulfil many deeds with Alan for the benefit of the community. The Chief offered them positions on the council and they accepted.

They often referred Richard Dering to as the wise man of the group. He came up with many ideas others had not considered immediately, but his wisdom did not venture far beyond this area. Richard was not much of a thinker. He was more of a take action person.

The Chief chuckled when he thought back to a time when Richard proved his wisdom. A storm had hit hard during one summer and Richard, being a soft-hearted individual, brought his small flock of twenty or so sheep into his dwelling to keep them safe. He was still cleaning sheep shit out for two weeks afterwards, and the smell of piss still faintly lingered in the corners of his bedroom.

Beside him sat Michael Forde, a lean man with dark, short-cropped hair. He was making eyes at several female serves who were returning smiles and looks of their own. Sybil often said that Michael was a man that would not have trouble finding a wife. The problem was, Barnard told her, Michael was having too much fun not being married. Tonight, by the looks of it, would be no exception.

The last man sitting at the table was Hugh Clarke. He was the Dogman of Woodmyst and possessed the knowledge of how to communicate with animals without words or whistles. A flick of the eyes or a tilt of the head, a movement with the hand or placement of the body instructed his hounds what to do and how to do it.

A good band of men, the Chief thought. He loved them as brothers. He was glad to have them as his close friends.

He leant back in his throne and sculled his mug dry.

The minstrels had played faster, merrier music. Some children and drunken folk had taken to the rug on the floor to dance. Others remained seated at their tables to laugh at the display.

The festivities picked up. Jollity and happiness filled the room as others stood to stomp their feet and clap their hands.

Some infants grabbed hands and spun around and around until they fell down. A few of the drunken dancers spun around and around until they threw up.

Ale was poured and spilt.

Music played loudly.

The fire blazed.

Laughter resounded.

"My lords! My lords!"

The music stopped as someone shouted from the door. The people froze.

"What is the meaning of this disturbance?" asked the Chief.

"Pardon my intrusion, Chief Shelley," a young guard called.

He wore armour complete with a sheathed sword at his side.

He was puffing from his haste. "We have company on the north-eastern border."

***

Chief Barnard Shelley rode alongside his trusted councilmen.

They crossed the open fields between the eastern wall of the village and the ridgeline of the hills, passing small farms on the way.

Ahead of them, perched on top of the hills, a lone figure stood. In the moon's light and stars, they saw the dark hooded cloak wafting back and forth as the cold, tender breeze swept down from the mountains and across the valley floor.

Something seemed unnatural about this figure. It didn't move, apart from the effect of the wind. It didn't retreat or attack.

It simply stood its place.

The Chief unsheathed his sword as they drew closer to the stranger.

His councilmen mirrored his action, revealing their own blades to the night.

The horses' nostril flared as they breathed deeply with each stride. The thunderous hoof-falls echoed across the surrounding hills as they ascended the mild slope towards the lone figure.

Still, it didn't move. Its identity remained hidden by the dark hood as it stood its ground.

Unmoving.

Unchanging.

Unnatural.

One horse gave a guttural cry of excitement as they flanked the figure on all sides.

It kept its composure. It continued to face the village as if oblivious to the men that had it trapped.

"Speak your purpose," the Chief ordered.

The figure remained silent. The cloak flapped softly as a sudden gust blew through the gathering.

"Speak, bastard!" the Chief barked.

Alan gazed at the figure, scrutinising the movement of the cloak in proportion to the positioning of the body.

"Are you mute?"

"Wait, Barnard." Alan slid from his horse.

"Be careful, Alan," cautioned Lawrence.

Alan gave him a quick sideways glance and a smile as he approached the cloaked figure. He paused when he was within arm's reach and cocked his head to the left, then slowly to the right.

In one swift motion, and without warning, he sheathed his sword and grabbed the cloak with his hand, ripping it off the figure and revealing what was beneath.

Tied to a wooden stake was the body of a slain man.

At least Alan assumed it was a man.

The skin had been peeled away and his arms had been taken along with most of the flesh from his torso.

It appeared to be a recent kill. The cuts were fresh and the blood wet.

Moist portions glistened in the moonlight.

The corpse's eyes turned upwards, staring blankly into the sky.

Torn from its hinge, the jaw was left to dangle wide open in a silent scream.

Two

The Great Hall emptied except for the Chief and his six councilmen, four elders, the mutilated body and two guards who stood sentry on either side of the large oak doors, now shut tight. The body laid upon a table near the fireplace, and the men gathered around it.

"Who would have done such a thing?" Michael asked as he stared at the flayed body. "What purpose does this serve?"

"Do you feel confused?" asked an elder, his cloak wrapped tightly around him as he drew nearer to the fire. "Do you feel a lack of control? Perhaps you even feel fearful, Master Forde?"

"I am not a coward, Eowyn," Michael objected.

"That is not what I said," the old man corrected. "I am merely stating that we, here in this room, are confused. We have no control over this circumstance. And, yes, I am fearful at this moment. I believe we all are."

Eowyn turned to face the men, who were all looking at him as he spoke. "If we are feeling this way, how do you think the people of Woodmyst are feeling? Word travels quickly in a village of this size. I don't believe one eye will close this night. And if any do manage to sleep, I don't believe their dreams will be pleasant ones."

"You are saying that those who have done this," Richard pointed to the body, "did so to simply scare us?"

"I believe so, yes," Eowyn replied.

"Task accomplished," Richard said. "I almost pissed myself up there on that hill."

“I believe it’s a warning of something to come,” said another elder, stroking his chin thoughtfully. “This is just the beginning.”

“We should send riders,” another elder suggested.

“No one leaves the village tonight, Frederick,” Alan said.

“I mean in the morning, of course. We should send riders to the other villages nearby.”

“Already done,” Barnard replied. “I ordered riders out when I first heard of this. We’ll also double the guards on the towers and check the bells to see that they are ready to signal if need be.”

The bells were long cast iron chimes that hung from the ceilings in the towers. Guards would hit them with iron hammers to produce a loud clang that resonated across the valley surrounding Woodmyst. It was a signal for farmers to abandon their crops and flocks in order to seek refuge behind the gates of the township, a signal for villagers to gather at the Great Hall for their protection and safety, a signal for the warriors to take their positions on the wall to defend their families and friends.

“The bells are fine,” Peter informed the Chief. “Lawrence and I went around to each tower four days ago. They are all fine.”

“Check them once more for me, please, Peter. Check that there are hammers in the towers. I need to be sure.”

“I will,” he promised.

“What about this one?” Hugh Clarke queried. They returned their attention to the corpse lying on the table.

“As far as I’m concerned,” the Chief said. “This one is a victim of foul play. We should build a pyre tomorrow and burn the poor soul.”

“Such a shame we do not know this one’s name,” Eowyn said. “It would be a better sending away if we could mention a name to the gods.”

“A sending away is better than rotting on the ground,” Hugh said. “Name or no name.”

“I’ll have the serves wrap the body in linen and green silk,” Barnard told the men. “We will send this one away as if it were one of our own.”

***

"From where did he come?" Catherine asked as she placed a loaf of bread on the table. "Who was he?"

"We do not know," Alan answered as he broke a piece of bread off. It was still steaming after not being out of the oven for very long. He took a mouthful. "Ooh! Hot!" he huffed.

"Break me some off, Da," pleaded a small blonde girl sitting across the table from him.

"Why?" he mumbled with a mouthful of bread.

"Because I want some," she giggled.

"Good enough." Alan broke off another piece and shoved it into his own mouth.

"Da!" she complained with a chuckle.

"You're teaching the girl bad manners," Catherine scolded.

"Mmph," he managed, chewing the chunks of bread in his mouth.

"Here, Linet." a boy, not much older than the girl, offered as he tore a portion from the loaf and handed it to her before taking a piece for himself.

"Thank you, Tomas," she said, and bit into the bread.

"Barnard wants a ceremony for the stranger," Alan told his wife. "We'll build a pyre today and hold the service before dusk."

"What will the elders say?"

"I'm not sure. We cannot tell if the stranger is a woman or a man. Perhaps there are words that can be said for this type of circumstance."

Catherine stoked the embers in the oven with a long poker and left the iron door open so the heat could fill the room. She then sat beside her husband and tore a piece of bread for herself.

"Perhaps," she said, "there are no words that can be said. Perhaps this poor soul will pass into the gods' care with our good wishes."

Alan nodded as he gave this thought. His eyes moved from his son to his daughter and then to his wife. He gave a wide grin before moving into her and kissing her on the nose.

"One can only hope that would be enough, my love."

***

Hugh Clarke walked with his dogs across the open fields towards the hilltop where they had discovered a mutilated corpse.

His four hounds jogged back and forth around him as he traversed in a direct path to his destination.

Now and then, the dogs ran wide to something of interest on the ground, sniffing the area, tilting their heads to listen to sounds carried upon the icy breeze before racing back to their master.

Waterfowl spooked by the hounds' movement fluttered from their hiding place in the tall grass and into the sky. One dog stopped to watch them fly across the sky some distance before landing to rest on the southern bank of the river.

Small flocks of sheep bleated and ran uphill to the north or towards the riverbank to the south. Stopping at a distance, they considered safe to watch the man and his dogs crossing their pasture. Hugh ignored them as he strolled on the grass, keeping his eyes firmly fixed on the hill where the cloaked, lone figure stood only a few hours before.

The sun had climbed a fraction above the mountains' peaks and felt warm on his face. The morning fog had retreated to the water's edge to his right, leaving soft, silvery dew on the lush green expanse about him.

He ascended the hill slowly as his dogs danced around and sidled up to him for a position of favour. He obliged them by patting them on the heads as they passed by him.

A short whistle emitted from his lips when he reached the place where they found the body. The dogs sat and watched him closely, obediently.

Hugh approached the stake that still pierced the ground. Peter Fysher had cut the ropes that held the carcass in place the night before. They now lay on the ground at the base of the wooden pole.

Hugh picked one cutting up and dangled it between his fingers and thumb. He pointed to one dog with his other hand. The dog rose and approached him. It sniffed at the rope and then at the turf. Nose to the ground, it headed north. As it drifted off, Hugh looked at the ground at the base of the stake.

Round hoof prints from horses and boot depressions from men were visible in the grass. Closer inspection told him his own group made all the indents. The horses had come from the village and the people from the horses.

The dog stopped moving a few paces away and sat. Hugh strode over and looked at the ground where a small patch of disturbed turf. Someone or something had ripped some grass out of the ground, exposing fresh dirt. Drag marks stretched a short distance across the ground here.

Blood stained the vegetation here about. But not enough, in Hugh's mind, to say this was where the body had been slain. He surmised this was where they, whoever they were, attached the body to the stake before being positioned on the ground, so it appeared to be looking down upon Woodmyst.

He searched a little more, calling the other dogs to him. They continued north a short distance but found no sign of tracks, blood or trail of any kind. To continue more would lead him into a grove that bordered the pasturelands from the hill all the way to the forest in the west. There would be no hope of finding any trail in there.

It was as if spirits had carried the corpse here and placed it on display before floating away.

***

Peter Fysher bundled the wood he had collected together with twine. So far he and Alan had gathered twelve bundles, each about the thickness of a man and half the height if they stood on their ends. They were placing the wood onto a wagon hitched to Alan's horse.

The sun climbed high in the morning sky. They must take what timber they had gathered back to the eastern gate of the village by midday. Afterwards, the men of Woodmyst would gather to construct the pyre.

"We need at least another twelve of these," Peter said.

"I know," Alan agreed. "We're running out of time." Alan finished tying another bundle and threw it onto the wagon. His horse tossed its head impatiently with a snort. "It's all right, boy. You'll be free soon." He rubbed his hand along the steed's neck as he moved towards a pile of cut timber the men had collected from the forest.

Alan laid two strips of twine onto the ground and started placing wood across them. Peter had got a head start and was stacking the wood several layers high. He brought the twine up and around the edge of the pile and tied the two ends together. This forced the wood to collect tightly into a bundle. He repeated the process with the other piece of twine at the other end of the bundle.

Peter hoisted his new bundle of wood onto his shoulder and carried it to the wagon while Alan continued to stack his branches. His thoughts drifted to the body they had discovered during the previous night. In particular, he wondered who was responsible for the act. Questions his wife had asked him during breakfast haunted him, and he also needed to know the answers.

"Who do you think killed this one and then left him on the hill like that, Peter?"

"I don't know." Peter placed two strips of twine on the ground. "I have heard stories from travellers from other villages about ghouls from the north."

"Ghouls?" Alan asked. "Why have you not spoken of these things before?"

"I just thought they were stories," he answered as he started piling wood together. "Like the ones we tell our children to make them eat their carrots and beans. I didn't think they were serious."

"What do these stories tell?" Alan hoisted the new bundle onto his shoulder and headed for the wagon.

"Well," Peter began, "about two years ago, I was in Oldcastle buying oats and barley. One of the peddlers there told me a couple of towns had been attacked by ghouls. He said they were places in the west within the realms of Melamwen and Kailibard."

Peter carried his bundle to the wagon and threw it on board. He grabbed two more pieces of yarn draped over the side of the wagon and returned to the pile of wood where Alan was stacking branches.

"The peddler told me the towns were destroyed and almost nobody left alive," he continued. "There was never a sign of the ghouls ever being there. No trail to follow. Nothing.

"But one thing made me think of these stories just now and that is the body we found. The peddler told me before the attacks, someone found a body. Perhaps a warning."

"You think ghouls did this?" Alan asked as he tied the last strand of yarn to his bundle.

"I don't know," Peter replied. "It is probably a coincidence, my friend. I've heard no one else mention such ghouls. The peddler may have just been spewing cow dung."

"I hope so," Alan said as he hoisted his bundle of wood onto his shoulder.

***

Many huts crowded the area between the back of the Great Hall and the wall that bordered the northern edge of the village. It was here where the serves that aided the Chief and saw to the menial duties within Woodmyst lived.

In one of these structures, two young female serves wrapped the body in fine linen, weeping as they did so. They never knew the individual they prepared for the pyre, but something within them both expressed great sorrow.

They applied clean, white cloth directly to the remains first. Starting at the feet, they slowly, carefully, neatly and tightly wound the material up each leg to the groin.

Many long pieces of cloth had to be used before they finally enveloped the head. They clothed the body in a scarlet robe made of silk and, with the help of two male serves, placed it upon a wooden stretcher before draping the hood of the robe over the corpse's face and boots drawn upon each foot.

The serves carefully placed sweet-smelling herbs around the body. An adornment of lightly coloured field flowers decorated the stretcher.

"Fit for royalty," the Chief complimented the serves standing around the body. "You should all be very pleased with yourselves. Go and take a rest. You deserve some time for yourselves."

They bowed their heads in respect and moved out of the room in silence. Barnard stared at the body for some time. He wished it would speak to him, if only to tell him from where it had come and why it had been left in such a state.

Eventually, he turned towards the door, where two guards waited for him.

"Stay and guard this one," he ordered.

Both guards bowed their heads as the Chief walked through the door, passing between them as he made his way back to the Great Hall.

***

The riders returned throughout the day with no knowledge of who the mutilated victim could have been. One rider, however, believed he knew where the individual had come from.

"I rode to Winterspring," the rider informed the Chief who sat in the Great Hall on his throne with the elders seated beside him, two on each side. "The elders there told me they saw smoke coming from Selidien, farther to the west. They were about to send riders to investigate as they had not had word from their neighbours for about a week."

A young female serve brought a pitcher with water. The rider gladly took the jug and sculled the contents, dribbling some down his neck. He lowered the pitcher and took a deep breath. "Thank you. My horse will..."

"Your horse is being seen to as we speak," the serve replied.

"My gratitude," the rider replied.

"Continue your tale," the Chief ordered.

"Well..." The rider returned his attention to the men on the platform. "I offered to accompany the riders. We rode in haste. When we arrived at Selidien, we found nothing but ashes and bones. There were no living souls, no livestock, no huts or storehouses at all. Except for the children."

"What was that?" Chief Shelley asked.

"They left the children untouched," the rider explained further. "Apart from being a little hungry, they were fine. Most of them had taken shelter in the farmhouses outside of what was left of the village.

"Apart from that, my lords, there isn't much to say. I accompanied the riders back to Winterspring before returning here. It would not surprise me if this unknown one came from there. Perhaps a prisoner."

"Take rest," the Chief instructed. "You have done well. I will send someone to fetch you when you are needed again."

The rider bowed, pitcher still in hand. The serve who waited for the pitcher to be returned to her bowed as well. Both retreated towards the giant doors of the Great Hall.

"Your thoughts, gentlemen," Barnard prompted.

"I believe we have already taken the best measure," said Nicolas, a thin, clean-shaven man. His staff rested against his thigh as he rubbed his hands together, trying to keep them warm. "Our defences are being prepared and fortified as we speak. I can not see what other action we can take for the time being."

"It also may be a coincidence," Eowyn interjected. "This poor soul may have been placed there as an act of jest by some very disturbed people who have moved on to their next target." He scratched at his beard for a moment. "But I think not. Nicolas is right. We should prepare the defences just in case."

"We should have the serves organise the stores," Edmond suggested as he leant back in his chair. "If these intruders return, we must be ready. We must bring our people into the village behind the safety of the walls. That means water and food must be readily available."

Chief Barnard Shelley nodded his agreement. With the rider's report still echoing in his mind and the possibility that the same marauders that attacked Selidien might be on their way, the Chief was deeply troubled for the safety of his people.

"Chamber serve," Barnard called. A young man standing near the gigantic fireplace in the centre of the room stepped forward and bowed. "Pass the word. Double the guards, call the citizens to the village and lower the river gates."

Three

Two enormous gates made of thick iron bars lowered into the water, one at the western boundary and the other at the east, where the river entered and exited the village confines, effectively blocking any intruder's attempts to access Woodmyst by boat.

The tower guards had been doubled, each armed with a bow and a significant supply of arrows. They struck hammers against the large chimes hanging in the tall structures. Loud notes resonating through the air called farmers and sheepherders to retreat behind the walls of Woodmyst.

They left the sheep and cattle to graze in the meadows as men and women grabbed clothing, food, and what weapons they had before making their way for the nearest gate. Dogs instinctively followed their masters, and horses led by the reins behind the village walls. Every able man was told to carry his sword. If no swords were available, farming tools would suffice.

The only men to remain outside the tall boundary of Woodmyst were those who were constructing the pyre. Here, Alan and Peter unloaded the wagon and placed the bundled wood under the enormous frame that was built for the stretcher that carried the body. Richard and Michael placed dry straw and kindling in layers around the bundled branches.

The frame stood at chest height in the field outside the western gate. This was the place for all pyres. It was symbolic as the west was the place the sun went to rest. So also, they believed the souls of men rested in that direction too.

"It's a good pyre," Richard said.

"Fire will be the judge of that," Peter replied, as he wiped his hands across the knees of his trousers.

"It'll take." Richard smiled.

"Indeed, it will," Alan agreed. "But we should retreat behind the wall for now."

"You're not afraid?" asked Michael. "With the help of Grolle, we four could take them on."

"I like your enthusiasm, my friend," Alan replied. "And yes, I am a little afraid. But my hunger outweighs my fear. My wife's cooking calls to me."

The men laughed as Alan gripped the reins of his horse before they all steadily made their way towards the western gate.

***

"Why don't the men of our village wear iron armour like they do in the other realms, Da?" Tomas queried as he sat on the kitchen floor, admiring his father's outfit. Alan tightened the straps of his brown leather harness with his gloved hands. It displayed the engraving of a bull's skull with its horns stretching across the breastplate.

"Iron is too noisy, my son," he answered as he lifted a vambrace and placed it against his left forearm. "If I run with iron armour, my enemy will hear me clanking and squeaking as I try to catch them by surprise. Leather," he continued as he strapped the forearm guard in place, "is reasonably quiet and allows me to move more freely. This is why the men of Woodmyst wear leather in battle."

Alan finished fitting the other vambrace to his right forearm before strapping his long sword's scabbard to his right side. He buckled a pouch belt around his waist and placed a battle cowl on his head.

"You look like a warrior," said Tomas with a grin.

"Not yet," replied Alan, before lifting his sword from the table. It was a simple, practical design with a double-sided blade, iron hilt and handle wrapped in brown leather. The leather had stained and frayed slightly with age and use.

He carefully slid the blade into the sheath, admiring the sound of metal against metal as it gently scraped along a blade guide that stretched from mouth to the base like a rail in the scabbard.

"My handsome man," Catherine breathed as she entered the room. She had been preparing herself in the bedroom and now wore a long burgundy dress with a matching hooded cloak. This was the attire for the womenfolk of Woodmyst when summoned to attend a pyre.

"My beautiful wife," he replied as he reached with his hand to touch her face. She stopped him short by taking his glove in her own before leaning in to kiss him deeply. Tomas and Linet both made a face to show their disgust.

"Touch me all you want after the pyre tonight, husband," she told him. "But not with those old pieces of cowhide."

He chuckled. Alan had forgotten that he was wearing his gloves. He nodded and turned to his children. "Fetch your cloaks. It is cold outside."

***

They had practically emptied the village for the ceremony. The inhabitants had gathered outside the western gate near the pyre. Only the tower guards remained at their posts, overlooking the area around Woodmyst.

Two young boys beat slowly on drums slung over their shoulders as they walked ahead of the procession. Their slow, steady rhythm kept the pace for those who followed them. Six male serves dressed in white hooded cloaks bore the stretcher that carried the slain stranger. They strolled along the road from the Great Hall's entrance to the western gate.

The four elders, robed in scarlet, closely shadowed them. Chief Shelley trailed behind with the six council members carrying flaming torches. All were dressed in their armour with battle cowls over their heads.

The gathering outside the gate parted as the procession made its way to the pyre, where the six serves hoisted the stretcher carefully onto the pile of wood. The body rested so the head was closest to the village while the feet were pointing westward.

All four elders gathered a small distance from the feet end of the body so they faced the village and the gathered witnesses. The serves moved into the crowd as the Chief and the council members filed near the southern side of the pyre.

Eowyn, one of the elders, held his hand high.

The drummers stopped drumming.

A solemn silence fell upon the already quiet gathering.

The sun slowly sank towards the treetops of the forest nearby. Slowly, a red tinge crept into the clouds that crawled across the sky towards the north.

"We gather to honour this poor soul," Eowyn began. "We do not know his name. Nor do we know from where he came. But we send him onward as one of our own. We follow the traditions set by our forefathers.

"His ash returns to Areang, keeper of the earth," the Elder announced as the council members stepped forward to light the pyre with their torches.

"His spirit will be guided by Haaen, lord of the sky," continued Eowyn as the flames took hold of the kindling lower on the structure.

"His memory will be mourned by Gwendra, guardian of life."

The fire grew larger and lapped the body resting atop of the lumber.

"His soul will be embraced by Grolle, shepherd of the dead."

As he spoke, the flames engulfed the pyre.

All heads bowed in silence as the pyre burned.

The sun sank below the tree line and the sky grew darker.

Lavender clouds drifted to the north as the smoke lifted into the sky.

Tears of sadness fell on the cheeks of women who shared Gwendra's pain.

Small children tilted their heads up, wrinkling their noses and scratching their faces at the confusion of it all.

The pyre crumpled as the fire ate away at the support beams of the structure. Sparks and embers flew into the sky as large flames ignited anew.

CLANG! CLANG! CLANG! CLANG! CLANG!

All heads suddenly lifted, and all eyes opened. Surprised and confused, many started murmuring, offering muffled questions to one another.

Barnard turned to his councilmen, wearing a perplexed expression.

"Where is it coming from?" he asked.

"From a tower on the eastern wall," Alan replied. "We need to get everyone who cannot bear arms inside the Great Hall."

"Do it," the Chief ordered. The six men started shouting and herding the crowd back towards the gate. They gave orders for men to gather weapons and for all others to make haste to the Great Hall as Barnard gathered his family and the elders before joining the townsfolk.

The chimes of the tower on the eastern wall continued as they shut and barricaded the western gate. Chief Shelley, his wife Sybil, along with Catherine Warde and Martha Fysher guided the elderly and others either too young or incapable of fighting into the Great Hall.

The four elders gathered what serves they could together so that they could give tasks to each of them. They sent some to gather and prepare food for the people, while they instructed others to supply the soldiers on the wall with arrows and water.

Alan Warde and Peter Fysher ran through the streets of the town towards the clanging peal that echoed across Woodmyst. Once they reached the base of the tower, they then entered a small doorway before ascending a ladder to a platform about halfway to the top. They crossed the platform to the opposite side, where another ladder led up to the viewing floor of the tower.

Alan was first to reach the lookout. A soldier was striking the chime with a hammer repetitively as another kept his eyes fixed towards the northeast. Alan placed his hand on the first soldier's shoulder as a sign to stop sounding the alarm.

The clanging ceased immediately as Peter hoisted himself onto the viewing platform. Both men approached the second soldier, who was still staring across the open fields outside the village walls.

"What do you see?" Peter asked.

"Hmm?" the soldier turned his head without moving his eyes. "My apologies. I can't hear too well. The alarm is still ringing in my head," he shouted.

"What do you see?" Peter repeated, increasing the volume of his own voice.

"On top of the hill," the soldier replied, pointing beyond the farmhouses and a flock of sheep some distance away. "In the same place where the body was discovered last night."

Alan squinted. The clouds were dark and obscured the hilltop. He could make out the sloping curves of the land as it gently swept its way from the rugged mountains into the pastureland near the village. Something stood on top of the hill.

He thought perhaps it was another body. It was motionless and robed in dark cloth.

But it appeared taller than the first.

"Do you see anything?" Peter asked.

"There is something," Alan replied.

The clouds parted and moonlight burst through, lighting up the pastureland and the hillside before them.

The sheep scurried towards the river as the shadow of the clouds retreated towards the mountains in the other direction.

A lone dark, hooded figure sat on a dark horse atop the hill.

The horse stomped its foot as the rider shifted his balance.

The cloak wafted in the breeze as the figure stared towards Woodmyst. Deep shadow obscured its face.

"By the gods," Alan whispered.

This time, there was no mutilated corpse.

There was only one rider.

Could it be that this individual was solely responsible for the body they had discovered the night before?

Perhaps it was a friend or family member searching for the mutilated individual.

Alan shook the thoughts away and hurried to the far side of the tower and shouted towards the ground where some soldiers had gathered, "There is one rider on the hill. Send horsemen to bring him in."

Within moments, five warriors on chargers were streaking across the pastures towards the hill. They drew their swords and held them high as they closed ground between themselves and the cloaked rider waiting upon the crest.

Suddenly, the rider snapped his reins around to his right and the dark steed raced towards the north and disappeared into the grove at the hill's edge. The warriors turned in that direction, but pulled their horses to a halt at the base of the hill.

Night was upon them and they didn't know what awaited them inside the wood where the dark rider had disappeared. Giving chase could prove lethal. They turned their horses back towards Woodmyst.

Suddenly, just within the line of trees where the rider had vanished, a flaming torch burst to life.

"There," called a warrior, pointing at the flickering light amongst the trees.

Another torch ignited nearby. Then came another, followed by another and another. Soon the grove was alive with points of light stretching from the hillside all the way along the northern border for as far as the warriors saw.

They were vastly outnumbered.

Without a word, the men kicked hard and sprinted their horses towards the eastern gate of the village.

"By the gods," Peter breathed. As he spoke, a clanging echoed across the village. Another tower on the western wall sounded the alarm. "What is it?" he called down to the soldiers below the tower.

"I'm not sure, my lord," one called. "We've just sent someone to find out."

"Hurry," Alan called to the warriors on horseback that were still racing for the gate.

The gate swung open and let the riders through, closing behind them as soon as they were within the safety of the walls.

"Barricade the gate," Alan commanded.

"My lords," a soldier from below called.

"What is it?" Peter asked.

"We've received word from the western towers," the soldier replied. "The forest is filled with torchlight also."

"They've surrounded us." Alan shook his head.

"Prepare for battle," Peter shouted. "Blow the horns."

One soldier on the viewing platform lifted a ram's horn from his belt and blew. A long trumpet call bellowed into the air.

Another in the next tower chorused the sound over. And so, it went until all towers had echoed the call.

"Ready the archers," Peter ordered. A soldier repeated the call from below. Men armed with bows and full quivers of arrows stepped upon the wall and prepared themselves for the order to engage.

The torches in the shrubbery continued to flicker. Alan observed them. He wondered if the army outside the walls might have left the torches in their place as a distraction so the men could move to other vantage points of attack. He also entertained the thought that perhaps only a few men were out there and that the torches were merely an elaborate trick to give the impression that hundreds of soldiers surrounded them.

The fear tactic was working. The look on the men's faces around him was enough proof of how afraid they were. He could only assume that the men and women below were feeling it too.

Suddenly, like an expanding wave, the lights extinguished, starting at the hill's end and sweeping westward towards the forest. Where dots of light brought fear of numbers, darkness now presented the unknown.

"Now what?" Peter asked.

Alan shook his head, "I don't know."

Four

Alan shivered as he stood watch on the tower. He continued to scan the area to the north in both directions. The moonlight produced a soft, silver glow on the top of the trees in the grove, which seemed to ebb and sway as the gentle breeze from the mountains moved through the branches.

A flock of sheep had gathered near the wall below the tower and bleated periodically as they huddled together for warmth. They sensed the danger and had moved to what they considered safer territory near the village.

The men on the wall were set on edge. Fear had gripped their hearts shortly after the torchlights in the shrubbery had winked away, leaving only darkness and uncertainty. Questions and summations had made their way along the walls, allowing the tension and dread to build as the night slowly drew on.

Who are they?

What do they want with us?

They are punishing us for taking the body in.

They are devils come to kill us all.

Both Alan and Peter attempted to calm the spirits of the men near them. The soldiers, archers and warriors listened and could control themselves for a time. But soon, that time would pass and they would make more questions and summations.

Both Alan and Peter felt afraid, too. It had been some time, hours in fact, since they saw the lights in the woods. Alan longed to be with his wife and children and he knew his friend shared the desire to be with his own family as well. A glance around at the faces of the men nearby standing on the wall exhibited the same emotion.

They all desired to be elsewhere.

Although they all wished to be with their wives and children, their fathers and mothers, the wall was where they remained.

They stood watch and waited.

And waited.

Young male serves dressed in armour would walk along the wall delivering hot cider every hour. It was a welcome sight when a young man carrying steaming wine skins climbed the ladder and appeared on the viewing platform.

"Cider, my lords?"

The men took the wineskins gratefully and devoured the contents in a few gulps. The cider warmed Alan's body from the inside out. It was a tremendous feeling.

"What hour is this?" he asked the serve as he handed the wineskin back.

"Fifth of the watch," the young man answered. "Three more hours until dawn."

"They're not coming," said one of the tower guards.

Alan moved his gaze from the soldier back towards the grove to the north.

"We stay on the wall tonight," he instructed. "And then we stay on the wall every night if we have to."

"Why don't they just attack?" the soldier asked.

"Because they want you to be afraid," Peter replied. "Are you afraid, boy?"

"I'm not afraid," the soldier answered as he handed his wineskin back to the serve. "I'm not afraid of them." He pointed towards the shrubbery outside of the village walls.

"Then you're as stupid as you look," Peter said. He polished off the cider in his wineskin and handed the empty vessel to the waiting serve. "I'm afraid. Anyone with any level of intelligence would be afraid."

The serve disappeared down the ladder and returned to his duties.

The men on the tower stood silently as they watched the northern tree line for any sign of movement.

None came.

"Three more hours until dawn," Alan repeated the serve's words. "This is proving to be a very long night."

***

The stars winked out, one by one. The icy breeze from the mountains continued to push the clouds southwards as they donned linings of deep purple. Waterfowl boisterously honked and splashed by the river's edge as the sheep moved back into the pastureland.

Dawn had arrived, finally.

Alan's eyes weighed heavily in their sockets. He had watched the grove all night, taking his gaze away from the area only when the serve had arrived with hot cider on the hour.

He turned his face towards the bleating sheep in the meadow. A low fog that smothered the ground like a chillingly grey blanket obscured them. The pointed roofs of a few farmers' huts penetrated the mist here and there.

As the light of the sun gradually filled the sky, more of the area surrounding Woodmyst became clear. The fog appeared to be moving through the grove and into the pastureland before flowing towards the river.

If the torchbearers from the night before were still amongst the trees, they now had something new to hide in.

The sky turned from purple to blue as more light filled the land. Alan scanned the terrain to the north and could still see nothing beyond the mist.

The sheep had moved on into the meadow and the cattle calls resonated from beyond the hill.

"I think they've gone," Peter whispered.

"What makes you think that?" Alan asked.

"The flocks are moving."

Both men had been thinking the same. Alan had noticed the sheep huddled by the wall during the night. Now they were out of view. Perhaps it was safe for the time being.

"Should we send men to investigate?" Peter queried.

"Let's wait until the sun breaches the mountains," Alan answered. "I would prefer more light before we venture in there."

The fog crept between the trees, creating confusing shadows.

In his mind, Alan saw men moving where there were only trunks of pine and maple. His heavy, tired eyes playing tricks.

"We should send people who have rested more than we," Alan suggested.

Peter grunted his concurrence as he nodded.

"My lords," a voice called from below.

Peter peered over the side of the tower. "What is it?"

"Chief Shelley has called for serves to take watch on the towers so that the men could receive rest," a warrior called back.

"Well, tell them to hurry up," Peter responded.

"Yes, my lord."

"Good news," Peter announced as he turned his attention to the others on the tower.

"We heard," Alan said as he continued to watch the grove.

Peter followed his gaze and stared blankly at the fog swimming between the trees.

"You think they are still there."

"I don't know," Alan replied. "They could be sitting there just watching us. Waiting for the right time to pounce. Taking the men from the walls might provide them with an opportunity to attack."

"I think the night has been long, old friend," Peter said and smiled. "You're starting to sound paranoid."

"Perhaps," Alan agreed. "If they are not there, then where did they go?"

"There are caves past the ridge." Peter pointed beyond the grove to tough, rocky hills that stretched into the northern mountains. "Some are large enough to house horses and men. They could have moved there during the night."

"True," replied Alan. "Let us hope that they have moved further north than the caves."

"That's what I'm saying." Peter slapped his friend on the back.

"They saw our walls and the men upon them and decided to go home."

It was a small hope that the four men on the tower shared, and their faith in it faltered as they continued to observe the north before they were relieved of their duty.

***

Peter Fysher returned to his hut, where his family awaited him. He undid his leather straps and leaned his sheathed sword against the wall before taking off his armour, draping the heavy clothing over a chair near the door. With a long breath of relief, he sat at the head of a table positioned in the centre of the main room.

His two girls, Agnes and Jane, sat on either side of him and watched him with worried faces. Martha, his wife, served up some stew from a pot on the stove into a bowl and placed it before him.

"How are you feeling?" she asked.

"Tired," he replied softly as he lifted a spoonful of stew. It was warm and tasted good. "What's this?"

"Some of that fowl you killed the other day," she answered. "It doesn't stew very well."

"Yes, it does," he said before shovelling another portion into his mouth.

Martha placed another bowl in front of Agnes, who quickly devoured the contents. Jane soon received her lot before her mother finally sat down to join the family. Both daughters ate furiously, but Martha simply sat and stared silently at her bowl of steaming stew.

Peter discerned there was a problem and stopped eating. He watched from across the table for what seemed a long time. Both girls eventually realised something was wrong and put their spoons down.

"What's the matter?" Peter asked. Tears stained Martha's cheeks and glistened in the firelight.

"I forgot to bake the bread," she answered.

"It's been a busy night," Peter reassured her. "We can live without bread."

"It's not about the bread, Father," Agnes interjected. For a ten-year-old, she had great perception. "She's scared. We all are."

"Hush," Martha instructed her daughter.

"I will not, Mother," she stood. "Why don't you just tell him?"

"Agnes," Martha smacked the table with her palm. Agnes compliantly sat back down and lowered her head.

"Tell me what?" Peter queried as he placed his spoon on the table.

A long silence followed.

"Somebody please tell me something," he said.

"Mother was crying," Jane started. "She cried so much and she grabbed us and took us home during the night."

"You didn't stay in the Great Hall?"

"We stayed for a while, but then we came home," Jane continued.

"Jane, enough," Martha commanded.

"Let her speak," Peter said. "Continue."

"Mother took some of the meat from the Great Hall and we came back here to make a stew," Jane finished.

Peter stared at his wife, who returned his gaze with watery eyes.

"Why didn't you stay in the Great Hall?" he asked her. "You would be safe there and well looked after."

"I couldn't just sit there and have serves looking after me," she sobbed. "All I could think about was you. I couldn't be there and do nothing."

He understood. She was always someone who liked to keep busy. It allowed her to occupy her thoughts with other things instead of allowing worries to take control.

Peter lifted himself from his chair and moved around the table to his wife. He bent low and kissed her on the forehead.

"I will be back up on the wall tonight," he told her as he crouched beside her chair. "I want you to be in the Great Hall. I'll talk to Barnard about placing you in the kitchen or anywhere you like. But I need you to stay there so that I don't worry about you and these two ogres." He glanced over to his daughters. They smiled back.

"Promise me you will stay there tonight."

She nodded and leaned into him. He hugged her tightly and kissed her cheek.

***

Lawrence Verney tumbled on the grass with his children outside the eastern gates of Woodmyst. He held his son Lor in his right arm and his daughter Sevrina in his left as he rolled to his left and right. Both children laughed hysterically as their mother Elara sat on a blanket nearby watching and giggling at the frolicking. Some cattle had gathered to scrutinise the strange behaviour the humans displayed as they grazed upon the grass by the village wall.

"You're attracting an audience," Elara called over to her family.

"They're just envious because they can't do this," Lawrence replied as he hoisted his daughter up to his bearded face. He placed his lips upon her cheek and blew as hard as he could. A long farting sound resonated across the pastureland, followed by loud cackling from Sevrina as her father lowered her back to the ground.

"You left slime on my face," she laughed as she wiped her hand across her face.

"And now for you," Lawrence announced as he jogged towards his wife.

"Oh no, you don't," she objected with a smile. She jumped to her feet and ran towards the wall. He was too quick and had her in his arms within a blink of an eye. He quickly pecked her on the face, neck, and head until she collapsed in a laughing fit.

The cattle retreated away from the humans as the children rushed over and tackled their father to the grass. He started tickling them furiously.

"They'll wet themselves if you keep that up," Elara said.

"You're right," Lawrence replied. He sat up and released his children, who both groaned their disapproval of ending the game.

"Father," Lor whined. "Please."

"No," he answered sternly. "Your mother is right. I've been tickling you for so long that it just isn't right."

They all looked at him, confused.

"Why should you have all the fun," he smiled, "while your mother needs tickling, too?"

"No!" she shrieked. Suddenly Lawrence and the children were upon her like ravenous, tickling wolves. She mingled her laughter with intermitted screams that echoed across the open grassland, momentarily startling nearby cattle.

Five

Alan Warde stretched out upon his bed with his wife. She snuggled against him as Tomas and Linet slept in their own cots in adjacent rooms. An occasional snore made Catherine lightly shove her husband in order to silence the terrible noise.

She had found it quite amusing that such a small physical act on her part resulted in quietening her husband. His breathing returned to normal, and she tried to return to her sleep.

Small birds chattered outside the window and distant sounds of village folk moving about reached her ears. She focused upon the birds and controlled her breathing as she placed her head upon Alan's chest.

His heart was strong, filling her senses with its constant rhythm.

She found her comfort zone again.

Her mind swam as her weariness swept over her like a gentle wave. Her thoughts blurred and interspersed with images of her children running and laughing upon the meadows during the height of spring.

Bright yellow daffodils and blue forget-me-nots peppered the open fields like colourful stars on a sea of green. Her children, like all children, pranced and ran through the pastureland for hours. As their laughter filled the air, they chased flocks of sheep but never catch them.

Orchards on the southern side of the river would be in full bloom with red apples clinging to branches and ready for the picking.

The pumpkin patches nearby would house large orange flowers and greyish green fruit lying on the ground.

The market would be active with smiling faces as bartering and sharing of resources took place in the streets of Woodmyst. Some bridled horses and loaded carts with supplies so they could trade with neighbouring villages.

These were happy times, and their memories brought happiness and peace to her as she slipped deeper into sleep.

Her children leapt and laughed with other children through the flowers of the fields as she watched from the eastern gate. They looked over to her and waved, to which she repeated the gesture in reply. Their smiling faces returned to their play as a sense of dread filled her.

Dark clouds blanketed the sky, and flashes of lightning streaked across the air. Her heart sank as she watched the children stop in their tracks.

She called to them, but no sound came.

Tomas turned away from her first and faced the hill at the end of the pastureland. He reached out his hand to his sister. Linet glanced towards her mother momentarily before taking her brother's hand.

Catherine called to them as thunder roared from the heavens.

Linet turned her face towards the hill and joined her brother's stare away from the village. Catherine moved her gaze across the meadow and saw all the other children doing the same.

They were facing away from Woodmyst.

They were staring at the hill.

None moved.

Not an inch.

She moved her eyes towards the hill to the lonely figure perched on top.

There stood a rider on horseback, cloaked in long black coverings, staring towards the village.

Staring towards her.

It raised a sword high above its head. The blade sparked and was suddenly alive with flame.

They lowered the sword towards the ground and the grass caught alight.

The fire swept towards the children like a rushing tide, engulfing everything in its path.

It swallowed daffodils, forget-me-nots, sheep, cattle, and farmhouses as it raced forward with a terrible booming.

Tongues of flame licked the staring children and melted their flesh from off their bones.

Catherine tried to scream, but still, no sound came.

She suddenly sat up in bed, breathing hard and fast and covered in sweat. A deep feeling of dread filled her as her heart thumped fast and heavily in her ears.

Gripping the side of the bed, she slowed her breathing and tried to bring control back to her body. Her heart slowed down and return to its regular rhythm. The beat left her ears, restoring the sounds of the world around her.

She turned her head towards her husband. He was oblivious to the experience she had felt.

Alan was still lying on his back, snoring again.

Slowly, she lowered herself back down beside him. She wanted to tell him of what she had dreamt.

Instead, she gently shoved him again. He fell silent once more.

Outside, the birds gently chattered as she closed her eyes again.

***

Chief Shelley reclined in a deep, cushioned chair in his upstairs dwelling above the auditorium of the Great Hall. He nursed a book in his lap and read quietly as his two daughters played with dolls on the rug at his feet.

The fireplace crackled as flames danced upon dried wood as he pored over verses and stanzas written about occurrences throughout the history of the area. He skimmed over stories of kings and queens, knights and warlords, good and bad harvest seasons to see if the story from Selidien was similar or shared by any others.

There were some with vague similarities.

Brief paragraphs about small villages burnt to the ground during winter were few. Linking them to anyone who could be held responsible was fruitless, as each story claimed there were no survivors.

In frustration, the Chief slammed the book shut with a snap.

"Good grief," Sybil gasped from the chair beside him. She had been hand sewing small fabric daisies into a dress for one of their girls. "I almost pierced myself, Barnard."

"Sorry, my love," he said bashfully. "I'm just concerned about our visitors."

"You mean the goblins don't you, Father?" asked Isabel, his elder daughter.

"Goblins?" he grunted. "There are no goblins, my dear."

Alanna, the younger of the two girls, swivelled on her rear to face him and crossed her legs. "Dorla said that they couldn't find any tracks when they tried to find the goblins."

"Dorla?" Chief Shelley furrowed his brow. "Who is this Dorla?"

"Dorla is the daughter of Farris, the stable hand," Sybil replied as she returned to her sewing.

"The one that looks like a toad?"

"What?"

"The ugly little girl with the big wart on her forehead?" Chief Shelley questioned.

Sybil gave a disapproving cluck and nodded as she rolled her eyes.

"Well," said the Chief as he set his gaze upon Alanna, "Dorla ought to keep her stupid thoughts trapped in her stupid head."

The girls giggled.

"Barnard!" chided Sybil.

"What?" he asked, wide-eyed and innocent. "She is stupid. There are no goblins."

"Who are they then, Father?" asked Isabel.

"Men," he replied. "Nothing more than men. They ride horses and light torches. These are acts of men. There is no magic or sorcery involved here."

"Will you catch them?" Alanna queried.

"Absolutely. Your uncles Hugh, Richard and Michael are searching for them as we speak."

"With the dogs?" asked Alanna with a wide grin.

"With the dogs." Chief Shelley smiled.

"They're not really our uncles, are they, Mother?" Alanna enquired.

"No," Sybil replied as she slid a needle and thread effortlessly through the fabric.

"Will you kill them when you find them?" Isabel quizzed her father.

"What sort of question is that?" Sybil rebuked. "Now you have them all worked up," she scolded her husband.

Barnard turned red with embarrassment. He wrung his hands together as he thought of something clever to say. Finding himself suddenly speechless, he withdrew to a simple apology.

"I'm sorry, my love," he said. "I'm sorry, my girls. I shouldn't have got you so excited about these terrible things. You're too young to discuss such matters as these. But to answer your question, dear Isabel..." He rose to his feet and held his fist to the sky triumphantly. "We'll slaughter the bastards!"

***

Hugh Clarke walked behind his dogs, crouching underbrush and climbing over fallen trees as they made their way through the grove. Richard Dering and Michael Forde, who both brought dogs of their own to help with tracking, trailed closely behind.

A small band of warriors weaved their way through the growth a short distance behind. All were searching for any signs of the invaders from the night before.

There was nothing.

Not one of them could find a scuff mark from a boot, a stone turned over, a hoof print or broken vegetation from a passer-by accidentally brushing against a plant.

The dogs continued to sniff at the ground, coming across several fresh scents of small game such as rabbits and foxes but nothing of significance to the troop in the undergrowth. Hugh grew frustrated but more embarrassed that his dogs were not living up to the reputation they had for being excellent trackers.

They seemed to sense his emotion, returning to him now and then to lick his palms. He gave them a reassuring scratch behind the ear before they raced off to continue searching.

"It's not the dogs," Michael said. "These things we hunt are devils."

"They're just good at covering their tracks, Michael," Hugh retorted. "The dogs are confused."

"How could they do such a thing?" Richard asked. "Could they be using other scents? Animals and herbs, perhaps?"

"You think they're out here cooking?" Michael quipped.

"I'm just trying to make sense of it," said Richard, as he watched a dog dart from left to right and back again.

"There's nothing to make sense of," Michael said. "We should have found some sign of their existence by now. They were right here. Hundreds of them. I'm telling you; they're devils."

"Stop saying that," Richard commanded. "We'll find something."

They trudged onwards through the shrubbery. The dogs continued to sniff around, running to the left and right to find a scent. Each time, they returned to the middle with no luck.

The troop had started at the base of the hill in the early hours of the morning and was making its way slowly westward through the grove. The sun was high in the sky by the time they reached an area next to the north-western tower of Woodmyst.

Stomachs growled with hunger and the water-skins were empty. Hugh whistled, calling all the dogs back to him. Eight dogs suddenly appeared by his side and sat obediently, waiting for instruction.

"I think we should call it a day," he suggested.

"We haven't made it to the forest yet," Michael pointed out. "We might find something there."

"The dogs would have picked up something by now," Hugh replied. "There's no reason to enter the forest. We need water and food."

"Not to mention sleep," said Richard. "We will be on the wall again tonight and must rest before darkness comes. It is already noon which doesn't leave much time."

Michael peered up through the trees to the glowing orb hanging high in the sky. Logic told him Richard was right. His stomach told him Hugh was also correct. Deep inside, he knew if there were going to be any trail, the dogs would have found it by now. The hunts they had been on many times before had shown him the hounds were reliable trackers.

He turned to see the tired faces of the warriors in tow. They all bore the same expression of hunger, weariness and thirst.

The numbers had it.

They would retreat to Woodmyst and take a rest before the night was upon them.

***

The townsfolk spent the day in Woodmyst preparing for the night ahead. Chief Shelley had ordered what serves were available to prepare food and dwellings in the Great Hall for the civilians of the village.

Bedding was laid out, and they arranged allocations in the auditorium for families. Tables were set in the centre of the room on either side of the grand fireplace.

The kitchen serves peeled potatoes and sliced carrots as they primed large pots of soup and baked many loaves of bread. The kitchen serves cleaned plates, polished cutlery and rinsed mugs.

Other serves poured cider into vats and placed over hot coals to prepare for the watchers on the wall during the long night ahead.

Eowyn, Frederick, Edmond and Nicolas, the four elders of Woodmyst, made their rounds throughout the village, reassuring the citizens of their safety within the walls and that there was nothing to fear. Some believed the old men. Others felt differently.

There was a strange heaviness on everyone's spirits, but an uncertainty to what this meant.

Gradually, as the day wore on, people made their way to the Great Hall, filling the allotted bedding spaces supplied by the serves.

Chief Shelley stood by the fire with his councilmen, watching with deep concern as people moved about.

"None that dwell in Woodmyst have faced an invading force before," he said quietly so that only those near him could hear. "The only fighting anyone in the village has experienced was when a call to the aid of the realm occurred many years ago. We were the last to see any battle."

He remembered a time of great confusion between the realms. The Kingdom of Rhigon was in a period of dissolution. The Great King Khadrr Morno had passed away, leaving no heirs to take the throne.

Each realm produced potential rulers of its own who believed it their right to take the throne and rule the kingdom. As a result, the realms did battle with one another and many lives were senselessly lost.

One of the last and greatest of all battles was between the realms of Haoilia and Aroria, to which Woodmyst belonged.

Thousands died upon the battlefield, including the two potential rulers.

In the end, all remaining realms and potential rulers agreed to let the Kingdom of Rhigon dissolve. Each of the realms softened their approach to politics, allowing the villages to govern themselves how they saw fit. Most opted to continue to trade and barter goods with one another, maintaining relations with their neighbours as Woodmyst did with her surrounding communities.

"Do you remember?" Shelley asked his councilmen, a lone tear spilling over his cheek.

"I remember," Richard replied with a shred of disgust in his voice. He looked around to each of the men nearby. "I remember all too well."

"That was a long time ago," Alan put in.

"Not for me," offered Richard before walking away towards the Great Hall's doors.

The Chief wiped his eyes.

"Richard," Michael called after him.

"Let him be," Shelley ordered. "It's time we all took our places, anyway."

Most of the warriors and soldiers dwelling in Woodmyst were too young to remember the war. None was old enough to have experienced actual battle.

Still all but boys, they paraded their armour proudly to adolescent girls, hoping to attract a smile and perhaps something more. Mostly, the method worked.

But the armour was still fresh and unaccustomed to battle.

Their swords had not penetrated more than the flesh of straw scarecrows during training.

There were only seven seasoned, experienced warriors in all of Woodmyst and each of them felt beyond his prime, complaining more each year as winter came to bite them in their bones.

The sun slowly sank below the trees in the west as torches were lit along the walls.

Archers took their places, and soldiers took watch on the towers. The gates were closed and barricaded as the sheep gathered near the wall once again. They sensed the foreboding dread that was felt inside the village and crammed together for comfort more than warmth.

A chill breeze swept across the open fields around the village as stars winked to life in the darkening sky. Wisps of purple clouds danced from the north to the south as stablemen steered horses and carts safely into barns.

The councilmen hugged their children and kissed their wives before leaving them at the Great Hall. Richard and Michael took the northwest tower while Peter and Alan returned to the northeast; the same tower they occupied during the night before.

Hugh took up position in the southeast tower, leaving Lawrence to take watch on the southwestern post. Two soldiers armed with bows and arrows and swords also manned each tower.

The last of the dusk light dissipated, and the moon raised her head over the hill at the end of the pastureland.

Framed by the light of the full moon was the lone figure of a cloaked man on horseback.

Alan felt a lump in his chest as his heart pulsed faster and faster.

Torchlight flickered to life from within the grove once again.

Hundreds of orange, flaming lights surrounded the northern border of Woodmyst.

The intruders had returned.

Six

"Now what?" Peter whispered as they peered towards the blinking lights amongst the grove to the north.

The ribbon of light flickered between tree and shrub, following the contour of the land from the base of the hill in the east to the forest in the west. Alan counted at least six to ten torches from front to back. So many flickering torches, too many to count.

Alan surmised they faced several hundred invaders, and that was if each of them held a flaming torch of their own.

The odds were against Woodmyst. The torches alone outnumbered the men, women, and children of the village by ten to one.

Peter and Alan shared another concern. They worried about the men under their command. Not one of them was a seasoned warrior. For the moment, each man wore a façade of bravado and professed a willingness to fight to the death.

Alan had heard such talk before. Many had declared how they would die for a cause, only to turn tail when the battle began. He hoped the men about him would stand true.

Peter wrestled with another issue. He moved his gaze along the line of flickering lights before turning to face his friend.

"What if they plan to just sit there all night?" he asked.

"Are you thinking they will simply repeat what they did last night?"

"I think last night was a scare tactic," Peter replied as he looked back towards the ribbon of light. "It worked.

We've now assembled upon the wall, armed and ready. I think they were hoping for that."

"What purpose would that serve?" Alan asked.

"I don't know." Peter shook his head. "To show our numbers and resources, perhaps?"

Alan placed a hand against the guardrail on the northern side of the tower and leant into it. He scanned along the northern grove carefully, watching for movement.

The full moon projected a silver sheen across everything in view. It also caused the shadows to appear darker than usual. It was among these shadows where the flaming torches were being held.

There were no sounds from the grove.

No commands were being given by generals.

Just the sight of flickering orange flames dotted for as far as the eye could see.

Perhaps Peter was correct.

Perhaps these intruders planned to sit in the grove to watch and bide their time.

But bide their time for what?

Alan surmised that if the story of Selidien and its destruction was to be repeated here, then perhaps the invaders were waiting to enact absolute devastation upon Woodmyst.

But for what purpose?

Senseless and total obliteration simply made no sense.

What threat was Selidien to these invaders?

What threat could come from Woodmyst?

They were a community of farmers, shopkeepers and families.

"What do we have that they believe they have a claim to?" Alan asked rhetorically.

"Maybe," said one of the tower guards, "this is a game to them. Maybe this is a hunt and we are the prey."

Peter took a long breath as he placed two hands on the guardrail and shook his head. He suddenly believed he understood how the fowl in the woods must have felt when the other councilmen and the dogs surrounded it during their hunt the other day.

"We could run to the south," the other tower guard suggested. "I'm not implying a coward's retreat. I'm thinking more about survival."

The men glanced over at him.

"They have us marked from the north," he continued.

"As far as we know, they have no one watching the south."

"As far as we know," Alan interjected. "Escape under the cover of darkness is not a good idea. Not for civilians.

"We may be hard to see, but so are they. It may be the very thing they're hoping for us to do. The one mistake that could cost our lives."

Peter turned his gaze southward and peered across the village rooftops to the wall at the far end of Woodmyst.

Open fields and orchards lay beyond. Farmhouses dotted the land here and about.

Eventually, any traveller heading that way had a choice to make; either turn west to enter the forest or continue south or east and climb the mountains that bordered the lands there. It was not a journey anyone could complete in a single night or day. With civilians in tow, it would take several days before they could reach the safety of a fortified village.

"They chose us," Peter announced. He turned back towards the flickering ribbon of light in the grove. "They've been watching us for some time. They know the lie of the land and planned whatever it is they intend to do. We can't escape."

Alan nodded.

"Then we fight," he affirmed.

***

The serves offered soup to the villagers inside the Great Hall. They placed stacks of bowls and a collection of spoons onto the tables in the centre of the room earlier during the day. They now brought several large pots of steaming broth through the main doors. Other serves followed closely with warm loaves of bread.

"Women and children first," Eowyn called from the base of the platform at the front of the room. "Please make a line to my right. More pots are being heated at the moment, so there is no need to rush."

Mothers with their children made their way over to him and formed a queue along the edge of the large rug on the floor. Eowyn turned to see the wives of the councilmen and Sybil, Chief Shelley's spouse, sitting at the long table upon the platform with their children. Only Martha, Peter Fysher's wife, was absent. She had opted to help in the kitchens with the serves.

"You too, ladies," the Elder insisted. "Your children are hungry as well. Line up here, please."

"We can wait," Sybil replied. "Let these people have their fill first."

"I insist," he pressed. "Bring the children and line up." He kept eye contact with her while holding a wide grin.

Sybil suddenly had a measure of dislike for this man. From her perspective, she was in a position of servitude and believed it would set a negative example if she and her family were to take from the table before the villagers had their fill.

From Eowyn's perspective, they were women with children and they needed to keep up their strength. If anyone were to complain about it, he would have very public words to say about them.

Reluctantly, Sybil stood, causing the chair she sat on to scrape loudly on the wooden floor. Keeping composure, she strode over to her daughters and took them by the hand. The three of them walked silently down the steps to the floor level of the auditorium and joined the end of the line.

"You should take the head of the line, my lady," said the woman queued in front of her.

"No, thank you." Sybil smiled. "There are no places of privilege or prestige in times like this. Tonight, we share this meal together as a family."

The other wives and children sitting at the long table on the platform joined her in the line. Catherine Warde placed a reassuring hand on her shoulder as tears welled in her eyes.

***

Chief Shelley paced back and forth in the armoury; a large building next to the Great Hall. He smelled the horses in the stables nearby and heard the murmurings of the men waiting for orders as they sat around in various locations in the room.

A runner opened the door behind him, allowing a sudden, chill breeze to fill the area. The man, clad in leather armour, stepped into the armoury and approached the Chief.

"My lord," he announced. "There has been no change. Lords Fysher and Warde have said the torches have not moved since they appeared over an hour ago."

Chief Shelley scratched his beard and furrowed his brow as he returned to pacing the floor.

"What are they waiting for?" he asked himself. He moved his gaze across the faces of each man in the room.

All were looking at him for instruction. They bore the faces of eager young men who wore confused expressions, yet showed excitement at the prospect of battle.

Jitters had hold of some, causing hands to shake and legs to vibrate. Some gripped the hilts of their swords tightly as they rested the tips of their blades on the floor. Others rocked and silently prayed to the gods for comfort, assurance, and guidance.

Chief Shelley thought about the torches amongst the grove. He wrestled with the idea that the invaders had merely lit them and retreated, leaving the flickering lights in order to give the impression that they were waiting. The chief pictured them in his mind, sneaking out of the brush to the north and returning to some camp they had established miles away. They were probably singing and dancing, joking and laughing about the fools at Woodmyst who were afraid of some candlelight.

"I want scouts to go into the grove," he ordered. "See what you can find and report back as soon as you can."

An armoured man crossed the room to Chief Shelley.

"How many would you like to send, my lord?"

"Send ten men," he answered. "Five to the west and five to the east."

"Volunteers?" the armoured man asked the others. All the men stood. The armoured man standing by Chief Shelley's side counted nine out of the crowd and instructed them to follow him.

The chief placed his hands against a table, pushed up against the wall, and breathed a long breath as the men exited the room. His mind was still wrestling with the invaders' tactics. Now, he didn't concern himself with the idea that the intruders had merely left the torches behind. He now worried that he may have just sent his men into a trap.

***

Word passed along the wall to the towers about the scouts and their mission. Alan didn't like the idea and voiced his opinion to the others on the tower with him.

"It's lunacy," he said. "We do not know how many could be waiting in there."

"I think that's the point, my friend," Peter pointed out. "We need to find out what is in there. That's why we have scouts."

"They could all be walking into doom," Alan sneered.

"Sometimes sacrifices need to be made."

"What sort of thing is that to say?"

"You and I both saw battle," Peter said. "We saw real sacrifice during the war. Necessary sacrifice."

"Not necessary," Alan argued. "Not necessary at all. Look what good it did. The kingdom stands no longer. No good will come of this either."

Peter silently surrendered. Arguments with Alan would simply go around and around on themselves. His friend's point of view was valid, but he felt Barnard was doing the right thing. The need to know was paramount.

"Where did they leave the village?" Peter asked the tower guard.

"They were lowered over the southern wall," he answered. "They intend to follow the river in both directions for some distance away from the wall before making their way towards the grove."

"Good idea." Peter nodded. "If they are out there, they'll be watching the walls, not the river and not the fields."

"Unless they have scouts, also," Alan cynically remarked.

***

Cautiously and quietly, five scouts slunk along the northern riverside. Their clothing was soaked through after crossing the river moments earlier. They kept low, concealing themselves from the view of anyone watching from the grove, staying behind the embankment that dropped steeply from the pastureland to the water's edge.

They drew close to a farmhouse not too far from the river. The lead scout halted and held his hand high for the others to see.

Stop!

Instantly, the other men froze in place. The lead scout slowly raised his head above the embankment to look.

The farmhouse stood silent, abandoned by its owners in favour of the safety behind the walls of Woodmyst. Its mud packed walls and thatched roof glistened silver in the moonlight.

Strong shadows stretched from the western edge of the house into the field. Beyond was open grassland with no protection from spotters hidden in the brush. The northeast tower stood some distance to the west of their position. The lead scout could faintly make out the figures of men standing upon the observation platform.

He moved his gaze along the ribbon of blinking light threaded throughout the trees until they reached the hill at the far end of the meadow. He calculated they had positioned themselves about halfway between the hill and the village.

His attention returned to the grassland between the farmhouse and the grove. He quickly deduced they would need to crawl on their bellies the entire distance in order to go unseen.

Signalling the men to draw nearer, he maintained his watch of the grassland and the torchlight beyond. "Head for the shadows of the farmhouse," he whispered. "Keep low."

One by one, the men crawled to the darkness along the western wall of the structure. They held the position momentarily before the lead scout spoke again.

"We crawl," he instructed. "Keep your bellies and your crotch to the ground. The grass should be long enough to hide you unless you let your fat arses stick up into the sky."

The men smiled.

They were nervous.

They were afraid.

The light-hearted comment from their leader eased their fears a little, but not much.

"Keep your swords sheathed," he instructed. "The moon is no friend to iron tonight."

With that, the lead scout moved first. He lowered his body flat to the ground and dragged himself with his arms.

Moving his legs only when necessary, he opted to drag himself along the ground.

Eventually, the five men crawled into the meadow.

They moved out of the cover of shadow and into the tall grass. The thick vegetation obscured their view of the grove as they deliberately and sluggishly inched their way further from the river and closer to the flaming torches.

Seven

Richard Dering stared into a dark pocket between the flickering lights. He thought he saw some movement, but wasn't sure if it had just been a trick of the brain.

He and Michael Forde stood upon the northwest tower for the second night in a row. Two tower guards were also on the tower with them, keeping watch over the area where the grove and the forest met.

A low mist had crawled from among the trees and spread itself over the open grassland. Richard wasn't sure if this was a good omen or not. On one hand, it offered cover for the scouts who were making their way towards the trees.

On the other hand, it offered cover for the invading force as well.

"Anything?" Michael asked his friend.

"Nothing," he replied, keeping his eyes fixed on one tiny speck of darkness.

"Do you think they're still there?"

"Every man on this wall is asking that question," Richard replied. "I'm not one to speculate upon such things."

Michael pulled his hood over his short-cropped hair and hugged his chest. "Have you ever noticed how the nights feel the coldest at the end of winter?"

"Not really," Richard answered. "I think it's just because you have a silly haircut and no meat on your bones."

"You think I'm thin?"

"The ladies call you sickly." A smile spread across Richard's face as he spoke.

"I'll have you know," Michael retorted, "that the ladies refer to me as many things, but not sickly or thin. They call me the staff of justice. The rod of pleasure. The pillar of ecstasy."

"The twig of smallness," Richard quipped.

"The phallus of floppy," said one of the tower guards.

The three men laughed, leaving Michael to scowl silently.

"My point is," he started.

"Not very big?" The other tower guard chuckled.

"My point is that I'm not thin," Michael quickly spat.

"That's not what *his* mother tells," said one tower guard, pointing to the other.

The men burst out laughing again. Richard had tears well in his eyes, wiping them away as Michael finally lost composure and joined the others.

At that precise moment, from between the flickering torchlights among the trees, something moved.

***

Martha Fysher carried a large basket full of freshly baked bread through a doorway to the side of the platform.

The serves and kitchen staff used the narrow passage into the Great Hall as a safer alternative to the main doors.

The passage led to a thin corridor that ran along the edge of the raised platform, hidden behind the interior panelling and tapestries hanging on the walls inside the auditorium. The corridor, just barely wide enough for one man, then continued on to another door that opened onto an alley where tiny huts contained the kitchens and food stores.

Chief Shelley had ordered the main doors to the Great Hall shut and barricaded. This left the only access in and out of the building through the long, narrow corridor to the tiny door that led to the alley.

For now, the door remained open for the kitchen staff and serves. Those bringing food, cider, ale and water inside, at the same time as others carried empty vessels and trays back out, experienced some difficulty when attempting to pass one another in the thin passage.

Still, they managed.

Martha took the warm loaves of bread from the basket and placed them on the tables in the centre of the room, by the fireplace that blazed bright orange light and immensely welcoming warmth.

She turned, intent on returning to the kitchens for what duties needed her attention, nearly bumping into Catherine Warde. She gasped as she gave a little jump in fright.

"Sorry," Catherine said, covering her mouth with her hand. "I didn't mean to startle you."

"It's fine," Martha answered. "I'm preoccupied with my thoughts."

"I was just wondering how you are holding up?"

"I'm fine," she answered. "I feel needed in the kitchens. I couldn't bear being here last night, just sitting and waiting."

Catherine nodded and placed her hand on Martha's shoulder. "You will let me know if you need my help? I could come back there and help you."

"You already are helping me." Martha smiled and nodded towards her two daughters, Agnes and Jane, playing with Linet Warde on the rug near the platform. "Keep them occupied while I'm out there. I won't be in the kitchen all night. We just got word that once we've served up tonight's portions, we're to retire into the auditorium and bolt the back door. Chief's orders."

"We'll keep a place for you with us," Catherine informed her.

"You are a good friend, Catherine." Martha hugged the other tightly with one arm as she kept hold of the empty basket with the other.

"As are you."

Martha returned to the opening near the platform with tears welling in her eyes, disappearing through it as Catherine looked on.

Martha rushed the length of the corridor, almost bowling over a young female serve carrying a steaming pot of soup in the other direction. The young serve was quick to recover and kept the contents of the pot from spilling.

"Sorry," Martha said, before continuing down the passage.

"It's all right, my lady," the serve replied.

Martha crossed the alley and entered the nearest kitchen building, where bread was being baked in several ovens. A large man with a white apron and four female serves were kneading dough and laying it onto large trays to be placed into the ovens.

"My lady?" The large man raised a questioning eyebrow.

"I'm fine." She smiled falsely. "What do you need me to do?"

"You could make another few loaves to prepare for breakfast," he suggested.

She nodded and headed for a barrel full of flour, content to keep active and her mind occupied.

***

Chief Shelley sat on a bench that ran along the wall inside the armoury with his head in his hands. His thoughts swam in circles as he weighed up whether the decision to send the scouts had been the right thing to do.

His wide eyes stared blankly at the floorboards beneath him as he pictured the faces of the men who volunteered to go over the wall. Each one of them had a family of his own. Some had a wife and children, while others at least had brothers, sisters, mothers and fathers.

It had been at least two hours since they lowered the scouts to the southern fields outside the wall. Shelley had gone to see them off and wished them well. He watched as they split into two groups of five and parted in opposite directions along the wall.

He kept his eyes on them until they vanished into the darkness of the night. Afterwards, he returned to the armoury and paced. When pacing became tiresome, he sat and stared at the floor. When nerves got the better of him and sitting became uncomfortable, he paced again.

And so, this was how it had been for what seemed an eternity.

Serves brought hot cider and food to him, only to have it politely turned down. Jitters invaded his stomach, and he didn't want to risk the possibility of a mixture of his nerves and food manifesting as violent illness.

The chief raised himself to his feet and started pacing again. He was increasingly impatient as he waited for word about the scouts' progress. He walked the length of the room to the back wall before spinning on his heels, turning to walk towards the door.

On the fourth turn back towards the door, he saw a soldier standing in the doorway. Chief Shelley paused and gave the soldier a quizzical stare.

"I have word, my lord," the soldier announced.

Chief Shelley nodded, Go on.

"Fog has rolled in and our spotters have lost sight of the scouts," informed the soldier. "I'm sorry, my lord."

With that, the soldier disappeared into the night, leaving Chief Shelley to gape vacantly at the open door. He sauntered to the long bench and plonked himself upon it.

His head returned to his hands, and his gaze fell to the floor.

He hoped his men were still alive, but his faith was wavering.

***

The mist had rolled over the five men as they edged slowly towards the grove's edge, concealing them from the eyes of any who watched the open ground of the meadow. Likewise, however, the mist also obscured the view of the grove from the scouts as they cautiously crept on.

An orange haze refracted through the fog, giving them a sign of how close they were to their goal. The lead scout estimated it was only a short distance to the nearest tree, but he couldn't see any if they were there.

Still, he crawled forward, inch-by-inch, trying desperately to remain silent and not disturb the surrounding grass. His men followed his lead closely, each keeping the next in view.

It wasn't long before the scouts saw the trunks of the trees nearby. They kept to the ground and dragged themselves slowly into the grove, hiding in the undergrowth.

The mist continued to blur their surroundings. The torchlight flickered and moved in the vapour, but they could see no clear sign of life. The men lay on their stomachs in silence, intent on listening for movement. Apart from the gentle flapping noise the flames made in a breeze, there was no other sound.

The lead scout signalled to the others that he was going to move further into the brush. The others nodded and followed with care. They moved slowly away from the line where meadow and grove met and deeper, deeper into the shadowy coppice.

Gripping fallen logs that had gathered moist moss over time, he pulled himself along the ground as he kept his eyes on the orange glow to his left and right. The blurry light separated into individual sources, allowing him to pinpoint the position of each of the closest torches.

He saw one flickering to his right, a short distance away. Another was ahead of him, a little way off. The closest stood to his left, almost within arm's reach. The mist, however, floated close to the ground and continued to hinder his view.

He was certain if he could lift his head slightly, the surroundings would become clear. But fear gripped him. If the torchbearers were to see him, they would cut him and his men down in an instant.

Risking it was a necessity. His mission was to find out if anyone was out here and he could not do this if he didn't lift his eyes above the line of the low-lying mist.

He turned his head back to signal his men.

One was lying near his feet, waiting and watching. The other men were out of view. The fog was simply too thick to see that far.

The lead scout signalled by pointing up. The other man nodded and, as the lead scout watched, he turned his head and repeated the signal to someone behind him. Giving the relaying message enough time to reach the last in line, the lead scout waited. Gently and deliberately, he lifted himself into a crouch before raising his head through the low cloud cover.

The torchlight became clear.

Small flames licked the air from the ends of blackened rods.

Tall, hooded figures held each of the rods, peering over the mist towards the walls of Woodmyst. As the scouts crept, they scanned around and noticed other figures standing between the torchbearers.

The lead scout lowered himself back below the cover of the mist. His men shadowed his motion.

The closest cloaked figure, holding a torch, turned its hooded head towards them. The dark void under the hood seemed to bore into the lead scout's life force, freezing his heart in mid-beat and causing a lump to form in his throat.

He turned his head to see all the other hooded figures glaring their way. Two of the dark ones suddenly cut their escape route off.

The men had no choice but to fight their way out, if they could.

They formed a tight circle with their backs to one another as they brandished their swords.

"They are here," called the lead scout as loudly as he could. "They are here. They are here."

The hooded figures moved towards them as predators fixed on their prey. Each slid a long, broadsword from a sheath hidden beneath their cloaks as all the torches suddenly extinguished, as if by sheer will.

"They are here," the lead scout called over and over from within the pitch-blackness in the grove.

***

"What was that?" Alan breathed as the torches in the brush winked out.

A muffled voice carried on the breeze made its way to them.

"I hear something," Peter said, as the voice called again and again.

"Can you make it out?" Alan asked. He turned his attention to the tower guards. "Anyone?"

They all shook their heads.

A distant clanging of swords suddenly replaced the voice. The exchange lasted only a moment before terrible screams of men resounded through the darkness.

"By the gods," Peter gasped. "They're under attack."

The screams went on and on for an eternity. The sound reverberated across the misty grassland below the walls. The sheep, sensing the horror, huddled silently.

Bloodcurdling cries reached the ears of all the men on the northern wall.

The screams eventually died away, replaced with deafening silence. It pained them more, not knowing what was happening in the trees beyond the wall now that they could hear or see anything in the field and grove.

They waited and watched for a sign of life or movement.

No one spoke.

As their eyes scanned the tree line, they silently prayed and hoped that at least one scout would step into the silver blanket the moon had laid upon all things beneath her.

No one came.

A sudden great, dark shadow flashed across them, covering a portion of the wall and moving on.

Alan moved his eyes to the silver orb in the sky and saw nothing.

"You saw that, right?" Peter asked.

"If you mean the shadow, yes," he answered. "If you mean the thing that made the shadow, no."

"Probably a bird," suggested a tower guard.

"Too big to be a bird in flight and cast a shadow so immense," the other guard replied. "I didn't hear anything. My guess is that it was very high in the air."

Peter nodded as he returned his attention to the tree line.

Darkness and silence.

Alan leant against the guardrail and shook his head as he stared at the grove.

The fear tactic was definitely working.

Not only were the invaders able to cause terror by simply lighting torches and putting them out. They now could cast shadows across the moon.

"Who are these bastards?" he asked.

***

Time passed slowly as hot cider made the rounds three more times during the night. Peter surmised this meant three hours had come and gone since the scouts disappeared into the grove.

The sheep had moved away from the wall a short distance and the moon had all but lowered itself into the western forest. Clouds collected in the sky over the north and east, obscuring the stars above the village.

"Dawn comes," a tower guard announced.

Alan turned his face to the east. The clouds bore the faint lining of the deepest red on their extremities. The sky beyond turned from black to purple as the light grew more and more bright.

He was thankful the night was over so he could return to his family once again. As quickly as he allowed that thought to run through his head, he suddenly remembered the scouts who had disappeared during the dark hours and realised there was work to do.

Mourning families would need to be consoled.

Frightened townsfolk would have to be reassured.

Another search of the grove would need to be conducted.

Still, in his mind, he couldn't help feeling the need to feed his own selfishness and run straight to his family when he was relieved of duty.

"What is that?" one archer nearby called. All the men on the tower turned to see the man pointing to the hill at the far end of the pasture-land.

Reluctantly, the men turned their heads to see what had the archer's attention upon the crest of the hill.

There, lined evenly apart, were ten silhouettes of men standing in a row.

"Not again," Peter breathed.

***

Flayed and stripped of their skin, ten bodies stood, bound to stakes and posted into the ground upon the crest of the hill. They had their abdomens sliced open, allowing their entrails to dangle from their bellies and collect on the grass as their feet. The dark ghouls had removed the soldiers' eyes, along with their tongues and the flesh from their thighs.

This puzzled Richard the most as he scrutinised the remains of the scouts. Why would the invaders remove the tissue from around the upper legs?

The other council members and Chief Shelley gathered near the bodies as twenty soldiers sat on horseback nearby. Some warriors kept watch of the surroundings for any movement in the grove, while others held the reins of the horses belonging to the seven men on the ground.

Chief Shelley held a hand against his mouth as he shook his head. His stomach turned at the sight of the dead men before him. He saw what had become of his scouts, the men he ordered into the field, and it made him sick to the stomach.

"I believe they were skinned alive," Richard said. "I hope they didn't survive the torture for too long. They cut their stomachs afterwards. Maybe after they were tied to the stakes here."

"What about their legs?" Peter asked.

"I don't know," he replied. "The muscles were removed before they brought them to this location. The lack of marks on the ground gives me the impression they were drained of most of their blood somewhere else."

The men's eyes moved to the bare white bone of the thigh. The cloaked ones had neatly cut away the flesh from hip to knee.

"Why the eyes and tongue?" Michael asked.

"Perhaps," Lawrence started, "removing the tongues was a means to silence these men. Removing the eyes may have been to prevent them from seeing the faces of their killers."

"What does it matter?" Hugh remarked. "If you are going to kill someone, why remove the tongue and eyes? It doesn't make sense."

Alan winced as he realised a possible, sickening answer to this question.

"By the gods," he shook his head. The others looked to him as he turned away and walked down the hill towards Woodmyst a short distance. He lowered himself to the ground and sat on the hillside, staring at the walled village below.

"What is it, Alan?" Barnard probed.

"It couldn't be." Alan continued to shake his head.

The other men turned to one another for an answer. The soldiers shared the same look of concern as the council members. They waited for an answer.

"Alan?" Chief Shelley crouched beside the seated man. "What is it?"

"They ate them."

Eight

The scorched ground outside the western gate sat as a reminder of the pyre held two days ago. The blackened turf stained the earth in a rough, circular shape and still emitted the stinging stench of smoke and ash.

Serves piled wooden beams nearby as carpenters constructed a new frame above the dark blemish to prepare for a new pyre. This time, it was to hold ten men. None of them was a stranger to the village. They were all men who had family within the walls of Woodmyst.

Several serves collected kindling and firewood from the edges of the woods. None dared to venture too far beyond the tree line out of fear of whatever may wait for them, just beyond the view of archers posted on the western wall.

The serves timidly bundled as many small sticks as they could carry and conveyed them to a pile close to the construction site near the gate. A dropping branch, a rustling breeze or a small bird calling from within the woods would cause the serves to jump in alarming.

On the wall, the archers stood tensely as they stood guard above the working serves and carpenters. Some had been on duty since the night before and longed to be released from their current obligation. Their eyes were heavy and the occasional yawn betrayed their stoic posture.

The morning was dragging on. The hours passed slowly and relief seemed to be a far off destination that may never come.

Still, the daylight hours were far more welcome than the dreaded darkness of the night. In the minds of all the men on the wall, the setting of the sun brought foul creatures that were bent on destroying them.

At least during the day, the invaders seemed to stay away, allowing the inhabitants of Woodmyst the chance to experience some normalities. But truly, no one in the village was experiencing normality. Everyone housed an element of fear and dread. The sun wasn't about to stop moving, so eventually, the night would come.

The carpenters and serves knew they had limited time, so they busied themselves building and gathering. Even with their minds occupied upon their tasks, they occasionally peered into the shadows of the trees.

***

The armoury's door had been closed and bolted shut from the inside. There, the four elders prepared the ten scouts for the pyre. They had laid carefully the bodies upon long benches and washed, as was the tradition. The four men had gently placed the intestines back into the abdominal cavities that were then sewn shut.

A mixture of water and rose oil was applied to the remains tenderly with folded cotton cloths. The elders took great care as they covered the men from toes to head with tightly bound wrappings. Once or twice, Eowyn shed a tear or two as he cradled the torso of the scouts so that Frederick could wrap the bandages around the back and abdomen. He had known each of these men as young boys and had watched them grow over the years.

They then fit the scouts in full battle dress with armour and battle cowls before being moved onto stretchers that rested upon the floor. Once they were placed on the litter, the elders tidied the outfits and straightened the clothes before placing each man's sword onto his chest with the blade pointed towards his feet. The final touch was to move their hands to the hilts, causing them to grip the handle in clenched fists.

The four men gathered to the side of the stretchers and knelt on the timber floor. They closed their eyes and silently prayed to the gods for the safe journey of their slain friends.

Eowyn allowed himself to sob as he remembered the ten boys running through the long grass of the meadow, playing with wooden swords and believing themselves to be invincible warriors. They vanquished the evil dragon daffodils by lopping off their yellow heads in one swipe, and they chased the terrible white barbarian sheep across the pasture from one end to the other. The elder smiled at the memory as tears streaked down each cheek, disappearing into his beard and trailing onto his chin.

His ears picked up the sound of the other three weeping as well. Several long sniffles and wipes of sleeves across faces later, the men rose to their feet and made their way to the door.

Nicolas unbolted the access and allowed the serves into the room. Twenty young men dressed in white entered the armoury and silently lifted the stretchers to waist height.

The elders, led by Eowyn, exited the room first, leading the procession towards the western gate.

***

The pyre gathered a few people. The chief had ordered that only the family of the fallen and necessary participants attend the ceremony because of the threat that lay outside the walls.

The council members and Chief Shelley stood to the side, allowing the immediate family of the scouts to take places of prominence. The wives of the married fallen and fathers of the ones who were not espoused held flaming torches in their hands. Their uncontrollable crying could be heard from within the walls of Woodmyst.

The village had grown quiet, and out of respect, they held an unofficial silence during the ritual. The only sounds to be heard were those from the wild birds, bleating livestock and children too young to understand.

Warriors carried the bodies one by one through the gate and into the open ground beyond the wall. Archers kept watch from above, scanning across the tree line for movement from within the woods and the grove to the north.

Each stretcher was raised upon the wooden structure and placed carefully on top. The armour of each scout gleamed in the sunlight as the sun floated high in the sky.

Eowyn stepped forward to speak the required words at the service.

"We gather to honour these poor souls," he began. This time he named all ten men and cried as he recited the speech.

The family members stepped forward and lit the pyre, placing the torches into the kindling. The gathering watched the flames engulf their loved ones and stayed until the flames had consumed all bodies.

Afterwards, the four elders moved along the line of family members and hugged each one as they offered comforting words.

Alan silently watched as they did this. He believed no words could bring comfort after seeing what had become of these men. He wanted vengeance.

The faces of the wives and parents of the fallen scouts simply wanted their husbands and sons back. But that was not something that even the power of the gods could muster. How could words remedy this?

Chief Shelley and the council members waited by the pyre as the elders escorted the families back inside the gate. The twenty serves stood nearby with large rods, waiting for the family members to move beyond view. Once they were inside the gate, the serves stabbed at the base of the pyre with the rods to hasten the fire within.

Some of the structure collapsed, sending sparks into the air. The smoke wafted high before being caught in a breeze far above the ground, sending it southward.

"Is this to become the routing for Woodmyst?" asked Chief Shelley. "Are we to be surrounded each night and light pyres every day?"

"Perhaps we should leave," Lawrence argued. "Let them have the village."

"They don't want the village," Alan interjected, as he stared blankly at the fire.

"What do they want?" Michael asked angrily. "Have you been talking to them?"

"Calm down, Michael," Peter said in a low voice, placing a hand on his friend's shoulder. "Use your wits, gentlemen. Alan is right. If they wanted the village, they could simply take it. We know they have the numbers."

"They want us," Richard said. "If we run, they will give chase. If we stay, we have a better chance of survival."

"Explain what you mean," said Michael grimly.

"They want us to run," Richard replied. "It's why they are using the scare tactics with the torches and leaving the mutilated bodies where we can find them. They are hoping we'll get scared and flee across open land to escape."

"The fear tactics are working, Richard," Lawrence said. "My wife and children are scared. I'm scared. I want to leave."

"If you leave, they will find you," Richard retorted. "You won't have the safety of the wall, the protection of our archers or the sanctuary of the Great Hall for your wife or children."

"I'll leave early in the morning and travel by day," Lawrence said.

"You'll be lucky to reach one of our neighbours before sundown," Chief Shelley said. "You have a young son and daughter who cannot travel quickly, a wife who would not allow you to travel lightly. That means you will need a horse and cart to carry you and yours out of here. You will be out in the open, and that is precisely what they want."

"But why do they want that?" Hugh asked. "I don't understand the reason for this siege."

"Food," Alan retorted.

"Food? Fine. Empty the grain stores and give them what we have. Let them take the cattle and the sheep."

"They don't want the grain," Chief Shelley said as he peered towards the woods, "and if they wanted the sheep and cows, they could just simply take them. They're all outside the walls. The livestock would be gone already if that was all they wanted. No, it's not any of those things that they want."

"Then what do they want?" Hugh asked.

Alan turned towards the western gate and started back towards the village.

"As Richard said. They want us."

***

Alan sat in a deep, cushioned armchair tucked into the corner of the living quarters of his house. Catherine brought him hot green tea in a small mug. It was something she gave him to settle his nerves.

When she had first offered it to him, many years ago when they started courting, he turned it down believing it was a woman's drink. Now it had become a custom in their home. He would walk through the door with a scowl upon his face, especially after a council meeting, and she would serve a cup of tea for him to sip as he sat in his chair.

He had to admit that after a few short sips and time to breathe, he often felt relaxed and able to move onward.

Today was not one of those days.

The frustration and confusion he felt was clearly visible in his friends and the village folk he passed in the streets on his way home. Fear was eating Woodmyst from within, and no one had an inkling of an idea of what to do about it.

He sipped his tea and closed his eyes as he held the potion in his mouth. It was bitter and warm upon his tongue. Savouring it momentarily, he swished it around his mouth before swallowing with a loud gulp.

Keeping his eyes closed, he allowed his thoughts to wander away from the worries that the invading force posed and onto the possibility of a peaceful life once again. He pictured himself farming, growing crops with his son Tomas and working the land in a way he had always dreamed since his days in battle were finished.

Alas, it was just a dream he entertained once in a while.

In reality, he was brought into the council almost immediately after the war and placed in charge of training the young men in the skills of weaponry and fighting. This had been his life for almost fifteen years.

Five years after he had returned home, he met Catherine, whose family arrived in Woodmyst when she was sixteen. Within the year, they married. Some within the village talked amongst themselves, saying that it was too long for a courtship. Others surmised Alan wouldn't marry Catherine because she was cursed with a barren womb.

The truth was, Catherine's father was not ready to relinquish his beautiful daughter to such a rough man who was not much younger than him. Eventually, it was his heart that Alan would have to win with the help of the chief, the elders, and the other councilmen.

Then came the delayed pregnancy. The gossip flared about Catherine and her barren womb again. Alan gave it no credence until he caught his wife crying into a pillow one night after a year of being wed. So, intent to not be precautious about getting her pregnant, he used every ounce of his being to plant his seed.

After introducing undeniable evidence such as morning sickness and a broadening stomach, the rumours of barrenness were quashed. Catherine held her dainty head high again and Alan wore a constant proud smirk that simply told the chinwaggers of Woodmyst, take that, you bastards!

One month before harvest came Tomas. He wriggled and jiggled his way out, excited to be in the world. His initial cry was more of a shout.

I am here.

Ever since Tomas has always been a defiant child by nature. He never overstepped his boundaries and always respected his elders, but he was courageous and willing to explore new concepts. Alan often found Catherine covering her eyes or looking away when Tomas was discovering his abilities.

From a young age, he would climb the wall in places where no ladder or device for ascending stood. He would jump up on horseback and entice the beast to gallop across the meadow. Twice, he had broken his leg from jumping from the mare's back. Once, he had almost drowned from diving off Woodmyst's mid-bridge into the river beneath it.

Luckily, fishermen nearby rescued him in time.

The elders, who had mended the boy's bones, had also treated his cuts, bruises, grazes and sprains. All had instructed Catherine to keep a tight rein attached. She had argued that he would simply chew through it to get away.

With age and learning, Tomas' explorations became more controlled and the element of hypothesising before experimentation helped him to control his actions. Eowyn had told Alan that his son was an intelligent student with great promise. Alan had thanked the elder for the kind words, hoping that Tomas might pursue an academic or agricultural path rather than follow in his footsteps into a life of battle and war.

Two years after Tomas came Linet. Little pudgy faced Linet with hair so blonde it shone like white gold.

With a heart bigger than she was, Linet displayed the traits of a deeply caring individual who always put others before herself. Alan would see her now and then, meet her friends' needs and desires at a loss to her own. Often, she would give a doll away to an upset little girl, pass a portion of her meal to someone her age that was still hungry, or simply give someone a hug if she thought they needed it.

He remembered times when she was still learning to walk: she would carry ants and small bugs from inside the house and place them somewhere safe outside before her brother would squash them with his boots. Sometimes she would miss one or two and Tomas would find them, smashing them into the floor with a gleeful chuckle. This always resulted in Linet screaming in horror at the sight, followed by streaming tears as she mourned the loss of an innocent insect.

Alan sipped his warm green tea and swished it around his mouth again. As he did so, Linet wandered in from outside, her golden blonde locks reflecting the light coming from the window. She carefully climbed onto her father's lap, embraced him around his chest, and buried her head into his neck.

All he could do was wrap his free arm around her and allow himself to smile.

***

Waterfowl swam about the reeds at the river's edge. Once in a while, they ducked their heads under the surface, leaving their short tails to waggle in the air before righting themselves again. Dragonflies and other flying insects hovered above the stream or crawled upon the weeds sticking out of the water here and there.

Lawrence stared, transfixed, as the small creatures carried out their daily rituals. When he had first arrived and sat down by the riverbank, the various animals had shied away from him. Slowly, they made their way back towards him to continue foraging among the reeds and lily pads that grew near the shore.

The ducks and geese were still hesitant to get too close to him. They kept themselves at a safe distance with a watchful eye on the man, ready to take flight if he made any sudden movement.

The sunlight shimmered upon the flowing water, casting specks of light across the surface, reminding Lawrence of the countless stars at night.

An icy shiver ran down his back as he cast his thoughts to the dark, gruesome evenings he had witnessed.

The vision of the first body they had discovered upon the hilltop still haunted his sleep.

The staring eyes.

The peeled face.

The endless silent scream.

He had awoken many times with that image etched in his brain. Even now, he saw it amongst the reeds, as rippled water created patterns and shapes that reminded him of the poor, unknown victim.

Then there was the cloaked figure that was watching from the same place the following night. The faceless silhouette upon horseback, hooded and concealed that rode into the grove when the village warriors drew near to him.

His own heart sank as hundreds of torch lights suddenly burst to life at that moment. It was then that he knew they were going to die. There were just too many invaders in the trees for the men of Woodmyst to deal with.

From that moment on, Lawrence struggled with his thoughts. He felt he had an unbreakable bond to the people of his village, but none more strongly than with the men of the council. He had fought in the Realm War with all of them and could not imagine ever abandoning them in times of need.

But now he had a family.

While his son, Lor, and his daughter, Sevrina, were too young to understand the dread that had befallen Woodmyst, his wife Elara comprehended it too well. Her tears had broken his heart, and he didn't know how to make her feel safe.

To her, the walls weren't enough. The shelter and fortitude of the Great Hall weren't enough.

She had asked him to consider taking her and the children to Ostwyn or Crystalvale where the walls were high; the keep was reinforced and actual armies lived. He had argued that they were more than a day's journey, but her sobs drowned out his words.

So now, wrestling within his mind, Lawrence sat by the riverside, alone. He knew it was too late in the day to begin a journey to any neighbouring village or city. The sun had passed noon and by the time he would have loaded the wagon and started on his way, he wouldn't reach the end of the southern orchards before darkness swept over the land.

He knew Richard and Alan were right in what they said about the strangers in the woods. They would catch anyone trying to escape Woodmyst, no matter what direction they ran.

It was a gamble in either case. The possibility of being attacked on the road south was just as much a possibility of dying in battle on the wall.

The sun bit at his neck. He lifted his hood over his head and stood to his feet. The waterfowl fluttered and squawked in fright, which disturbed the insects resting upon the reeds.

Lawrence turned towards the eastern gate and started trudging back to the village. His mind still weighed up the benefits of staying against those of leaving. He ignored the internal battle and decided. He would pack the wagon, ready to leave in the morning.

He thought by making a stand, the conflict within would be over. Instead, the voices shouted louder at each other. It seemed just like the outcome of the Realm War; there would be no victors today.

Nine

Chief Barnard Shelley took time to visit the blacksmiths of Woodmyst. He had a list of demands to be filled as quickly as possible. The list comprised mainly the forging of a thousand arrows, a hundred daggers, and long blades. He was adamant that functionality should take absolute priority and that appearance should not even fit within the equation.

The blacksmiths understood.

"What item would you like us to work on first?" the lead blacksmith asked. He tucked his long dark beard behind his leather apron.

Behind him, large bellows, operated by young men, kept the coals hot. They pulled down on large wooden handles, causing the bellows' air sacks to squeeze air into the ovens. The roar of air rushing into the fireplaces reminded Barnard of thunder as the coals flared bright red with each blow.

Nearby, a blacksmith hammered a rod of iron on an anvil. Each hammer blow resounded a loud clang and send red sparks flying as he flattened the hot rod at one end.

Holding it by tongs at one end, the blacksmith lowered the rod into a metal bucket of water. A loud hiss screamed out as steam burst from the water.

"I'd like all of them," Chief Shelley replied, as he watched the rod being lifted from the water for inspection.

"No disrespect intended, but we're limited in ore, my lord," the blacksmith responded. "We could probably fulfil your order of arrows, but not get to all the blades. Alternatively, we could possibly produce half the blades but you will have no arrows."

"Surely the armoury still has swords, my lord?" asked one of the other blacksmiths.

"It does, but the blades are dull and brittle," the chief replied.

The lead blacksmith scratched his beard. "I have an idea."

"Please," Barnard invited.

"Get the serves to bring the swords and daggers," he began. "We can sharpen them on the stone. Any that are too brittle to last the night, we can reforge and use some old scrap from our stockpile. They won't be as strong as a proper sword, but they will still cut and stab."

"Good enough," Chief Shelley agreed.

"That will leave the ore to be used on arrows," the lead blacksmith told him. "Our apprentices can fulfil that part of the order by nightfall. The senior staff will look after the blades. That will require some skill to be a success."

"Thank you." The chief shook the blacksmith's hand before turning to leave.

Barnard made it a few steps from the blacksmith's storefront before a young female serve stopped him.

"My lord?"

"Yes," he answered with a smile.

"The cooks have sent me to inform you that the soup stock is too low to cater for our needs tonight," said the serve.

"What do they suggest?" Chief Shelley queried as he continued to walk along the road.

The serve kept pace alongside. "They request we butcher two of the cows. One for tonight and the other for tomorrow."

Chief Shelley pondered this momentarily as he walked. Eventually, he returned his attention to the young woman by his side. "Tell the butchers to prepare two of the heifers," he instructed. "The larger parts of meat for roasting and the tougher portions for mincing. Then tell the cooks we will have roast meat tonight and prepare pies for tomorrow."

"Yes, my lord," she replied before scurrying away ahead of the chief.

Chief Barnard Shelley watched her disappear into another street that led back to the Great Hall. He then moved his gaze across the many stalls about him. Most were empty. The street itself seemed almost deserted.

He knew the reason for this was because most men who worked the markets were also standing on the wall during the previous night. It made sense that these men would favour rest over work.

The chief deeply appreciated their sacrifice. Closing their stalls to protect their loved ones and the wellbeing of the village tugged at his heart. Still, he would prefer to see smiling faces and busy streets before the need for men to stand upon the wall each night.

Although it had been only three days since this turmoil had befallen his beloved Woodmyst, he longed for it to be over and for all things to return to normal. But could it ever be normal again? Ten scouts had lost their lives for the sake of the village. For the sake of the chief.

Chief Shelley shook his head.

How he wished he had never given that order.

***

Richard, Michael and Hugh had walked around the outside of the village walls together. None of the three men could sleep with the images of the ten mutilated scouts branded into their thoughts.

Richard saw them every time he closed his eyes. He needed to find something to occupy his time, and when Hugh suggested taking the dogs for a walk, Richard offered to accompany him within a heartbeat.

The two men and six canines then sought Michael out and invited him to join them as well. He was also experiencing difficulty coping with the occurrences of the previous three nights and jumped at the opportunity for distraction.

The three council members decided not to invite the other village leaders, as they had families and were possibly busy with their wives and children. The chief was always busy, so they left him to his duties as they ventured for the western gate.

The dogs bolted across the open ground, sniffing and leaping over one another, careful to not move too far from Hugh and his watchful eye. Once outside the gate, the men turned north and scanned the wall as they strolled through the tall grass.

They looked for weaknesses and places of easy access.

The walls were tall and made of steep stone and wood. A few archers stood atop the entire length, and they posted a man in each tower. At night, they practically crowded the walls with warriors. It would be near impossible for anyone to get as close as they were to the wall.

Still, it could happen.

Richard pointed to the north-western corner of the wall, just below the tower structure. The other men followed his gesture and peered at the area.

"What do you see?" asked Michael.

"The corners could be scaled," he informed them. "Where the stones overlap. Someone could use the protrusions to grip with their hands and feet."

"We have archers and guards posted here," Hugh said. "Do you believe they could do this?"

"How many of us are there compared to them?" Richard asked. "If they outnumbered us, they could divert our eyes just long enough to allow one or two to get to places such as this."

Michael stood facing the wall, right at the point where the northern wall met the western. He moved his eyes along the line of both tall barriers and saw many small protruding stones along the lengths of their entirety.

"We need to pay more careful attention to the entire structure," he said. "The wall is old and we have not been keeping her in the best of conditions. And Richard is correct. We don't have the numbers to watch everything that happens out here. It's not just the corners that present climbing holds."

"Shall we continue?" Hugh asked as he started moving east, keeping the wall on his right. The dogs bounded to their master's side, stopping briefly for a pat before running ahead.

"We could concentrate our numbers in this section," Michael offered. "After all, the woods here and the grove are where they seem to muster."

"Seem to," Richard replied as his eyes moved along the wall. "For all we know, there could be thousands of them in the southern orchards."

"Do you truly believe that?" Hugh asked.

"No. But I've been wrong before."

"There, there and there." Hugh pointed to three places on the wall. "I bet you little Tomas Warde could climb those with his eyes shut."

"I wouldn't take that bet," Michael replied. "That boy could climb polished marble columns."

The men watched as the dogs vanished into a dense patch of long grass. Now and then, a furry, brown face would pop into view with ears pointed towards the three friends before disappearing again.

Richard smiled as he watched the canines bounding and leaping. One ran towards the tree line a short distance where it squatted. The men averted their eyes to the wall, looking for weaknesses and noting their position as they continued to move along the expanse.

"Why do you think they are focused on this area?" Michael asked. "I mean, you may be right, Richard. They could have men waiting in the south, but their efforts seem to be strongest here."

"Perhaps the river poses a problem," Hugh said. "The three closest bridges to cross are within the walls of Woodmyst. The next bridge to the west is beyond the woods, at least twenty miles away. The river is just as wide there as it is here. And there are no bridges to the east."

"No," Richard replied. "But the watercourse thins out to a stream beyond the hills. There are rapids, which make it dangerous to cross but not impossible. Let's not forget that these aggressors gathered on our north. The river turns from that direction before reaching us. Surely, they must know the northern territories if they come from that way. Therefore, they must know of places to cross safely."

The men pondered this as they continued to stroll along the northern boundary of their village. The realisation that their new enemy may surround them on all sides, at all times, was in the back of their minds, but discussing possible strategies of the enemy wasn't something they had done for many, many years.

Not since the Realm War.

Richard remembered a time on the front line of the battlefield; long before any of the council members were leaders of their community, long before any of them had married or had children. Before they had made Barnard Shelley chief of Woodmyst and any of them had been regarded as responsible, they were soldiers.

***

Fireballs, fired from catapults, streamed through the dark sky above and smashed into the earth, crushing the foot soldiers committed to combat beneath the barrage. Archers fired flaming arrows randomly into the field from both sides, unknowing whether they struck friend or foe.

The seven men, part of a troop of twenty, and one dog moved in unison across the expanse of mud, blood and fire, slashing and hacking anyone they came across. In such conditions, it was impossible to differentiate between their own and enemy's armour.

Survival was far too important to care about such trivial things.

"Wait," Michael called to his friends.

The troop stopped and raised their shields.

"Look," he called, pointing to the sky. A great fireball rocketed through the sky towards them. "Go left."

The men scurried to the side.

The fireball crashed into the ground, sending sparks in all directions. Two of the troop members had fire strike them on their backs. Alan tackled one to the ground and rolled him in the mud, extinguishing the flames immediately.

The other man fled, causing the flames to grow and engulf him as he ran. Eventually. he fell, screaming as he writhed in pain. The screams stopped when the body finally lay still.

Barnard moved his gaze from the burning corpse to lock with forty enemy soldiers just beyond. He gave a loud cry and ran for them. The troop followed and rushed towards their foes.

Swords clashed as the two forces met.

The men fought wildly, stabbing, slashing, and hacking madly at one another. Barnard fought the hardest, taking three men on at the same time and dropping them to the earth within moments of engaging.

Hugh blocked and parried with a swordsman of equal skill. Realising he had no chance with a long blade, he quickly pulled his dagger from his belt and moved in close to his opponent. In one swift motion, he pushed the thin blade up through the chin until he hit bone and twisted.

Blood dribbled from the lips of the enemy soldier as his eyes rolled back in their sockets. The man fell in a crumpled heap onto the ground before Hugh moved onto the next.

Five of the enemy soldiers turned and ran in the opposite direction after seeing what happened to their allies. Hugh glanced down to the hound, which immediately gave chase.

The dog closed the distance rapidly. It nipped the ankle of a lagging escapee and sent the man tumbling. His sword flew from his hand and landed out of reach.

Before he had time to react, the canine had its teeth buried deep in the soldier's throat, ripping, tearing violently at the man's flesh.

The fallen warrior gargled his last breath as the dog tore an enormous chunk of meat from the soldier's neck.

"Good dog," Hugh said as he caught up to the hound.

The troop finished the remaining enemy, losing another two of their own. Now they were nine.

"Some escaped and headed for those trees," Hugh announced, pointing to a forest some distance away.

Barnard turned his face towards the battle and thought about his options for a moment. Fiery arrows streaked across the air and plunged into ally and enemy alike.

Giant balls of flame fell from the sky and exploded among groups of men battling on the field.

"We give chase," he instructed.

***

Richard brought his thought back into focus.

He didn't know why his mind returned to that particular moment. There were many instances where swords had clashed during combat, but that was one battle he had tried so desperately to forget.

He closed his eyes tightly and willed the memory from his brain.

"There," Michael announced.

Richard opened his eyes to see his friend pointing to a section of the northern wall. Some stones sat at odd angles and stuck out of the wall slightly.

There stood another possible climbing place.

"Perhaps we should get hot oil to pour over the wall," Hugh suggested. "Just a precaution."

Richard's mind returned to the forest in his past and what lay beyond its borders.

Ten

The potato peelings piled high in the barrel beside her. They had placed her and seven serves on preparation duty, beginning with the worst job of all; peeling the vegetables.

The small blade in her hand slid along the surface of the dirty, brown mass, lifting the skin to reveal white flesh beneath. She observed how quickly the serves could do this compared with her efforts.

"You've had practice, I assume?" she asked the young woman sitting beside her.

"I do this every day, my lady," the serve answered. "If you don't mind me asking, why are you here?"

Martha smiled as she plopped a freshly peeled potato into a pot of water before reaching for another from the pile of dirty vegetables on the floor.

"I just need to keep myself busy."

"I understand," the serve replied as she dropped a spud into the pot and retrieved a new one. "An idle mind can drive you mad. That's something my father always says."

"Wise words," Martha said as she slid the blade across the potato's surface. She noticed the young woman next to her was already more than halfway through peeling and well on her way to finishing. Martha had barely taken two strips off the spud in her hand.

"Don't worry, my lady," the serve said. "You'll get quicker with practice."

Martha smiled. She didn't want to get quicker. She wanted to be home in her bed each night, knowing her family was safe with her in their house. She'd rather peel potatoes slowly as she talked with her husband and then sit by his side after their meal as they watched their daughters play together on the floor.

Sitting in the kitchens wasn't something Martha desired. What woman would want this for herself?

She was thankful to her husband and the chief for allowing her to work during this precarious time, but she didn't want it. Having her family divided as Peter stood watch upon the wall and her children were under the care of others was not her desire.

She wanted her family together, in their living room, eating and laughing together as it was before the strangers came.

Still, she smiled outwardly as she peeled potatoes with the seven serves. Inside, she screamed for familiarity and ordinariness again.

A few male serves carrying freshly cut portions of meat entered the room and stacked them onto a large wooden table nearby. Fresh blood spattered and smeared across their chests, stomachs and shoulders of the men's coverings.

"This is for the roasting tonight," said one young man. "We've got more to bring to you. Chief Shelley requires the meat to be seasoned before you take it to the fireplace for cooking."

"Ooh, spuds tonight," said another.

"How many cows is this then?" asked one of the female serves as she dropped a peeled potato into the pot.

"This is just part of one," said the first man. "We butchered two. Looks like we might need to bring some inside the gate for safety though."

Martha gave the man a quizzical look. "What do you mean?"

"Some cows have gone missing, my lady," he explained. "Probably just spooked by what's been going on. You know. But the head butcher thinks these ghouls might have stolen them. Who knows?"

"I guess the ghouls get hungry, too," said the other man. "How many spuds are you cooking tonight? Can I get three?"

"Shut up about your spuds." The first man gripped the other by the arm. "Come on. We have got more meat to get."

With that, the men left the room.

"Those poor cows." The young woman by Martha's side shook her head. "I forgot about them being out there the whole time. Who knows what those things out there are doing to them?"

"Probably the same as us. Eating them," suggested another serve with a chuckle.

***

"Why wasn't I informed?" Chief Shelley turned his face towards a serve standing behind his throne in the Great Hall. Surrounding him were the four elders in chairs.

The large tables that spanned the platform during meal times had been stacked and placed to the rear of the raised area, beside the hidden stairwell that led to the living quarters above. Five serves stood before the stacked tables.

Martha stood on the rug in front of the platform, facing Chief Shelley. Three female serves of varying ages were behind her, preparing the grand fireplace with firewood.

"This is the first I have heard about it, my lord," one serve replied, stepping forward. "Would you like me to investigate?"

"Absolutely," the chief replied. "Who knows what else might be missing. Get someone to take stock of the sheep as well."

"Yes, my lord," the serve replied with a bow before he walked off the platform and towards the large doors at the front of the Great Hall.

"Thank you for bringing this to my attention, Martha," said the chief. "Please let me know if you hear any other news such as this."

"Of course, Barnard," she replied. She hurried through the passage to the side of the platform and vanished from the view of the men.

"Our livestock." Chief Shelley shook his head.

"We had to expect something of the sort," Edmond said. "The cattle have no protection outside the walls."

"Are we able to bring all the livestock into the village?" Nicolas questioned.

"And put them where?" responded the chief.

"Chief Shelley is right." Eowyn leant back in his chair. "There simply is no shelter large enough. The only answer would be to let them roam the streets during the night."

"That would not be wise," Frederick put in. "Our soldiers and runners will need the streets clear of obstructions."

Chief Shelley listened intently to the words of the four men. Each had a valid point, but Frederick won the argument. The streets needed to be vacant during the night.

"The cattle and sheep remain outside the walls," the chief instructed. "We will simply need to bear the loss."

"And if they all disappear?" Edmond asked.

"We'll need to survive on grain and vegetables," Chief Shelley answered, as he turned to the remaining serves behind him. "Boy," he called to one.

The young serve stepped forward and bowed.

"Take a horse and cart out to the orchards to collect potatoes and pumpkins," Chief Shelley ordered. "Gather as many as you can to help you. We are on borrowed time. Be back before sundown."

"Yes, my lord," the lad replied as he bowed.

Chief Shelley rubbed his hand across his forehead as the boy left the room.

"Do you think that will be enough?" Nicolas queried. "Pumpkins and potatoes?"

"I have no idea," the chief retorted. "I know that if they starve us out of supplies, terrible things could occur."

***

As farmers worked in the southern orchards to gather what crops they could, shepherds and herders counted the livestock dotted upon the eastern pastureland. Dogs were used to steer the cattle and sheep together in small groups.

When final tallies were made and double-checked, the counters gathered by the eastern gate to combine the score.

After careful deliberation, the men agreed they were missing five cows and seven sheep.

The serves delivered the news to Alan, the lucky councilman given the duty of overseeing the counting. He had never experienced something so uninteresting to do in his entire life. Watching the grass grow would have provided a much-needed adrenaline rush compared to the excitement he experienced during the afternoon.

The final count and summation were written upon parchment and handed to the council member. Alan rolled the vellum into a scroll of sorts and entered the gate. He rushed through the streets of Woodmyst, intent to bring the news to the village chief.

Politely, he greeted those who stopped him in the streets. Fortunately, there weren't many who did this. Most of the men were still resting up in their homes after standing watch on the wall during the night before.

Alan made his way to the Great Hall and entered. He passed by the monolithic beams and under the watch of carved dragonheads as he rounded the grand fireplace.

The kindling had been lit and was now being cared for by two serves that started placing larger pieces of wood. Alan glanced to the ceiling out of habit and checked to make sure the panels that acted as a flue were open. The smoke from the fire was drifting upwards and disappearing through the vents into the open air beyond.

He climbed the steps to the raised platform where the chief and four elders sat. Without saying a word, Alan handed the rolled-up parchment to Chief Shelley and stood back to wait for a response.

The chief eyeballed him; his expression perplexed as Alan handed the parchment over. He unfurled it and read it silently as the elders watched on.

"By the gods!" he exclaimed before reading the notes again. "Five cows and seven sheep? How could that go so unnoticed?"

"The men have been tending the wall, Barnard," Alan replied. "They've neither had the time nor the energy to fulfil their regular duties."

"Still," the chief said, shaking his head, "that's quite a number to have simply disappeared."

"I'm surprised it isn't a larger quantity," said Alan.

"They could have been spooked and run off," suggested Nicolas.

"Do you truly believe that?" Alan asked.

The old man scratched his beard and lifted his eyebrows.

"They will take more," Alan opined. "We would do the same if we were the aggressors. May I suggest we butcher a few cows and sheep, salt the meat and put it into storage? It won't last more than a week, but I honestly think if any of us is still alive by then, we would be rid of these strangers."

The four elders puzzled over Alan's words. Chief Shelley grimaced, understanding their meaning.

"In other words," he said, "you think we'll be dead before then."

Alan cocked his head. "Not without a fight."

***

Several farmers hacked at the hard ground with spades and hoes in a desperate attempt to gather as much of the crops as they could. Drenched in sweat and exhausted, they lifted potatoes and pumpkins from the soil and piled them into the cart that one serve drove.

The crops had barely filled the wagon more than halfway, and the workers feared they wouldn't be able to add much more to the stockpile. Most of the crops were still immature and not ready for harvesting.

Still, they took what they could.

The sun was dipping towards the western horizon. They had another three hours of light left at most. The serve on the cart looked at the load and the faces of the surrounding workers.

"Do you think we can gather much more?" he asked a well-weathered farmer nearby.

"There's not much left that we can call edible," the farmer replied as he dug his spade into the dirt to lift a few small spuds from the ground.

The serve looked around one last time before setting his eyes upon the sun in the sky.

"Pack it up," he called out. "This will have to do."

The farmers and workers collected what reaps they could and placed them into the wagon. The serve flicked his reins and the mare towing the wagon leisurely moved forward. Slowly, the men made their way back to the village.

***

The blacksmith apprentices forged arrow tips and fixed them onto long, thin shafts of wood. On the rear end of the arrow, they fitted three small triangular sheets of metal instead of the traditional feathers.

They were roughly halfway through filling Chief Shelley's order. The senior blacksmiths instructed the apprentices to deliver what arrows they had made to the armoury. The sun was gradually lowering towards the top of the western wall and night would be upon them before they knew it.

The apprentices loaded up a hand wagon with finished arrows and several resharpened blades the older smiths had been working on. Two of the younger men pushed the cart carefully through the streets as another two walked ahead, clearing the path of obstruction and holding traffic back as they progressed through the village.

Eventually, they came to the building that housed the weaponry. With the help of a few male serves, they unloaded the wagon. They divided arrows and slid into leather quivers that hung from hooks above racks of bows. Swords and daggers were sheathed and positioned upon the large, long tables in the centre of the room.

The young apprentices returned to the blacksmiths' store with the hand wagon as the serves continued to prepare the armoury for the night watch.

"How goes it?" Peter asked as he entered the building.

"I think we've got it under control, my lord," answered a serve.

Peter observed, as helmets, chest plates, and shields were neatly placed upon the benches that ran along the walls. They filled wineskins with water and set them beside each pile of armour. It was a tedious job for the serves, but it made the mustering of the soldiers move quicker if each warrior could access his equipment easily.

Peter inspected the equipment and the work the serves had done. He lifted a helmet or two to check for rust or wear and tear on the leather straps. The councilman briefly examined the blades on the table before he moved to the new arrows.

He lifted one from a quiver that hung upon the wall. He touched the tip before carefully running his finger along the sharp barbs on the sides. His eyes moved to the tail, in particular the metal feathers.

"This is new," he said as the serves watched on. "Do we know if this works?"

The serves looked to one another for an answer.

"Let's find out," Peter suggested as he lifted a bow from a rack. He positioned himself alongside the serves and pointed the arrow into the room, to the rear wall.

A broad axe hung in the centre of the wall and posed the perfect target. He aimed just above the axe, intending to hit the wall in that spot. Tightening the muscles in the small of his back, he positioned the arrow's nock onto the string and pulled back to his shoulder.

With a quick movement of his fingers, he released the arrow, allowing it to zip through the air with a loud whistle. A sharp clang informed the men that Peter had missed his mark, but not by much.

It was where the arrow had landed that surprised the onlookers more than Peter's ability to shoot.

The tip had penetrated the wall less than an inch lower than where he had intended to land it. In order to do so, it had passed through the axe's blade first.

"By the gods," a serve gasped in disbelief.

Peter chuckled merrily.

***

Catherine Warde watched on as her daughter Linet giggled and played with Agnes and Jane Fysher on the rug in their living room. She sat in a rocking chair as she darned a pair of Alan's trousers, smiling as the sound of laughter filled the room.

Tomas wasn't able to cope with what he perceived as constant cackling. Feeling outnumbered after his father left to conduct certain duties, Tomas opted to venture to the stables, where he would rather shovel clumps of manure.

At least that's what he told the group of ladies before accusing them of sounding like angry poultry and storming out through the door. His mother had ordered him home before sundown and he had shouted a promise as he ran down the street.

Upon arriving at the stables, he noticed two men pouring grain into the feeding troughs. Another three were brushing horses down as they whispered to the large animals. The smell of straw and manure filled his senses.

"May I help?" he asked politely.

He waited to be handed a brush or a scoop to dig grain from the barrel and pour into the manger. Instead, the burly stable master appeared from within a stall and sauntered over to the young boy.

"You're Alan Warde's son, are you not?"

"Yes, sir," he answered with a smile. So, this man knows who my father is and who I am. "My father is Alan Warde."

"Well then," the horseman smiled, "if you're half the worker your father is then you can help us a great deal." He reached into a nearby stall and retrieved a shovel that was leaning against the wall. Steadily, he held it out to the young boy who took it despondently. "Shit needs shovelling."

All the men in the stables laughed.

Their chuckles tempted Tomas to throw the shovel down and run back to the annoying giggling of the girls at home. At least there, he knew they weren't laughing at him.

However, he knew this would disappoint his father, who was a leader in the village. He didn't fully understand what being a leader entailed, but he understood it was so important that other people were watching what you did.

He gripped the handle of the shovel in both hands. It was too large for him. A broad smile stretched across his face, and he locked eyes with the stable master, lifting his head proudly.

"Where do I begin?"

After an hour of scooping mounds of brown turds into wooden buckets and asking many questions, he had cleaned out three stalls and learnt that they would use the collected waste for fertiliser on the orchards. He struggled with the shovel as he worked and had broken a sweat during the exertion.

He filled twelve buckets to the brim with steaming manure, and he was working on topping another off. Tomas didn't know horses could hold so much within them.

"Does this get done every day?" he asked.

"Shovelling?" quizzed a stable hand.

"Yes," Tomas clarified.

"Every day," the stable hand replied. "We load the buckets and take them to the farms."

Tomas scraped the blade of the shovel across the dirt and lifted another scoop into the bucket standing beside him.

"That's a lot of manure," he said. "Every day?"

"Every day," the stable hand reaffirmed.

After another hour, the hefty stable master told him to go home. Tomas protested until the hefty man informed him the sun was falling beyond the western wall.

The boy remembered his promise to his mother to be home before sunset. He thanked the stable master for letting him stay and turned to run home.

He suddenly turned and locked eyes with the burly man one more time.

"Can I come back tomorrow?"

The beefy horseman peered at him curiously. "D'ya like shovelling turds, son?"

Tomas nodded his head, yes.

The man looked around at the faces of the other men in the room, who all either shrugged or nodded their approval of the lad.

"We bathe the horses tomorrow just after sunrise," the stable master informed him. "If your father and mother give you permission, you are more than welcome here."

"Thank you," Tomas called as he turned and ran off into the street.

His feet moved so quickly he felt he was flying. The grin on his face had grown so wide it almost hurt.

He couldn't wait to get home and tell his mother and father what he had been doing. His excitement and joy were so overwhelming that he almost didn't see the people and other obstructions on the road. It was as if by instinct that he avoided hitting other villagers as they moved about in the street.

He bolted along the path that led to the door of the house and flung the door open.

The girls seemed to be still sitting and cackling in the same place they had been when he left, but his mother had moved to the stove at the rear of the room. Tomas' eyes suddenly met his father's look from the padded chair in the corner.

"Where have you been and why are you so happy?" Alan quizzed.

"I've been shovelling shit and I want to do it again tomorrow," he shouted with glee. "Can I?"

Eleven

With the sun sinking into the forest to the west, many of the villagers made their way towards the centre of town. Women walked with their husbands, some hand in hand, others with children in tow. Their destination was the Great Hall.

Most of the villagers walked slowly in an attempt to spend as much time as they could with their loved ones. Once they arrived at the Great Hall, they would say their farewells and separate. The women and children would enter the building while the men departed to the armoury to prepare for the night watch.

Until then, and for as long as the sun still illuminated the sky, they would stay together.

The closer they came to the centre of the village, the more people they encountered. Children following their parents saw this as an opportunity to meet up with their friends. Some raced ahead to the Great Hall and played in the road until their fathers and mothers caught up with them.

Ushered inside by their elders, the children didn't stop their frolicking but behaved in a much more subdued manner. It was as if an unwritten law was engraved upon them whereby, they understood that inside and outside behaviour are different.

As four female serves turned the roast beef hung on a spit, the fireplace was roaring ablaze. The smell of cooking meat was inviting. Women, children and old men gathering in the building wagged their chins about how much they were looking forward to the night's meal.

For a moment, they all forgot about the threat from outside the walls and what the young men may face during the watch on the wall.

People clustered into groups around the Great Hall. Bedding had been made up during the day and places allocated to families. Children, too young to understand and oblivious to the happenings within the village, clambered over the furniture and wrestled on the floor.

Adults grouped chairs into tight circles near their allotments and discussed the occurrences of the day before moving onto the topic of the week. Who were the outsiders?

As more and more people arrived, the children's games grew louder and the circle of chairs became larger. Old men and women talked about the weather and how the rain must be upon them because their bunions were aching.

The men of the village who were young enough to stand watch waited for their wives and children to enter through the giant doors of the Great Hall before continuing on their way to the armoury. It was a short walk along the street to the building where the town's weapons and armour were stored.

Once there, they would enter the door to the large room with benches lining the walls and large, long tables in the centre. The men would find a pile of armour on the benches and put it on before selecting the weapon of choice.

Archers, specifically trained for the role, would take a bow from the rack against the far wall and a leather quiver from the hanging hook above. Pikemen, usually unskilled, grabbed long spears from a bracket positioned in an adjoining room. Swordsmen, the more disciplined of the soldiers, either brought their own blades or took from the pile of sheathed blades upon the tables.

Slowly the sun sank out of view, turning the sky from orange to pink, to a deep mauve. Some stars winked awake in the eastern sky, signalling to the men that it was time to take up their positions. The pikemen and swordsmen made their way to positions beside the eastern and western gates, while the archers climbed upon the walls of Woodmyst.

Alan and Peter found themselves on the northeast tower once again. The air was chilly and the exhaling breath of men appeared as thick mist jetting from men's nostrils and mouths. Stamping his feet and jumping brought little warmth to Alan's bones as he shivered slightly in the evening air.

His wife had robed him in a bearskin after he dressed for battle. She told him the night air would be cold and probably would take him before any arrow or blade did. For her comfort more than his, he agreed to wear the skin over his armour.

He was glad he did.

"That gets shared about tonight," Peter said, acknowledging the brown furry garment hanging over his friend's shoulders.

"Go kill your own bear if you want one," Alan replied with a wry smile.

"Bastard," hissed Peter, as he wrapped his arms about his chest and stamped his feet.

The deep lilac glow in the sky drifted into the west as the light from the sun vanished. Stars twinkled to life across the expanse above as a scroll of dark clouds swept in from the north.

The sheep instinctively made their way towards the wall for safety. Alan believed the timid creatures were far more intelligent than he'd thought. The cows, however, were still out in the pasture and now sat much lower on the scale of smart things.

He scanned the meadow for any sign of the livestock and saw a few white dots on the side of the hill in the east.

The lack of light made it difficult to spot anything, but the specks that were so far away moved and behaved like cattle.

At least he thought they were cattle.

Waterfowl frolicked upon the water's edge, which set some archers nearby on edge. One pulled back on his bowstring, arrow loaded.

"Don't shoot," Peter called. "We don't need to waste ammunition on ducks. Besides, they're too far off for you to hit."

"Sorry, my lord," the archer called back bashfully, lowering his bow.

Peter eyed Alan, shaking his head as if to say, silly young boy, playing soldier.

Alan replied with a look of his own, raising his eyebrows, he's just scared.

A light mist rose from the river as thunder echoed in the distance. All eyes moved in the direction of the sound.

Silent flashes of light danced among the clouds hanging above the mountains. The men's countenances fell. It was bad enough having to stand watch upon the wall.

Now a storm headed their way.

The warriors longed to be home near the warmth of a fire, in the embrace of their women and within earshot of their children's laughter.

Gentle, distant thunder rumbled through the mountains and across the meadow as it bounced between sky and earth. More light flickered and flashed in the gathering clouds, causing hearts to sink.

"Let's hope it doesn't rain," one of the tower guards said.

"It will now," Alan replied, "won't it?"

"What do you mean?" the guard asked.

"You had to mention it," Peter informed him. "If you say something like that, then it will happen. It's just the way things are. I hope it doesn't rain, results in rain. Got it?"

"Sorry." The guard furrowed his brow confusedly before smiling. "I still hope it doesn't rain."

The other tower guard laughed. Alan grimaced and shook his head as he continued to scan the trees for any sign of movement.

"I heard your son may have found his calling," Peter said.

"What do you mean?" Alan asked as he leant upon the guardrail.

"The stable master told me he's good with a shovel," chuckled Peter.

"Bastard." Alan shook his head.

***

Lawrence stared blankly towards the area where the grove joined the forest. His thoughts trailed off to the loaded wagon he had stored behind his cottage, not too far from where he stood.

His intent was to leave Woodmyst at dawn with his family and head south to one of the larger cities. A calming peace filled him when he informed his wife of his decision. She shared his relief. But now, standing upon the north-western tower, his mind wrestled with whether he should tell his friends.

Hugh stood nearby, moving his eyes from the peak of the north-eastern tower, across the grove and over the façade of the forest to the west. The mist had crept silently from the river to the road outside of the western gate. His eyes followed the road to where it disappeared into the dark shadows cast by the forest trees.

The trees seemed to form a tunnel of sorts, reaching their branches over the road in an arch to create a shadowy passageway beneath. A thick fog rolled through the growth in that place, obscuring the view of anything beyond the tree line.

Dull thunder echoed from the mountains as Hugh turned to his friend. Still staring blankly at the same place, Lawrence scratched at his long red beard as he pondered what to do.

"You appear troubled," Hugh remarked.

Lawrence seemed to snap back to reality. He turned his face towards the other and smiled. "I'm just tired," he lied.

Hugh sensed the untruth in the statement and kept his eyes on Lawrence who lowered his gaze and returned to staring at the trees before him.

"Are you sure that's all it is?"

"Mmh," grunted Lawrence in the affirmative, avoiding conversation as if it were the plague.

Hugh let his eyes remain on the other man for a moment longer. The answer didn't satisfy. But he knew Lawrence well enough to know not to pursue with questions.

It was early in the night, and he had plenty of time to revisit the topic.

The thunder rumbled a little louder as lightning flashed through the clouds gathering above.

Hugh winced as a drop of rain hit him on the cheek.

***

"That's terrific," Richard called out sarcastically.

A light sprinkle fell from the sky, placing a fine film of water over everything. The towers had rooves, but the viewing area was still open to the elements. The precipitation was falling at an angle that defied the shelter above them.

"This is going to make it an enjoyable night," he said to the two guards with him.

"Why didn't they build an awning on this thing?" asked a guard at the shelter above him. "Something that extends over the sides a little."

"You're a carpenter, Lewis," said the other guard. "Guess what your job will be tomorrow."

"I'll inform the chief first thing in the morning." Richard smiled.

"Thank you very much," Lewis spat at the other guard, who laughed in response.

The sprinkling gained velocity and turned into a steady rain. The icy breeze from the north blew the rain into the viewing platform. Instinctively, the men moved to the southern edge in an attempt to keep dry. They kept their upper bodies away from the shower, but their trousers were soaking the water in.

Richard turned his head to see how the archers on the wall were holding up. Each man was holding his position and had pulled his hood over his helmet for some reprieve from the falling rain.

The lightning above and the low thunder was a sign to Richard that this was only just beginning. The worst was yet to come.

Suddenly, as if something tore the air around them open, a loud ripping sound rocketed through the sky from above the forest and past the tower towards the southern orchards. The men on the wall and in the tower turned their heads to follow the source of the sound but saw nothing.

An abrupt gust of wind almost knocked Richard off his feet. The rain changed direction momentarily before resuming its original pattern.

Something big had moved by them.

Something that owned the skies.

***

The deafening sound reminded Michael of fabric being torn, except it was moving around him from the west towards the south. He squinted as rain sprayed over his face, trying to observe the cause of the resonating noise.

A giant black shadow zoomed between the silhouette of the southwestern tower and the forest. Michael had trouble keeping his eyes on it as it lifted high into the sky as it drew nearer to the orchards.

A sudden flash of lightning illuminated the creature as it reached the lower clouds in the air. It was monstrous.

In the tiny moment Michael could view the beast, he noted the features he saw. A pointed head sat upon a long neck, which led to a thick torso. Two membranous giant wings with three long, bony fingers stretched out from its shoulders. The last thing he saw was a long tail trailing behind as it flapped its wings and suddenly vanished into darkness as the lightning subsided.

A terrible roar of thunder shook the tower the men stood upon. The sound of thunder diminished and the creature bellowed a guttural call that echoed across the sky. Michael's heart raced and pounded in his ears. He continued to stare in the direction he had last seen the flying beast.

"By the gods," gasped a tower guard. "What was that?"

Twelve

"Did you hear that?" gasped a guard standing beside Peter.

All eyes moved towards the south where a great yawn had bellowed through the air. Something terrible was calling out from that direction.

"See anything?" Peter asked.

"Nothing," Alan replied as he peered towards the south-eastern tower. He could barely make out the forms of the men standing upon it let alone anything beyond.

The sky was pitch black, and the rain created a haze over everything between their position and anything beyond the first row of rooftops nearby.

Peter peered down the exterior of the wall to the sheep huddled against it. They acted skittishly, turning their heads towards the direction from which the noise came.

Nervously, they huddled and struggled against each other in a mad attempt to get to the centre of their group.

He strode to the other side of the tower and looked down to the small band of soldiers gathered below. They were glancing up to the wall and then to him for someone to explain what was happening.

It seemed a mass confusion infected them all. No one had the faintest idea of what made the gut-wrenching sound. All they understood was that something new had presented itself.

Something tremendously terrible.

Something to be afraid of.

Clanging from the north-western tower broke the silence and snapped everyone back to reality. All eyes shifted to the direction of the chime.

Peter dropped his gaze to the men below the tower and called out for a runner to be sent.

A soldier obliged by tearing off full speed along the road.

Peter kept his eyes upon the north-western tower while Alan stared off towards the south. It was at that moment when one guard realised their attention had been divided.

Some were looking south as others looked west.

But nobody was watching the east.

The guard moved to the guardrail and panned his gaze across the dark expanse of pastureland. He could no longer see the mist from the river. The rain had washed it away.

The steady pour obscured his view of the meadow before him but the hairs on his neck stood up, and he knew he was being watched.

The sheep below stopped moving and averted their gaze from the south towards the east. They sensed it too.

Breaking through the air, a high-pitched whistle sounded as a blackened arrow zipped through the air and landed deep into the guard's heart.

He stood motionless for a moment, not believing what had happened.

Slowly he turned to the others upon the tower with him as he raised a hand to the rod sticking from his chest.

Alan was still staring to the south as Peter and the other guard looked to the west.

The wounded guard opened his mouth to speak. He had the wind knocked out of him, and all he could manage was a barely audible wheeze. "My lords?"

All eyes moved to the guard who stared at them wide-eyed and confused.

He fell, pierced through. Motionless, the guard bled onto the wet platform. The falling rain washed his blood through the wooden boards.

Alan stared towards the grassland.

A sudden flash of lightning revealed scores of hooded figures standing upon the field. There were too many to count.

Peter turned his eyes a moment too late to see the crowd outside the wall. Darkness met his gaze, but he knew someone was out there.

"Ring the alarm," Alan ordered the guard.

The guard complied immediately, hitting the small mallet against the iron chime that hung from the rafters.

Now, two towers signalled the town of danger.

"Archers ready," Peter called to the men upon the eastern wall.

The archers loaded their bows.

"There are many," Alan informed his friend.

"How far out?"

"Perhaps fifty yards," he replied.

"Fifty?" Peter breathed, finding it hard for anyone to be able to hit a target like a guard so precisely at that distance.

Alan nodded.

"Aim, fifty yards," Peter shouted.

"Aim fifty yards," another called further down the line.

"Are you sure you want to do this?" Alan asked, yelling over the sound of the clanging alarm. "Our men are shooting blindly."

"They can't retreat that quickly," Peter answered.

"Loose!" he called.

The eastern wall sent a barrage of arrows into the night sky. They flew at great velocity, silently heading for their target fifty yards away.

Alan signalled for the alarm to cease. The tower guard held the hammer to his side as they waited and listened for any sound to come from outside of the wall.

They expected to hear the screams and cries of injured men. Instead, they heard ringing in their ears that resonated from the clanging alarm and the sound of pattering raindrops.

Another high-pitched whistle resounded through the air. An archer, some distance down the eastern line from the north-eastern tower, was punctured through the throat with a black shaft. He stepped back towards the edge of the wall. Some men attempted to stop him but he toppled to the ground below.

"By the gods," Peter hissed.

"They see us, but we don't see them," Alan said. "They can pick us off one by one."

As if to credit Alan's point, another arrow struck an archer further down the line. This one broke through the bridge of the man's nose and dug into his skull.

"I'm at a loss, Alan," Peter confessed. "What do we do? Should we send soldiers out to meet them?"

"No," Alan replied. "That's what they want."

Lightning bounced in the clouds above, enough to shed some light upon the meadow. Alan briefly saw many hooded figures moving about. Some were closer to the village, others further away.

"Send another volley," Alan suggested. "Stagger the targets. Some closer, some further out."

"I don't understand," Peter admitted.

"They're moving about," Alan explained. "The darkness is their cover and they're using it to vary their positions."

"Archers ready," Peter called. Someone once again repeated the order further along the wall. "I hope you're right," he said to Alan.

"So do I."

"Vary your targets," Peter ordered. "Thirty, fifty, sixty yards."

He waited for the order to be relayed along the barrier. "Loose!"

Arrows flung into the air and the warriors crouched behind the protection of the wall and waited silently in anticipation for a result.

They were not disappointed.

Several screams and roars bellowed across the field.

None sounded like the calls of men.

"What was that?" the tower guard cried.

***

The tower guard in the north-western tower dropped the hammer to the floor. The clanging alarm pealed into the night air, overtaken by the sound of pelting rain. He faced towards the east and peered across the rooftops to the wall at the opposite side of the village.

Lawrence and Hugh were giving their full attention to the tree line. The sudden silence caused Hugh to turn his head to the guard.

"Why did you stop?" he asked.

"I think something is happening on the eastern wall."

"What?" Hush quizzed, stepping away from the guardrail and closer to the guard. He scanned the eastern horizon but saw only flashes of lightning in the clouds and rain.

"I don't know, my lord. There just seems to be movement along the top of the wall. I think they're engaged with the enemy."

"A runner from the eastern wall, my lords," a voice called from below.

"What news has he?" Hugh called.

"Nothing, my lord. His orders are to find out why we sounded the alarm."

"They must have sent him before whatever is happening over there started," Lawrence suggested.

Hugh nodded in agreement. "Tell him we have spotted torches in the trees," Hugh called down. "Now there is just one remaining."

He stared through the rain at one flickering light that stood alone where the grove met the forest. It hadn't moved in some time.

"Perhaps this one is a distraction," Lawrence proposed.

"Should we send some of our archers to the eastern wall?" one of the tower guards asked.

"No," Hugh replied. "We don't know how many are out there. The eastern wall could be the distraction while they gather their forces here. We can't afford to thin our defences in any place."

"We should find out what is going on over there," Lawrence said.

Hugh strode across the platform and peered over the side to the soldiers below. "Send a runner to find out what is happening on the eastern wall," he instructed.

"Yes, my lord," the voice below replied.

Within moments they heard the patter of two sets of feet running through the street as the runner from the far wall returned to his post with a runner from the west.

Lawrence locked his eyes upon the flickering light just within the trees. He sensed something was out there watching them.

A chill ran up his spine as he thought about the imminent threat upon the village's borders. His mind pictured the loaded wagon once again, and he knew he was making the right decision to leave.

"What's on your mind?" Hugh asked.

"Nothing," he responded. "I'm just concerned about whoever is out there and what they want with us."

It wasn't entirely a lie. He was concerned about the invaders. Hugh didn't need to know he and his family were leaving in the morning. He would keep that news to himself.

He wasn't sure why he wanted to keep it to himself.

Was it out of pride?

Perhaps he just didn't want to argue with his friends about the reasons why he should stay.

Maybe it was shame.

Regardless, he would hold on to his secret and leave telling none of them.

With luck, he would be upon the southern mountain pass before anyone realised he was gone.

Until then, he focused upon the flickering light within the tree line and pondered why these foes had chosen Woodmyst as their target.

It wasn't as if they were a wealthy village. They fished and farmed. That was all.

The miners in the cities to the south had more wealth with what jewels they dug from the ground. They had gold, rubies and diamonds to spare.

Woodmyst had milk, wool and crops.

The comparison was baseless.

There was nothing here to warrant invasion.

Yet here they were.

Invaders surrounded them and held them at siege in their own homes.

The lone light flickered, wafting in the breeze slightly as the rain fell steadily all around. Lightning flashed above, sending thunderous roars to the ground.

Lawrence let his thoughts return to the wagon.

Thirteen

Leaning over the eastern side of the tower as far as he could, Michael moved his eyes between the archers on the wall to the meadow on the northern side of the river. The enemy was there. They hadn't crossed the water to attack the southern end of the structure.

"Keep watch of the river," he called to the tower guards. "I can't see these bastards through the rain. If anything large makes a splashdown there, I want it taken down immediately."

Lightning opened the sky with a bright white light and illuminated the pastureland. The men on the south-eastern tower saw an enormous mass of hooded figures near to the wall on the northern side of the waterway.

Darkness veiled everything again as a clap of thunder shook the tower. Michael saw spots before his eyes as they tried to readjust after the sudden flash of light.

"Dammit," he called. "I can't see a thing."

"A report from below says they're targeting archers, my lord," a guard called from the far side of the tower platform.

"Keep to the cover," Michael hollered along the wall to the archers nearby.

Part of him wished he was with Alan and Peter in the tower at the far end of the wall. At least there, he would be in the thick of the action instead of waiting for something to happen at his current posting.

Then there was the flying creature.

No one had seen hide or hair of it since it climbed into the clouds above. For all he knew, it was still up there waiting for an opportunity to attack. This bout on the north shore could well be the occasion it was looking for. All eyes were scanning the other side of the river when, perhaps, they should have been looking to the south.

Michael kept this in mind and occasionally turned his face towards the air above the orchards for any sign of the monster in the sky.

He pointed to a few of the archers on the southern wall, who were craning their necks in order to see what was happening beyond the river, and yelled to one of the tower guards. "Tell them to keep watch over the plantations. We'll worry about the east."

The guard turned to see the men neglecting their duty and swore.

"Keep watch on your quadrant," he barked.

The men quickly returned to their watch as Michael panned his eyes across the expanse between the hill and the wall between the river and the grove.

He could make out the silhouette of the trees and mountains in the distance. The hooded invaders, however, proved to be more difficult to locate.

The cover of darkness, the steady fall of the rain and the irregular flashes of lightning worked in the enemy's favour.

They could be anywhere.

***

"Make sure the eastern wall is well supplied with ammunition," Chief Shelley called to the men bustling about in the armoury. "And get some cider and water over there."

His anxiety was obvious as he pointed and shouted, paced and commanded his men from the rooms within the armoury. News came constantly of the exchange of arrows on the eastern wall. The need to make sure his men were well supplied became his mission in life.

The chief's biggest trepidation was the imminent return of the flying beast he had heard. He didn't need the reports from the runners to understand the village was under serious threat.

Several serves and soldiers hurried themselves loading sacks, baskets, wooden boxes and their pockets with whatever they could hold. There were arrows, canteens of water, hot cider, loaves of bread and hooded cloaks being sorted into piles.

Some men left, carrying the supplies to the men on the wall as others returned with lists of demands and needs.

"They need more covers," shouted a serve as he burst through the door, sopping wet from the rain.

"We're running low, my lord," another yelled across the din to the chief.

"Take what you can," Chief Shelley instructed.

The men gathered together the cloaks and blankets piled up on the tables and ran back into the downpour. The chief turned to a soldier who was loading a box with arrows, ready to be transferred to the archers upon the eastern wall.

"You," he called.

"Yes, my lord." The soldier stood at attention.

"Go to the Great Hall," Chief Shelley instructed. "Find my wife and tell her we need as many blankets as can be spared. Go!"

The soldier disappeared into the darkness beyond the door.

The chief took overloading the arrows as others around him continued with their duties. Some gave him a sideways glance as they observed their leader partaking in lowly work.

He noticed their stares and shot a quick glance at each of the onlookers.

"I wasn't always chief, gentlemen," he said. "I was once a soldier, like you. Filling boxes with arrows is not beneath me."

More soldiers and serves entered the door as he finished loading the box. He slid it across the table to a man.

"Take that to the wall," he ordered, as he reached for a fresh box to load.

***

Peering from the southwestern tower, across the orchards in the distance, Richard kept his eyes peeled for any enemy warriors who may try to flank them. Apart from the close call with the monster in the sky, the night had been uneventful at his posting.

The increasing sound of excitement from the east held his curiosity. He turned towards the direction of the noise.

The distance alone was enough to prevent any view of what lay beyond the wall. The steady downpour of rain added to the obstruction.

He forced himself to keep his eyes on the area between the forest to his right and the fields directly ahead of him. Ignoring the noise of shouting that echoed across the village, he scanned the trees slowly, lingering his gaze for a moment longer in certain areas when flashes of lightning illuminated his view.

His eyes flicked towards the clouds every once in a while. The hairs on the back of his neck continued to warn him of the threat from above. Lightning reminded him of the magnificent beast that had rushed past him earlier.

Richard thought back to the alarm from the northern towers. He had since discovered why the chimes rang in the northeast. The reason for the clanging in the north-western tower still eluded him.

A runner had been sent to investigate the reason for the sound but had not returned. Richard refrained from sending another as the hostilities in the eastern barrier had begun by the time he realised one of his men was missing.

He decided he would wait until first light to send men out to find the missing runner. It was most likely another group had sequestered the man and was performing duties elsewhere.

Richard was a little annoyed, but understood most of the men under his command were not trained warriors. Most were farmers, shepherds, and store owners.

If he found the runner again, he would simply remind him of his duty and leave it at that. There was no need to reprimand him for not fulfilling his military duty, especially if he was not military personnel.

Lightning flashed in the clouds above the field exposing the rows of fruit trees and tilled ground to the south. A few small houses dotted the landscape here and there.

There was no movement on the ground.

No hooded figures to threaten them.

Nothing but immature crops and farmland.

Still, Richard's eyes widened in fear, and he froze in place.

High above the harvest fields, nestled amongst the swirling clouds, was the dark form of the winged beast.

For a moment, Richard watched, as it seemed to glide around in a tight circle before the lightning dissipated and allowed the darkness to sweep back into place.

With the ability to see the view before him diminished, he found he could move once again.

"It's back," he called. "It's back. It's back."

One of the tower guards lifted the hammer and struck the chime hanging from the rafters. The alarm rang out across the village drawing the attention of nearby eyes towards the source of the sound.

"Stop," Richard ordered. The guard continued to strike the alarm over and over, unable to hear his commander through the clamour. "Stop," Richard repeated as he grabbed the man's hand. "Stop!" He kept his eyes trained towards the direction of his terrifying vision.

A long, guttural roar bellowed from the black sky above the orchards.

"By the gods," the guard gasped as he dropped the hammer.

"Ready yourselves, men," Richard called along the two walls by the tower. He wished he could recall the words he had spoken. How was anyone going to prepare themselves for what horrors this creature may bring?

A tremendous flash of light revealed the creature silhouetted in the sky, diving directly for the village. It moved at such an intense speed that Richard saw the air and vapour about it swirling like a ship leaving its wake in the sea.

Darkness filled the sky as a deafening thunderclap erupted and the monster called out once more.

Richard placed the palms of his hands against his ears as the giant beast raced by his tower on the left, right above the southern wall.

The archers ducked as a great gust of wind followed the creature, knocking one guard over the side of the tower and two archers from the wall. All three landed in the lane below that passed between the wall and some houses below the tower.

Richard kept his eyes upon the enormous shadow that moved by as it continued to glide towards the Great Hall.

"Oh no," he wheezed.

***

The soldier stood as straight as he could, both arms extended as Sybil Shelley loaded him up with blankets that were stored in an oak chest to the side of the raised platform. "Tell my husband this is all there is."

"I will, my lady," he replied as she took the last blanket from the chest and draped it over the others.

"And tell him his daughters miss him."

"I will, my lady." The soldier nodded.

"And that his wife loves him."

"I will, my lady."

"And to stay safe." She smiled with troubled eyes.

"Of course, my—" the guttural roar of the flying creature calling from outside interrupted him.

The Great Hall shook from the force of the thing above as it swooped past the building, just skimming the rooftop with its long belly.

The soldier buckled at the knees and ducked instinctively. He glanced over to Sybil who was upon her knees holding her hands over her head.

Screams and gasps echoed through the large room as people dived for cover or froze where they were.

Small children hid behind the closest adults and bawled as the monster called into the night again. The sound was terrifying.

***

The enormous creature rose into the night sky and turned towards the northeast. It beat its giant membranous wings once, twice, propelling it higher and higher. Peter and Alan turned towards the flying beast as it called into the darkness, disappearing into shadow and cloud.

Flashes of lightning and thunder filled the air as the rain continued to fall steadily to the ground.

Both men stood transfixed. Their eyes locked upon one area of rain clouds.

"We don't see any movement, my lords," the tower guard called.

They snapped back to reality. There was an enemy out there.

"What did you say?" Peter asked.

"The invaders," the guard replied. "They're either hiding or gone."

Alan peered over the edge of the tower. The sheep still huddled together beneath the structure.

He moved his eyes towards the pastureland and still found it difficult to see anything beyond the falling rain.

"How can you tell they're gone?" Alan quizzed. "I can't see anything."

"Me either," Peter agreed.

"The lightning," the guard informed them.

Both men looked to the guard for more clarification.

He must have sensed their confusion.

"Each time the lightning lit the sky we saw them moving about."

Alan felt like a fool.

"And you can't see them now when the lightning flares up again," he said. "Can you?"

"No, my lord," the soldier replied. "It would seem they have gone."

Alan kept his eyes towards the east, waiting for the sky to light up again. It seemed every time he wanted the lightning to appear, it would purposefully test his patience.

He felt as if he was waiting for something to happen that never would.

"I bet they used that beast to distract us," Peter suggested. "That big bugger probably had every man on watch looking at it as it flew over the village."

"I don't doubt it," Alan put in. "If that was their plan, it worked. I was watching the monster as it passed by."

"As was I," Peter confessed.

"And I," the guard declared.

Keeping his eyes upon the meadow, Alan waited for the lightning.

His patience eventually paid off. Although he felt as if he was watching and waiting for an eternity, only mere seconds had passed.

Sudden, bright light bathed the pastureland.

Cattle gathered about halfway between the wall and the hill to the east. Steep-roofed houses protruded from the long grass here and there. The river continued to flow on the southern side of the meadow, and the grove bordered the north.

The tower guard was correct.

There was no sign of the enemy.

They were gone.

Fourteen

The rain had set in and continued to fall steadily. A grey veil blanketed the sky in all directions. The storm had long since passed and the morning had arrived. The long grass appeared to be tinted with a fresh tinge of green and the meadow flowers opened up to expose their bright colours to the world.

Waterfowl frolicked along the banks on both sides of the river, squawking and splashing. The sheep huddled in the open field allowing the rain to wash over them as the cattle chewed cud, seemingly oblivious to the conditions.

As serves and soldiers collected the fallen warriors from the walls and streets of Woodmyst, other kept watch and scanned the meadow for the enemy.

They saw none.

Not even the dead.

The watchers upon the wall shared their confusion, remarking how it was impossible for there not to be a sign of their foe ever being on the pastureland. Arrows had hit the cloaked figures during the night, producing screaming and calling from the darkness.

Now, as the watchers scrutinised the expanse of grassland before them, there was no evidence of a violent exchange between themselves and the invaders.

No bodies.

No blood.

Not even a stray arrow.

"We should send the dogs," Peter suggested to Alan. "Their noses might pick up a scent."

"I have a feeling they won't find anything," replied the other. "But you are right. We need to get out there and conduct a search before we lose any track in this rain."

Peter called down the side of the wall for dogs to be fetched and soldiers to conduct a search from the gate and up to seventy yards out.

Within moments, a line of twenty soldiers and five dogs walked carefully from the wall's edge towards the east.

The dogs buried their noses in the grass as they moved forward. The men scanned the surface for any mark or trinket the enemy had left behind.

Alan watched intently as the line of men moved slowly and deliberately away from the village. He couldn't believe the invaders' capability for mobilising and disappearing so swiftly.

They were there only a few hours ago, and now it was as if they had never been.

While others around him asked where they could have gone, he questioned how they could muster and gather everything so speedily and simply vanish.

He wondered if they had retreated to somewhere nearby and were watching and waiting for the cover of darkness to return so that they could attack once again.

He respected their strategy.

It was patient and slow.

It created fear and intimidation.

It produced confusion and anxiety.

It was tearing the village apart from within.

They wouldn't need to do too much in order to become victorious and triumph over the inhabitants of Woodmyst.

All they needed to do was watch and bide their time.

Last night, Alan believed, was part of that strategy.

The enemy selected specific targets, thinning the defences of the village.

Then they unveiled the greatest weapon they had; the great beast of the sky.

Without directly attacking the village, it invoked fear by simply calling across the clouds and flying past the onlooking soldiers on the wall.

Clever, Alan thought.

The line of soldiers had moved to about fifty yards out from the wall. The dogs kept sniffing the ground, and the men continued scanning the area.

They found nothing and, Alan believed, nothing ever would be.

***

Running at full speed, Chief Shelley headed for the Great Hall. He ducked and weaved by weary soldiers who sluggishly made their way along the street. It wasn't a long trek to the enormous building from the armoury, where he had spent most of the night.

He bounded up the steps that led to the enormous doors, now opened after an endless night of battle. The town's people secure inside couldn't wait to be free of the building. A desperate need to get out and find their loved ones who stood upon the wall overcame them and they packed at the door and caused traffic blockages on the steps.

The chief pushed and wriggled his way through the throng in order to get inside. His desperation to get in matched those wishing to get out.

Once inside and away from the crowd, he scanned the room from one side to the other. Some families sat around the edges of the auditorium while others made their way to join the mass at the door.

Glowing embers from the grand fireplace sent a thin shaft of smoke towards the ceiling. Strips of roast meat hung precariously from the spit hanging in the fireplace, appearing dry and inedible.

Chief Shelley looked past this, towards the raised platform where he and his family sat for village banquets.

The area was bare and those who he came to see were not there.

Briskly, he walked past the warm embers and dry meat, up the stairs to the platform and to the staircase at its rear. He quickly ascended the staircase and entered the living quarters above the auditorium.

There they were.

Sitting on the floor, playing with dolls, were Isabel and Alanna. They chatted and giggled, oblivious to their father's presence. Near them, resting in a deep-cushioned chair, Sybil was sewing.

"Thank the gods," the chief breathed.

Sybil rose to her feet, dropping her needlework to the floor.

"Father," the girls chorused as they ran across the room and wrapped their arms around his waist. He placed a hand on each of their heads before reaching an arm out to his wife. In four strides, she was in his arms, holding him tight.

"I've never been so afraid in my life," she admitted.

"Me either," he replied.

The four of them held each other in a group embrace for a long time before letting go.

After some time, the girls returned to their dolls, Sybil returned to her stitching, and the chief sat in his chair alongside her watching the children.

"What are you going to do?" Sybil asked.

His mind returned to the terrible sound of the beast roaring in the sky. It shook his innermost being to a place beyond fear when he had first heard it. Now, as he remembered it, a slow shiver ran down his spine.

"I don't know how we can fight against that thing," he acknowledged. "I don't know how we..." He stopped and looked at his daughters, who were playing and giggling on the floor. Lowering his voice, Chief Shelley continued, "I don't know how we can survive."

She sighed. He appeared tired and older, worn out.

He shouldn't have to bear this load, she thought.

"Call a meeting," she suggested.

"I was going to talk to the council members and the elders today," he replied.

"No," she said. "I mean the entire village. Let everyone stand and say their piece, if they wish."

He leant back in his chair and scratched at his chin thoughtfully before nodding. It was a good idea. After all, this assault upon Woodmyst affected all of its inhabitants, not just the council.

"You are a treasure to me," he said.

"And I will remind you of that every day." She smiled.

"Am I a treasure to you, father?" Alanna asked.

"You both are," he replied as he stood to his feet. "A treasure more precious than gold and rubies."

Sybil watched him curiously. "Where are you going?"

"To call a meeting," he answered her. "We'll banquet for lunch and call all available people to attend."

He descended the stairwell to the raised platform and approached the serves in the auditorium. They were tidying up the mess from the night before. Linen was being folded and bundled for the laundry. The serves gathered food scraps, plates and cutlery into baskets to be taken to the kitchens for cleaning.

"Serves," the chief called to the group of young women and men busying themselves throughout the Great Hall.

They all stopped what they were doing and faced Chief Shelley standing upon the platform.

"Could you please send word to all available serves that there will be a banquet at lunch," he instructed. "We will need the tables set and food supplied. Make a simple meal of bread, beef and mead. Nothing fancy. All places are to be set with food on plates and in place before anyone arrives. The time will also serve as a town meeting. You are all invited to attend and I want to begin in six hours from now when it is one hour past noon."

The serves started a conversation of who was to pass the message on while the others remained to clean the Great Hall. Chief Shelley returned to his family as two young female serves dashed through the doors to pass the word.

***

The search for the lost runner had begun. Soldiers searched both within and beyond the western wall of the village. Some had taken to walking the perimeter outside the barrier, while others carefully combed the streets and yards near the structure.

Richard checked the tavern, hoping his instincts were wrong. The last thing he wanted to do was reprimand a man for neglecting his duties, particularly if that man had grabbed a jug of mead.

The tavern was empty. Not even the keeper was present. Richard assumed that, like him, the tavern keeper was engaged in obligations that had spilt over from the night and into the daylight hours.

He moved his attention to the streets again, searching back lots, alleys and hidden pockets between buildings that he didn't know existed until now. Each time, emptiness or discarded, festering food scraps he wished he hadn't uncovered confronted his senses.

The search gradually worked its way from the base of the south-western tower towards the river. Some men in Richard's charge headed towards the markets where the sound of hammers striking anvil and iron resounded through the streets.

Deciding to stick closer to the wall, Richard took a few men to search the area along the path he thought the runner would have most likely taken. In his mind, the runner would have navigated through the twisting lanes of Woodmyst, crossed West Bridge over the river that snaked through the village before heading for the north-western tower.

The search party lifted wooden pallets, moved large barrels and knocked upon doors as they edged closer and closer to the river.

It was as if the man had simply vanished.

After what Richard had witnessed during the night, a disappearing man didn't seem all that far-fetched.

As families returned to their homes after spending a terrifying night in the Great Hall, he heard the children referring to the invaders as the Night Demons. He hoped the missing runner hadn't suffered at their hands.

His mind returned to the first victim discovered upon the eastern hill. The poor soul; skinned, left fastened to a stake and garbed in clothes similar to what the enemy wore.

He then remembered the scouts left outside the eastern gate in a similar manner; men he knew. Richard forced the thought away as he focussed his attention back on the search.

As he explored through the streets, a male serve dressed in traditional white approached him. "My lord."

Richard paused and faced the young man. The soldiers nearby stopped searching also and gathered around.

"Keep searching, men," Richard gently instructed. "We need to find him. I'll join you soon."

The soldiers quickly returned to the search.

"What is it?" he asked the serve.

"Chief Shelley will hold a banquet at one hour past noon," the serve informed him. "It will also be a chance to hold a town meeting. He wishes all council members to be present."

"Inform Chief Shelley I will be present as soon as I find my lost man and after we hold pyre for the men who were slain last night," Richard replied. "Tell him I think it would be good for the banquet to also serve as a time for remembering our fallen friends. Thank you."

"My lord." The serve bowed before turning away.

Richard shook his head. "A banquet," he said. "I swear all that man ever thinks about is eating."

A flashing image of a murky swamp, deep in his past, flooded his mind. Low branches of old willow trees dangled their foliage towards the gloomy marsh. Twisted mangroves dug into the damp earth around the water's edge. Vines and weeds laced the dirty liquid's surface as insects and frogs called through the dank, thick stench that rose from beneath.

"My lord?" a soldier asked, forcing Richard to snap back to reality.

"Nothing," he replied. "Keep searching."

The search party moved within sight of the bridge. A few side streets and alleys lined the area between the water crossing and themselves. The soldiers moved along each access carefully, deliberately, turning over everything that they believed a man could crawl under or hide beneath.

Richard peered into an alley where a soldier was pulling some large planks away from a wall. Beneath them was a large object, slumped and dark.

Obscured by shadow.

As the soldier moved the lengths of timber, more and more light exposed what lied beneath. Richard kept his eyes on the spot. He hoped to the gods it wasn't his lost runner, but wanted the search to be over. Selfishly, he wanted to be in his home, sleeping in his bed. The looks on his men's faces informed him they also wanted this for themselves.

He then thought of the missing man's family. How would he explain their loved one had passed away under a pile of boards leaning against the wall?

More light fell onto the area as the soldier moved the planks to the side.

Lying on the ground was an overturned barrel with an old blanket on top.

Richard felt a sudden sense of relief intermixed with frustration.

He was glad it wasn't his missing runner underneath the leaning planks, but annoyed that the search needed to continue.

"My lord," a soldier called.

Richard snapped his head around to the source of the sound.

One of the other soldiers stood atop West Bridge, pointing to where the river flowed out through the western wall.

Richard ran towards the soldier, his other men in tow.

They arrived at the pointing soldier's side together, one man almost slipping over. Together, they carefully scrutinised the area.

The water was higher than usual and flowed rapidly after the rain. Boats tied to small docks bounced and knocked against the platforms as the river ebbed and swayed beneath them.

Iron bars blocked the causeway, allowing only water to pass through. It was a defensive structure that had been lowered on the chief's command in order to prevent enemy forces from entering the village.

The gates prevented men from entering, but also stopped large objects from exiting. Forced up against the bars by the pressure of the rapidly flowing river, were small branches, a fishing boat, baskets and other debris. Amongst them was the form of a man.

Richard saw from the clothing that it was his lost runner.

The men felt their hearts sink and leant against the guardrail of the bridge. One lowered his eyes and silently prayed while another simply shook his head.

Tears welled in Richard's eyes, falling upon his cheeks, only to be swept away in the rain.

Fifteen

The scent of manure and straw was an inviting aroma. Something about it made Tomas feel he was where he belonged. He didn't want to live in the stables, but definitely felt this was where he would like to spend his spare time.

He had filled three buckets with horse crud since he arrived at first light. The stable master had instructed him to be cautious around the animals. Tomas didn't need the warning. It was clear the evening's events spooked the horses.

An occasional loud noise or shouting passer-by caused the beasts to stamp their hooves and nod their heads in protest. A gentle word and a touch on the nose from a stable hand settled them somewhat, but Tomas saw the fear in their eyes. The workers inside the building tried to keep as quiet as they could for their benefit.

By mid-morning, Tomas had filled eight buckets with round, grassy turds and placed them onto a wagon. His next task was to unfurl bundled hay and lay it in the mangers. As he did so, the burly horseman followed him, pouring buckets of water into troughs.

"Master Lytton," one of the stable hands called softly.

The stable master lifted his gaze to the other man. The stable hand pointed to the door where a serve was waiting.

Tomas kept watching as the horseman strode across the floor, past three stalls, where curious horses followed the man with their eyes as he walked by.

"I'm sorry to intrude," the serve said a little too loudly for the horses.

The brown mare in the stall Tomas currently occupied stamped its feet unhappily. The boy turned to the beast and placed a hand upon its neck.

"There, there," he whispered.

The horse replied with a low nicker.

"Quiet," the stable master instructed the serve. "The animals are scared. Try to keep the noise down."

"I apologise," replied the serve softly. "I bring word that a banquet and town meeting will be held one hour after noon. Chief Shelley would like as many of you that can be spared to attend. Again, I apologise for my inappropriate behaviour."

"It's all right, lad," the stable master replied. "Go about your business."

The serve took his leave as the horseman returned to the stall where Tomas stood. The boy had stayed with the mare during the conversation between the stable master and the serve. His hands remained on her neck, moving occasionally to pat her lightly along her nose. The mare had half-closed her eyes and lowered her head for him to reach more towards her ears.

"She likes you." The horseman smiled. "I think she has claimed you as her own."

Tomas grinned from ear to ear.

He resumed loading hay into the manger as the hefty man picked up a bucket and poured water into the trough.

Tomas looked to the door and back to the stable master.

"What is it, lad?" the stable master questioned. "Do you have some grand concern about the town meeting?"

"Hmm?" Tomas grunted. "No. Not that. I was just wondering why the serves do what they do."

"What do you mean, do what they do? It's their job, lad."

"No, I mean, they're not slaves or forced to serve. They could be shopkeepers or farmers or even work here. I don't understand why they are servants."

"Well," the stable master started, thinking of the best way to respond. "Why are shopkeepers, shopkeepers? Why are farmers, farmers? For the same reason, a serve is a serve. They choose to be. They put themselves in the service of Woodmyst and in reward, they are given shelter, food and clothing. When they become too old to serve, others serve them. It's been a long tradition of the realm, not just our village, for centuries."

"But why choose that for work over some other job?" Tomas asked as he spread the last of the hay.

"I see what you're asking," replied the burly man as he placed the bucket on the ground and stretched his back, twisting this way and that. "They mostly become serves out of family tradition. Some are serves because there wasn't any other work available."

"Can they become something else if work becomes available?"

"No. Once you swear to serve the village, you are a serve for life. There is a binding contract between the elders and the serves that cannot be broken. Punishment for abandoning your obligation as a serve results in banishment from the village with only the clothes on your back."

"No food or water?" the boy queried.

"Nothing," replied the stable master as he lifted his two empty buckets and turned to leave the stall. "You leave with only that which you truly own."

"But the clothes belong to the village," Tomas objected.

"Let's call it a parting gift," the beefy man replied. "Civilised people don't leave a person naked to walk the wilds, lad. We can, at least, make sure the needy have coverings."

The mare watched wistfully as Tomas followed so that he could retrieve more hay for the other horses.

"I don't think I'll ever want to be a serve," he said.

The big man chuckled quietly at the boy's words.

***

It had been a long time since anyone had called a town meeting. Those who could recall the last time an assembly such as this remembered all too well the reason for the gathering. It resulted in most of the men from the village being called to duty for the realm. The overall consequence was many of their men not returning home afterwards.

Chief Shelley had this memory in the back of his mind as he sat upon the platform with his family and the families of his councilmen. This time they weren't being called to fight for the realm in some distant land.

The threat was on their boundaries.

The danger was at home.

He allowed the gathering to enjoy the meal and had asked the serves to join them in the auditorium for the banquet. It was the first time the serves had the honour of sitting within the walls of the Great Hall to partake in a feast. Usually, they served the meal and ate in the rooms near the kitchens behind the building.

Not today.

Perhaps never again.

The appearance of the flying monster had caused the village leader to re-evaluate their circumstances. He honestly did not know how to defeat such a creature.

He looked towards the rafters of the Great Hall, to the heads of the carved dragons that supported the beams. The resemblance was not identical, but appeared very near to the beast.

How the enemy could have tamed a dragon was beyond his comprehension.

No one had claimed to see a dragon since the days before the Realm War. The stories of such animals boasted they were wild and unpredictable. There had never been any tale that mentioned the ability to train them.

Yet, here one was that seemed to work in league with the invaders.

How could this be?

Raising his mug to his mouth, he gulped down the mead from within and lowered the empty vessel back to the table. Sybil noticed and placed a hand on his knee. Slow down.

Nodding his acknowledgement, he scanned the room carefully to gauge if the gathering was ready to begin the meeting. He surmised they were as their conversations grew increasingly louder, indicating the feasting was over.

He glanced in both directions along the table, checking that his council was ready to begin. They signalled their reply, all except Lawrence who, along with his family, was absent from the table.

A quick look around the room, in case the man had sat with friends elsewhere, informed him that the council member had not come to the meeting. Shelley didn't see the point in waiting for him. They had finished the meal, and it was now almost two hours past midday. There were still preparations for the night to be made and who was to know how long the meeting would last.

He stood to address them all.

"People of Woodmyst," he shouted. "People of Woodmyst," he called again, ensuring their undivided attention.

Silence flooded the giant room as all voices ceased and eyes moved towards the platform.

"People of Woodmyst," Chief Barnard Shelley continued. "I have called this meeting to discuss our options concerning the current plight. We have had to hold yet another pyre today. I predict we will need to hold another tomorrow.

"For whatever the reason, we have an enemy on our lands. We do not know who they are or why they have chosen us, but nevertheless, they are here and it doesn't look as if they intend to leave anytime soon."

He glanced down at the table in front of him, looking for his full mug of mead. It remained empty after his last interaction with it. Returning his gaze to the villagers, he continued addressing them.

"I am going to be honest with all of you; I plan to fight them and die if I have to. I plan to stand until the end—"

"Easy for you to say, Barnard," a man called from his seat. "I haven't seen you upon the wall with the rest of us."

"No!" Alan stood and shouted back angrily. "You haven't seen him up there because he's running tactical operations from the armoury, sending you much-needed supplies while you're on the wall. No, you haven't seen him on the wall. But you have seen the rest of us up there with you and we support him wholeheartedly."

Chief Shelley looked along the table to his friend, who was lowering himself back to his seat. A curt nod signalled his gratitude to Alan, who simply raised his mug in reply before draining its contents.

How he wished he had some mead of his own right now.

"Last night was our first proper night of conflict," the chief informed the assembly. "I have no doubt we will face something similar, if not more intense, tonight. We need to be ready.

"I believe we should stand and fight. If you have any other solutions to our shared problem, then now is your chance to speak your mind."

Chief Shelley sat back down next to his wife, who returned her hand to his knee under the table hidden from view.

A thick silence fell over the room, as eyes looked this way and that as an intense moment passed as the gathering waited for someone to stand and say something.

"I have something to say," called a woman's voice from the back of the room.

All eyes turned to see who the speaker was. Some grumbled their disapproval of the utterer, wanting to leave the Great Hall to prepare for the evening. Others turned in order to listen more intently.

Chief Shelley leaned in his seat to see past the fireplace, which obstructed his view of the owner of the voice. The attempt was in vain, as the hearth was simply too wide.

"Please speak your piece," he called to her.

"Why can't we just leave?" she asked. "I look along your table and see that one of our council members is missing."

Where are you, Lawrence?

Chief Shelley took a deep breath and tried desperately not to glance down the table to his missing friend's place.

"I know we did not count him as one amongst those who were on the pyre," she continued. "What I have heard is that he has left the village with his family. I don't mean any disrespect, Chief Shelley, but some of us simply don't want to be here, and I'm guessing Lawrence Verney didn't either. We're scared and we want to go."

She sat back in her seat and started sobbing. The man beside her placed his arm around her, and she buried herself into him.

"We can't leave," a man from across the room called out. "My apologies, Chief." The man stopped. "I'm not sure of the formalities."

"Please continue," the chief replied.

"We can't leave because we don't know where the Night Demons are," the man said.

Richard was reminded of what the children had called the invader earlier in the day.

Night Demons.

It would seem that the designation for the enemy was spreading to the adults, or perhaps had started with them only to be overheard by the youths.

"They only come out at night," someone else shouted.

"We don't know that," continued the man who was speaking. "They've attacked us at night, but they could be sitting out there watching the village as we speak. They could be waiting in the forest for us to escape, only to cut us down as we run. We're safer here, behind the walls. They haven't made it in yet."

"But they have a dragon," called another. "You're all fools if you believe the walls are going to stop a dragon."

"They won't stop a dragon." Peter stood to his feet. "Nothing will. I can't begin to know how these Night Demons, as you call them, could ally with such a terrible creature. But they did.

"If it can get inside the walls, so can they. So, if nothing can stop the dragon, then nothing can stop the Night Demons. That being the case, leave Woodmyst."

Shocked by his words, all eyes at the table fell upon him. Chief Shelley couldn't believe what his friend was suggesting to the people of his village. Peter, however, hadn't finished.

"But our friend there has a point. What if these bastards are watching and waiting for you to run? Perhaps you and your children will be skinned just like our scouts were, and placed on pikes outside the eastern gate for us to find tomorrow.

"Now let us consider what our other speaker said. They only come out at night. Let us believe for a moment that this is true. That perhaps the sunlight causes them pain. Fine.

"The hour is late. You won't get much farther than the far end of the orchard before nightfall. With your family in tow, and even with the fastest steeds pulling your wagon, they will be upon you before you knew it.

"So, leave if that's what you want to do. Nobody will stop you. But don't expect us to come to your rescue. I will not put any man at risk when there is an enemy surrounding us. No way."

With that, he plonked himself down and raised his mug to his lips.

Chief Shelley stared at his friend in silence. The words were blunt and to the point. He didn't believe he could have put it in such a way, as it would have tested his diplomatic standing that he had worked so hard to accomplish over the years.

"Barnard," Sybil hissed in his ear.

He snapped back to reality and moved his eyes to the staring crowd. They all gawked at Peter. Some who shared his sentiment raised their mugs, while others clapped. Those who didn't agree simply shook their heads or whispered unkind words amongst themselves.

Chief Shelley stood to his feet and called, "Any more speakers?"

Some mumbled for a moment, but none stood to take the floor.

"Very well," the chief announced. "Meeting adjourned."

***

High upon the southern slopes, on a thin winding road leading into the mountains rolled a well-laden, rickety wagon with a red-bearded man, his wife and their two children. He steered the gelding carefully along the track as his children stared back towards the only land they had ever known.

They had travelled in silence for some time, and the need to speak was becoming overbearing. Finally, Elara broke.

"Where will we spend the night?" she asked. "We're not as far as we thought we would be by now."

"We'll move some of the load and put the canvas over the cart," Lawrence replied. "It'll be one night and then we'll make the other side of the range tomorrow. We should be in Dweagan in a day or two after that."

"But what if they come for us during the night?" she questioned nervously.

"They won't," he answered confidently. "They gathered on the northern side of the village. We won't even be worth their consideration this far south. We'll keep moving until dusk and set up camp. It will be fine."

He smiled and leant over to kiss her.

She glanced over her shoulder and saw her son and daughter still looking back. Woodmyst was well out of view and the tail end of the plantations was a distant blur.

Turning to face forward, she saw the grey rock faces of mountains with protruding thickets of pine trees here and there.

"You heard your father, Lor, Sevrina," she said, trying to assure herself that they made the right decision. "It will be fine. We're going to find a new home and start all over again."

The children continued to keep their eyes facing away from their parents. It wasn't a longing for Woodmyst more than it was a protest about being made to leave their friends.

Lawrence understood this and let them be. He believed they would eventually grow out of their unhappiness once they settled in their new home.

Far away from Woodmyst.

Far away from death.

It will be fine.

It will.

Sixteen

It stopped raining, but the clouds had remained in the sky, threatening more precipitation at any moment. The sun's light refracted through the grey blanket, signalling dusk by presenting a red tinge to the cover as she sank closer towards the horizon.

A few men, positioned upon each wall, watched and waited for any sign of their foe, and for the long-expected relief that was due to take their place any time now. Most of them had been on the wall since the night before. The desperate need for sleep was overpowering as some felt their heads dip now and then as they tried so hard to keep their eyes open.

Arriving early to his position, Richard had climbed the tower and given the guard his release. The guard was most grateful and immediately descended from the tower to make his way home. He wanted to rest, but knew that if the night ahead was like the previous one, he would be back upon the wall before sunrise.

Richard moved his eyes over the tree line of the woods on the western border. The foliage's colours appeared bright as it usually did after the rain had fallen. As if new life emerged, or a fresh canvas just had paint applied.

He admired the scenery as he listened to the birdcalls ringing from within the forest. It was hard to believe that something that appeared so beautiful could harbour a sinister enemy who had practically held them at siege over the previous three nights.

The lush green landscape before him faded as a memory of another forest returned. Soft sounds of birds happily chirping drifted away as he recalled the snapping of branches and rapid footfalls in the scrub as he, and eight others with him, ran and ran.

***

The nine men burst through the undergrowth at high speed. Twigs and thistles scratched at the bare flesh around their faces as they ran after the five enemy soldiers who had turned to flee from the fight upon the field.

The dog barked as it spotted one escapee running along a dry riverbed. The man stumbled upon the smooth stones and fell to his knees. A crunch was heard, followed by a cry in agony as the soldier fell onto his side, gripping his knee in his hands.

"There," called Barnard, pointing with his sword past the fallen warrior to another four men climbing the embankment on the far side of the stony ground.

The band of nine hastily moved across the ground. Alan drew his sword as they drew closer to the injured man.

The warrior's eyes locked onto his and widened in fear.

"No," he called. "Please, no."

But it was too late.

Alan dug his blade deep into the enemy soldier's chest. The man went limp and lay still upon the dry riverbed as Alan withdrew his blade and continued after the other runners.

They climbed the embankment after the four fugitives. The dog reached the peak before the men and yapped towards something out of the nine men's view. It remained at the top, waiting for them but turning in circles impatiently, urging the humans to hurry.

Once at the top, they were confronted with a marshy area overgrown with weeds and fungus. Some willow trees enfolded the area, draping the surroundings with long foliage that dangled from twisted limbs.

The four runaways were a few yards into the swamp, splashing and falling awkwardly as they used every ounce of strength to escape their pursuers.

The nine men waded into the water and pushed their way through the growth that laced the surface of the march.

Richard felt the soft ground beneath the murky water, swallowing his feet and attempting to suck his boot away from him as he tried to move forward.

The chirp of the crickets and the croak of the frogs stopped, as if they knew what horrors were about to follow.

They could only hear the buzzing of flying insects over the sound of the sloshing ripples that the men made as they waded through the thick liquid.

The escapees stopped running.

They understood they had no chance of escape.

They turned towards their hunters and dropped their swords into the marsh.

The blades glinted momentarily before sinking below the weeds and out of view.

"W- we surrender," one of them announced as he raised his arms. His allies followed suit and lifted their hands as well.

Barnard stepped forward slowly and measured the men visually before plunging his sword into the first warrior's face.

"I don't care," he hissed.

The words stunned the other enemy soldiers. This wasn't how one treated prisoners. There were rules.

But before they could protest, the blades of Alan, Peter and Michael cut them down.

The silent bodies fell into the murk with a loud splash that caused the growth on the surface to ripple outwards in an odd circular pattern. When the water finally settled, there was no sign that the enemy soldiers had ever been there.

"So," Barnard said chirpily, "where are you two from then?"

The two men that accompanied the troop looked to one another, silently deciding who should speak first.

"Well," one started. "I'm Travis from Selidien and this is Lewyn from Rhendalith."

"Travis from Selidien and Lewis from Rhendalith," Barnard bowed slightly, "welcome to our little group from Woodmyst."

The men started slapping each other on the shoulders, smiling and laughing as they stood thigh-deep in murky water.

Richard looked on in disbelief.

Had he truly seen his own friends do what was just done? And now, they were acting as if they were meeting in a tavern.

He shook his head and spoke.

"Wh—"

CRACK!

All nine men snapped their heads around to the source of the sound.

The dog gave a muffled woof as it stared towards a place where the land rose back out of the marsh.

A pair of large yellow eyes were looking straight at them. The tiny figure they belonged to was half-hidden behind the trunk of a willow tree. Afraid.

The dog stepped forward and growled.

The creature ran in the opposite direction.

It wore tattered rags about its body and moved similarly to a man. Richard saw, in the quick moment that he had, that it was hairless and had no ears. The creature reminded him of a frog or a toad of sorts, except it ran on two legs.

His curiosity got the better of him, and he moved towards the shore.

"Where are you going?" Peter questioned.

"I need to know what that thing is," he replied as he waded through the marsh.

"Can't let him go alone," said Hugh as he followed the other with the dog in tow.

The remaining men looked at one another. Barnard simply shrugged and waded after the other two men.

Eventually, the nine made it to the bank and climbed ashore.

They stared dumbfounded at the sight before them.

Mud huts, grouped together at the bases of several trees, like miniature cave-like constructions with openings big enough for men to fit through.

Wicker baskets and crude wooden tables sat beside the buildings. Wooden plates with fruit possibly gathered from the surrounding forest sat upon tables. Some contents laid spilt upon the ground. Several small campfires continued to burn unattended.

The dwellers of this primitive village had hidden in haste.

Richard scanned the black doorways of the mud structures.

Staring back at him from the darkness within were several, fearful yellow eyes.

***

The leaves lost their luminosity as the sunlight disappeared behind the forest. In places, the sky turned to lilac, and the canopy cast dark shadows into the undergrowth.

Richard forced his memories away, replacing them with thoughts of the here and now. Men had arrived upon the wall, ready for the night watch.

Returning his observation to the scenery outside of the wall, he scanned the area from the river's edge, past the forest and to the southern plantations. Occasionally, he moved his eyes skywards for any sign of the flying monster.

Only dark, looming clouds and dimming scenery met his gaze. But in the recesses of his mind, he saw yellow eyes staring back at him.

This terrible memory just wouldn't leave him be.

Seventeen

Chief Shelley climbed to the viewing platform of the south-eastern tower, where Michael and two tower guards conducted lookout duties. He crossed the well-worn boards to Michael's side, where he placed his hands upon the guardrail and began scanning the environment for any sign of the enemy.

"You shouldn't be here," said Michael as he stared towards the river before moving his eyes to the chief on his right. "You should be in the armoury ordering runners around and making tactical decisions."

"They don't need me for that," Chief Shelley replied. He would rather be anywhere than upon the wall, but the words of one man during the town meeting had resonated with him. I haven't seen you upon the wall with the rest of us.

So here he was, attempting to prove to the watchers upon the wall, perhaps even more so to himself, that he was just as brave and ready to fight as they were.

The fact was the serves and soldiers were quite capable of running the operation from the armoury without him. He had felt out-of-place over the previous nights. Filling boxes with arrows, sending supplies to the walls and barking orders all night for men to collect and distribute blankets could be done by any man, woman or child, for that matter.

Now, as he stood upon the tower overlooking the land outside of the village walls, he felt unprepared, and even more out of place. His hands shook slightly as he gripped the guardrail in an attempt to settle his nerves.

Noticing his friend's edginess, Michael closed the distance between himself and the chief.

"Calm down," he whispered. "You are supposed to be our leader." Michael tilted his head towards the two guards on the platform facing towards the south. "If they see you like this, it will make them second guess every decision that is made tonight."

Chief Shelley took a deep breath and exhaled slowly.

"I'm sorry, Michael," he replied. "It's been a long time since I've had to fight. We've had it too good for too long. We got lazy and soft."

Smiling wryly, Michael shook his head.

"You got soft," he said. "I, my friend, am in my prime. And as far as having it too good; well, that is a state every man longs for. As far as for too long, it's never long enough. Except when the ladies require some Michael Forde time. Then length is adequate and fulfilling." He clasped his hand upon Chief Shelley's shoulder as he bore a glorious smile.

"Is that all you think about?"

"Well, there was that one time I thought about becoming a minstrel," he chuckled. "But the flutes they use just weren't as much fun to play with."

"Disgusting." Chief Shelley laughed. The tower guards had overheard the latter part of the discussion and snickered as they kept their eyes to the south.

Faint outlines of tilled ground and cottages could be made out in the distance. The neat rows of trees and a discarded plough leaning against a barn slowly dissolved into shadow as the light in the sky faded.

Night had come.

"You'll be fine, Barnard," Michael assured his friend, stepping in close to do so.

"Thank you, Michael."

***

Standing upon the north-western tower, Hugh Clarke felt slightly vulnerable and alone. Two tower guards accompanied him, but the absence of Lawrence Verney had become all too real after he had climbed to the tower's platform.

Selfishly, he considered the lack of banter he and Lawrence had exchanged. He then thought about the solemn manner of his friend on the previous night and how there really was no mocking or teasing at all.

Something had been troubling his comrade.

Something so disturbing that it had changed his disposition.

Lawrence was usually a cheerful man. He would joke and tease and take it just as good as he could give it. His bravery and fighting skills always awed Hugh. Usually first into the fray, Lawrence would take the enemy on headfirst and, more often than not, walk away unscathed.

So, why the change in mood?

Why wasn't he here?

What had happened to him and his family?

Hugh folded his arms and leant against the guardrail as he stared blankly to the place where the grove met the forest. He remembered his friend had held his gaze towards the same place during the night before. Maybe gazing to the same spot would see his questions answered.

They were not.

Peering up to see if the answers were to be found in the stars above, he only saw pitch-blackness and nothing. The clouds had obscured the night sky for a second night.

At least it wasn't raining.

The evening was still and silent. Even the men upon the wall were still and nervous as they peered into the shadows of the trees beyond. There were no murmurs or whispers that he heard from his position on the tower.

Turning his head to his right, he saw the archers upon the northern wall tucked behind the battlements along the wall, peering cautiously out towards the grove through the crenels. The design along the top of the wall had always reminded Hugh of teeth, with gaps between each just large enough for an archer to aim and shoot through.

They were not tall enough to protect a man.

The attack upon the eastern wall had proved this point during the night before. They lost several archers who stood taller than the defensive barrier to enemy arrows. Now, the men upon the wall crouched uncomfortably behind each battlement in fear for their lives.

Turning his face to the left, Hugh saw the men upon the western wall were using the village's defences similarly.

No one was taking any chances tonight.

The disadvantage for the men along the wall was that they could not clearly view the entire environment surrounding them. This could provide an opportunity for a surprise attack.

Given that darkness had enveloped everything in sight, a surprise attack was a considerable possibility.

Hiding behind the battlements left effective viewing to those upon the towers. While the towers provided cover from the platform to the guardrail, such as Hugh leant against, the men upon them were more vulnerable during an attack than those upon the wall.

The protective barriers of the towers were thick planks of timber, smothered with a few layers of grey mud found on the river's banks. When the mud dried, it became hard like stone.

The protective layering of mud, however, had not been up kept for several years. Parts had flaked off and exposed the weather-worn planks beneath, which had become rotten and weak.

Hugh made a mental note to bring this up with Chief Shelley in the morning. For now, he and the tower guards would have to make do with what they had.

"There," one of the tower guards whispered and pointed.

Moving his eyes to the place the guard gestured to, Hugh saw a lone small flame flickering among the trees of the grove. It reminded him of the single torch from the night before that stood where the forest and the grove joined.

Tonight, the light flickered some distance to the east. Hugh calculated it sat about halfway between the two towers on the north wall.

Was this, as with the night before, a distraction from an attack elsewhere on the village defences?

Perhaps this was the enemy's rallying point.

He was about to call for the alarm to be sounded when he heard clanging from the north-eastern tower.

"Send a runner," he ordered. "Tell them we see it too."

One of the tower guards moved to the village side edge of the tower and shouted down to soldiers beneath,

"Send a runner to the north-eastern tower and inform them we see one torchlight in the grove."

The sound of the alarm brought restlessness to the archers on the nearby walls. Murmuring began, and fear crept in.

"Steady men," Hugh called encouragingly. "It's just a torch."

Inside, he felt his heart bursting through his chest.

The sound of a man running along the damp street resonated to the top of the tower as the runner sped towards the east.

Hugh felt knots forming in his stomach. The sudden urge to throw up gripped him. He fought the impulse off and gripped the guardrail.

***

"Stop that infernal racket," Peter shouted over the clamour.

The tower guard lowered the hammer and stepped back from the chime.

"From now on, we send runners to herald the news," Peter ordered. "My ears can't take much more of this."

"Agreed," said Alan as he stared towards the solitary torch flickering in the grove.

"What?" Peter wriggled a finger in his ear.

"I said I agree with you," Alan replied a little louder.

"Mm." Peter moved to beside his friend and scanned the grove for any other movement. He believed the single torch was a ruse. The enemy, in his mind, was assembling elsewhere for an attack.

Alan wasn't so sure. The invaders had used this method on the previous night. Each time they revealed themselves, it differed from the preceding time. He believed tonight would be something new. Something unexpected.

"Where are they?"

"Why are you in such a hurry to see them?" Alan asked.

"I hate all this waiting," Peter admitted. "They hide, we seek. They light some torches; we soil our trousers. Why not just come out and fight?"

Alan looked sideways at the other. "You really want them to come at us head-on?"

"At least we will see them coming," Peter replied.

"What about the dragon?"

Peter stared silently at the flaming torch in the grove for a moment, considering Alan's words. Fighting an enemy upon the ground was workable. He understood ground battle. Defending against an enemy that used the sky was new to him. He truly did not have an answer to his friend's question.

A long silence passed as the two men kept their eyes peeled for movement amongst the trees. Peter slowly scanned the grove towards the hill in the east.

Another torch flickered in the trees, where the ground gently rose.

He wondered how long it had been there. Certainly, they would have seen it before when they had first noticed the lone torch near to where they stood. One of the first things he had done afterwards was to scan the horizon for more lights. That was right before the guard started striking the chime, almost deafening him.

"There," he said. "Another torch."

All eyes moved towards the hill to see the spectacle. As they did, a vast number of torches burst into life within the grove.

"Didn't we see this strategy already?" asked the tower guard.

"Perhaps they have only three that they keep using again and again," Peter suggested.

Alan kept his eyes on the grove. He felt on edge.

Hairs on the back of his neck stood rigid and an icy shiver moved down his spine.

Intuition told him something bad was about to happen.

"Archers ready," he shouted.

Peter buckled at the knees and crouched behind the tower's fortification. The tower guard instinctively followed suit as the archers loaded arrows into their bows.

"Archers ready." The order echoed down the line of both the eastern and northern walls.

"What do you see?" Peter asked. "What is it?"

"Torches in the woods," Alan replied.

Peter thought his friend must have been losing his mind. They had all seen the torches in the woods. To call for archers seemed a little premature and illogical at the least. It was no use firing off your ammunition unless you could actually see your enemy.

Yet, here was Alan, about to do just that.

"Prepare to fire," Alan bellowed.

The archers nearby pulled back upon their bowstrings, creaking loudly as the tension increased.

The order resounded along the walls again.

"Hold," Alan called, standing tall upon the tower, exposed to the enemy.

"Alan, get down here," Peter ordered.

"Hold," he called again, ignoring his friend.

Movement in the trees directly north of the tower caught his attention.

One of the flickering torches moved towards him, moving left and right as it rounded the trunks of trees and ducked under low branches.

It emerged from the tree line and into the open ground between the grove and the wall. Holding the torch high and facing towards Alan was a dark, hooded figure.

It dropped the torch to the ground, reached beneath its long, tattered cloak and brandished a curved sword.

A great guttural roar belched from beneath its hood, resonating along the wall in all directions.

Others echoed the call in thunderous unison as hundreds of hooded warriors burst from the grove wielding swords of their own. They left their torches on the ground amongst the trees.

"Fire," Alan commanded.

Arrows filled the air, streaking towards the hostile mass. Many bolts found targets, sending many attackers to the ground before the battle had truly begun.

But the first volley barely made a dent in the enemy. Scores and scores of them ran swiftly to the wall; more swiftly than any man could run.

Alan kept his eyes on the first hooded figure that continued to stand near the tree line of the grove. The warrior held his hand up, signalling for someone to hold their ground.

Realising the signal wasn't for the encroaching force, Alan surmised there were others still in hiding. He scanned the grove quickly and could see only the dying torches discarded by the attacking warriors.

"Archers ready," Alan called along the lines. The order echoed along the wall as the archers stood to take aim at the closing enemy. Bows were loaded and strings were pulled.

"Fire!"

A volley of projectiles flew.

Many enemy soldiers fell to the ground as copious arrowheads pierced their flesh.

Stepping over their fallen comrades, the warriors continued to close the gap between themselves and the wall.

Alan saw this was going to result in hand-to-hand combat.

"You had better get ready, Peter," he advised. "We're going to fight them head-on."

Eighteen

"What the blazes is going on over there?" Chief Shelley bellowed.

The sound of many beasts calling from the north boomed over the rooftops to where he stood. His intuition informed him they were under attack.

"Send a runner," Michael called to the men below. He then addressed the men on the walls. "Keep your eyes upon your quadrants. We don't want those bastards sneaking through here."

All archers kept their eyes fixed upon the expanse beyond their section of the wall. The din from the north ate at their curiosity, but their self-discipline overcame the urge to crane their necks for the chance of a look at what was happening in that direction.

The chief stood rigidly, anxiously awaiting word. He saw the torchlights in the grove blinking out one by one as the flames died. What he couldn't see was the source of the sound, obscured by the wall.

He wanted to know what was happening.

He needed to know.

"I have to get over there," he said, heading for the ladder to descend the tower.

"Where are you going?" Michael yelled. A few quick glances from the archers nearby, and the tower guards stabbed at him like tiny daggers. You may have overstepped the boundaries this time, Michael.

"I need to be on the north wall," Chief Shelley replied. "That's where the attack is."

"Yes," Michael agreed. "The attack is upon our northern flank. But what about the attack upon the east and the south?"

"There is no attack here, Michael."

"How do you know?"

"Look about you," shouted the village leader, as if stating the obvious.

"Do you even remember what it was like to be in battle?" Michael asked. "Do you even remember what tactical manoeuvres are?"

The chief paused and listened to his friend.

"We need you here, Barnard," Michael continued. "They could be fortifying their positions on our flanks as we speak. This attack in the north is only part of their offensive. No one exposes their entire force, or their best warriors in one sweeping blow. Never. And you know this."

Chief Shelley lowered his head bashfully.

He still wanted to be on the northern wall, but Michael was right.

The worst was yet to come.

A great thundering roar from the clouds erupted above them. The beast had returned.

Looking to the sky, Michael searched for the creature. The dark clouds concealed it from sight, but the deep sound of its wings beating through the air showed from which direction it approached.

The sound grew louder and louder, filling the hearts and minds of the men upon the wall with dread.

Chief Shelley swore as the clouds opened like a veil, revealing the creature descending through the vapours towards them from the south. It carried an object of considerable size in its talons.

It swooped low outside the southern wall and dropped the object onto the ground. The article landed with a sickening crunch before the creature lifted itself back into the sky.

The archers and the chief trailed the dragon with their eyes as it disappeared into the clouds with a terrifying call. Michael kept his eyes upon the object that had fallen not too far from the wall.

It was a crumpled wagon with its cargo strewn about. Amongst the clutter lay two bodies, a man and a woman, twisted and lying awkwardly like discarded rag dolls.

"What is it?" Chief Shelley asked, looking at the mess outside the wall.

"Lawrence and Elara Verney," Michael replied.

The chief stared blankly at the bodies lying in the misshapen heap.

Things had just become extremely bad.

But the worst was yet to come.

***

"Volley," Hugh shouted to the archers on the north wall. They leant over the battlements and fired at the onslaught of enemy warriors near the base of the wall.

"Volley," he called to his left, where the archers upon the western wall replayed the actions of the men upon the adjacent barrier.

The call appeared to be in vain.

They hit several of the warriors, who fell into the grass below the men of Woodmyst. Many others had scrambled up the wall towards them.

Remembering the stroll around the structure with his friends and his dogs, he visualised the many places they had spotted where someone could advance upon the wall and climb to the top. Right now, the enemy was using these very places to their advantage.

"The Night Demons are climbing the walls, my lord," shouted an archer.

"Prepare for hand-to-hand combat," Hugh called out as he drew his sword from its sheath.

A scream from far along the northern wall, somewhere out of view, informed him that the wall had been breached. Following the scream was the clanging of swords. The noise of iron grew louder as more of the enemy reached the top of the fortification.

The sound echoed towards the south. There were breaches in that direction as well. Hugh ran to the edge of the tower and looked over the side to the men below.

"The wall has been breached," he hollered. "Send word to all men to ready for battle."

Runners sent word to other sections within the wall. News spread quickly of more and more areas of the barrier that had enemy soldiers upon it. Soldiers on the ground moved rapidly to meet them if they ever made it into the village.

The archers fought hard, but were inefficient swordsmen; so much so that some had not bothered to carry a blade, thus becoming the first victims of the Night Demons.

Swords clashed and blood spilt on both sides. The dead and dying bodies of the enemy were thrown back over the wall in the hope to knock some of the advancing climbers back to the ground.

Turning towards the ladder, Hugh was tempted to descend the tower in order to climb the wall, where he intended to face the enemy. A sudden movement in the corner of his eye caused him to turn.

Climbing over the guardrail, a hooded figure lifted itself upon the platform and drew its sword. The tower guard turned in time to parry the enemy's blow with his own blade. Hugh couldn't leave now.

He lifted his sword and stabbed at the demon. With a simple swing of its weapon, Hugh found himself half spun around and facing the wrong way.

The Night Demon was terribly strong, and he realised he had underestimated its power. He wouldn't make that mistake again.

The tower guard slashed downward, over and over. The invader blocked and parried each strike effortlessly with one hand. Hugh lifted his sword and attacked from the side.

The curved sword met his and held the blow in mid-strike. The tower guard saw this as an opportunity and brought his sword down again.

A dagger came flashing out from beneath the cloak and slid deep into the tower guard's throat.

The guard's eyes grew wide, shocked at what just happened. He moved his eyes to Hugh, who wore an expression of disbelief.

It was so fast.

So fast.

With a final twist, the dagger withdrew, spilling blood down the front of the tower guard's uniform.

Hugh felt sudden rage fill his every being.

He swung and hacked over and over, changing his angle of attack with each strike.

The demon blocked and parried each blow, but Hugh was unpredictable. A few strikes got incredibly close to the warrior.

Backing up towards the edge of the wall, the invader was running out of ground. Its confidence dwindled as Hugh continued to attack.

At last, his sword dug into the enemy soldier's shoulder. The curved sword fell to the floor with a loud clang.

Recoiling his sword, Hugh didn't wait for that dagger to appear again, so he struck once more. The blade sliced into the demon's flesh a mere inch to the side of the first cut.

The hooded figure roared, sounding like a wounded pig squealing in agony.

Hugh pulled his sword from the demon and used his boot to push him over the guardrail and off the tower.

The warrior fell to the ground, where it hit with a stomach-turning thud.

Hugh looked down the side of the tower to where his enemy's body lay. It rested at an awkward angle, unmoving. His eyes then shifted to two more hooded figures climbing the wall towards him.

Nineteen

Cradling Linet, Catherine Warde hummed soothingly to calm her daughter's nerves. The quiver in her voice had worsened as the night progressed. She rocked gently as she sat on the edge of the bed, hoping the movement may help Linet fall to sleep.

Gripping her mother's clothing with one hand, Linet stared wide-eyed up to Catherine's face as she sucked her thumb; something she hadn't done since she was first learning to walk.

Catherine moved her eyes down to meet those of her daughter. The fear in them must have been apparent as Linet tightened her grip, pinching the flesh on her mother's waist beneath the blouse.

The distant sound of clashing steel made its way into the Great Hall as the fighting outside intensified. The runners had informed the elders, who were inside the auditorium with the villagers, that the battle was confined to the walls for the time being. Ground troops were ready to defend the streets if need be. For now, the archers and tower guards were keeping the Night Demons at bay.

Catherine kept looking at Sybil Shelley, who shared her concerns and fears. Their husbands were in the towers, exposed to the onslaught they heard.

They offered prayers to the gods. They sang songs of triumph. The elders gave words of encouragement as they moved about the room.

Still, there was a sense of hopelessness amongst the women and old men of Woodmyst. No matter where Catherine looked, she saw defeat and fear in everyone's eyes.

Even in the eyes of the elders.

Tomas, however, didn't show such emotion or sense of downfall. He stood, listening intently to the sound. From his position, standing by the grand fireplace, he presumed the battle was located in the northern region of the wall.

His thoughts weren't for his father and his wellbeing during battle. If Alan Warde were to fall, it would be because that was his fate, according to the gods. He also didn't share the concerns of his mother about the safety of his sister and himself. They were in the Great Hall, which was built to withstand the worst of the winter storms that swept in from the mountains with intense violence and were barred shut from the inside by a great beam across the doors.

The stables, however, were not built as sturdily and they were easily accessible. There were no beams across the doors, or locks to keep intruders out. So, Tomas listened to calculate how close the battle was getting towards the horses.

In his mind, he pictured the mare acting skittishly, needing the hand and soft words to ease her fears.

"Tomas," Catherine called gently. "Come."

He held a hand up. *Wait.*

Cocking his head, hoping to catch the faint jingles of blades striking one another, Tomas ignored his mother's summons. He lowered his face to peer into the hearth, where the flames danced upon glowing embers.

A sudden scream from a horse caused his heart to jerk.

Fearing his mare was being hurt, he turned to face Catherine. Her countenance fell even more when she saw the look on his face.

She stood, still holding Linet tightly against her. The little girl voiced her objection to the movement with a long whining groan.

"Tomas," Catherine pleaded. "Please don't."

The boy felt torn, but compelled.

"I'm sorry, Mother," he said before turning for the passage beside the platform.

"Tomas," she called after him. He disappeared through the doorway and started along the corridor.

Many faces turned to either the door where the boy had gone, or to Catherine, who stood holding her daughter, unsure of what they had just witnessed. Sybil came to her side. She put her arms around Catherine and stared at the now-empty door where Tomas had vanished.

"Shall I go after him, my lady?" a female serve asked.

"No," Catherine replied. "It's no good putting yourself in danger. Besides, he's long gone."

"We'll pray for him and his safe return." Eowyn placed a hand upon Catherine's arm. "Knowing the boy as I do, I'm sure he'll be fine."

***

Cautiously, Tomas crept past the kitchens where some soldiers were instructing the serves inside to abandon their post. The cooks were objecting as they were still to preparing food and cider for the night watch.

"There is no night watch anymore, you fool," a soldier informed the cook. "Can't you hear that? They're fighting on the walls right now."

"Put out the flames and get yourselves inside the Great Hall," another soldier commanded them. "All people who cannot wield a weapon must be inside. Those are Chief Shelley's orders."

"Fine," the cook snorted. "We take what we can. Grab anything that is prepared or that can be done inside, over the fireplace. We will not waste our supplies. Is that fine with you?" He looked at the soldiers.

Tomas moved silently past the open doors, right behind the heels of the soldiers, and into the shadows between the kitchens and the rear of the Great Hall.

"Fine with me," the soldier replied. "We'll even help you carry it in. How's that sound?"

"Bastard," Tomas heard the cook say as he moved away.

Thinking he was in the clear, Tomas raised himself to full height and hurried away from the kitchens.

"Tomas," someone called from behind.

He froze.

"Tomas Warde," the voice called again. He turned slowly to face the one who called to him. "What are you doing outside? It's not safe."

Standing before him was Martha Fysher, her hands on her hips and a furrow on her brow.

"You get yourself back inside immediately," she ordered.

"I can't," he replied. "I have something I need to do."

"What could be more important than staying alive?" she asked.

"Keeping someone else safe," he answered.

"Keeping someone..." she repeated, not comprehending his words. "Don't be silly. Your mother and sister are in there. How do you think she will be feeling right now? Quick. Come with me."

"I'm sorry," he said. "I have to go." Turning, he ran into the shadows, hearing her call after him as he vanished into the night.

***

Screaming, hollering, clanging and shouting made its way across the village rooftops to Richard's position upon the southwestern wall. The battle was happening on the far side of Woodmyst.

He saw enemy warriors moving about on the north shore of the river, but spotted none in the southern regions. The woods from the southern bank of the waterway through to as far as he saw to the plantations appeared devoid of any movement.

Still, he instructed his men to be vigilant and not take their eyes from their quadrant. He, however, couldn't help himself, and scanned the top of the wall on the opposite side of the village.

From his position, he saw the flashes of steel reflecting light as blades swung through the air. Men moved along the wall quickly, randomly. There was no coordination amongst the friendly soldiers.

It didn't look good.

"My lord," a tower guard called.

Turning, Richard faced the guard but didn't need to speak to the other. He saw what had gripped the guard's attention, and it brought a lump to his throat.

The beast was swimming in and out of the clouds above the orchards. Its giant black mass pushed the vapour away, causing it to spiral in giant puffs as it sped in and out of sight repeatedly.

"By the gods," Richard whispered as he watched the magnificent animal turn in a tight circle above the plantations.

"What is it doing?" a guard asked.

It vanished into the clouds momentarily. The clouds swirled slowly, like a forming whirlpool, before the dragon floated back into view. Descending lower and lower, it drew close to the farmland.

Richard kept his eyes on the churning clouds. He thought he saw something there, but wasn't sure if it was merely a trick of the brain or shadows at play.

He believed he saw a large, dark mass moving just beneath the surface of the mists. He hoped to the gods he was simply seeing things.

The dragon swooped back towards the sky and bellowed a deep, guttural call. It turned towards a small farmhouse and swooped towards it.

Opening its mouth, it spat a long jet of flame at the tiny structure.

"Oh no," gasped a tower guard.

The archers' eyes grew wide with fear. One of the tower guards fell to his knees.

They watched as it instantly engulfed the tiny structure in flames. The beast turned back towards the stirring clouds and roared.

It was answered in kind, by something not seen.

Something hidden in the vapours.

Richard's fears had come to fruition.

There were two dragons.

The second dragon burst through the clouds, unveiling itself to the watchers of Woodmyst. It descended swiftly towards the ground, directly for the orchard trees.

Opening its mouth, it sent a great jet of fire that shot through the air and immersed the trees in flames. It swooped towards the sky and turned sharply to repeat the process. If any trees weren't aflame before, they definitely were now.

The first dragon directed its attention upon burning the tilled ground and the crops within. Before long, all the fields were burning.

The creatures continued to circle the area, dowsing the ground in flame and heat. Farmhouses and barns, discarded ploughs and carts were all burning.

It appeared to Richard like a sea of flames and smoke.

So intensely it burned that it cast a brilliant orange glow upon the swirling clouds above.

The great dragons continued to circle and spit jets of fire towards the ground.

All the men on the southern wall could do was watch in awe.

***

"Those are our crops," Chief Shelley cried. "You bastards."

His hands had formed into fists. He pounded the guardrail in frustration as he watched the two dragons circle in the air above the plantations.

"Unbelievable." Michael gawked at the spectacle before him. The vision was both beautiful and terrifying.

"Two dragons."

"Dragons?" the chief snapped. "You're admiring the damned dragons while our fields burn."

"The fields were going to burn, regardless," Michael spat back angrily. "Any invading force would attack supplies. It's how they did it that has my admiration."

"You admire...?" Chief Shelley turned to the other, wide-eyed and unable to believe his friend's words. "They are the enemy. We're not here to admire them, Michael. We need to find a way to destroy them.

"They're on our flanks," the chief pointed across the rooftops, "on all sides. We're surrounded."

"But we're not dead," Michael replied as he peered towards the giant beasts circling above the burning orchards.

"Not yet," Chief Shelley admitted. "But if we don't get hacked to pieces by those Night Demons over there, or burnt to ashes by those things up there, then we get to starve. And you remember what that's like, don't you Michael?"

Fury filled Michael, and he pulled his gaze away from the flying beasts to face the chief.

"I don't need to be reminded of that," he spat. "None of us do."

Chief Shelley fell silent. His friend was right. That was a long time ago and a deep shame they had all carried unwillingly.

He moved his eyes back to the burning fields. Michael had moved to the southern edge of the tower and leant against the guardrail, his eyes following the circling giants in the sky.

Suddenly, the whole ambience of the men upon the tower transformed. A quiet atmosphere fell upon them both. Chief Shelley had no words to say to his friend, except to apologise.

"I'm sorry, Michael," whispered the chief. "I don't know why I said that."

"Never again, Barnard." There was anger in the other's voice.

"I promise," he replied as he stood next to his friend. "Never again."

***

Running along the street, avoiding any contact with soldiers or runners, Tomas drew closer to the stables, where he intended to stay with the steeds during the battle. The din of the scuffle was much louder here, as the stables were closer to the western wall than he recalled.

He found the stable door open and heard upset horses over the sound of clashing iron on the wall. Slipping inside, Tomas closed the door behind him and turned to face the chargers.

Many calmed a little upon seeing him. Still, their ears twitched and twisted as the battle noise continued outside.

"It's all right," he softly called to them. He grabbed the grain bucket and scoop and made his way along to each stall, placing the feed into the mangers. Food was used to calm the people's nerves in the Great Hall. Perhaps food, he thought, would ease a horse's spirits too.

Some approached him, sticking their noses over the gates for a rub. He complied and spoke soothingly to them as he did so. Others stayed to the rear of their pens and shook in fear. He scooped food out for them, say something comforting and move on to the next.

His father had told him to never approach a sick, injured or scared animal. They more often than not attack in order to defend themselves. So, heeding to his father's words, he left the timid beasts alone.

Eventually, he came to the mare's stall. She was waiting for him. He scooped some grain out for her and rubbed her muzzle. The mare gave a soft nicker as she buried her nose into her feed trough.

"It's all right," Tomas spoke softly to her. Her ears twitched as the sounds of battle surrounded them. "I won't let them take you. I'll be here all night."

She lifted her head and nuzzled him, rubbing her head against his chest. He lowered the bucket of grain and the scoop to the ground and rubbed his hands across her cheeks and mane.

Her nose returned to the grain as he continued to rub her neck. All the while, he spoke soft words to her, and she answered with gentle nickering.

Twenty

Alan moved down to the wall-walk where he confronted the enemy head-on. He had noticed how the dark, hooded warriors continued to scale the wall at great speed and were taking the archers by surprise.

In a rash decision, he clambered over the side of the tower and dropped upon the passage behind the battlements of the defensive structure.

"What are you doing?" Peter called after him.

"Stay up there," commanded the other. "Keep watch and tell me what to do."

"That makes sense," called Peter. "After all, you just told me what to do."

Alan approached a cloaked figure from behind. It was engaged in a struggle with a young archer. It was clear to see that the Night Demon had the advantage over the young man, so Alan stepped in to assist.

He swung his heavy sword with both hands from his right, hitting the warrior in the back, just below the shoulder blade. The weapon dug in deep. The enemy soldier squealed with an inhuman call.

The archer brought his blade down into the figure's head. A spray of blood hit Alan in the face as he heard a very loud crunch of splitting skull. Both men pulled their swords from the enemy and tossed him back over the wall.

"Do more of that," Peter commanded.

"Thank you so much," Alan called back.

Another hooded warrior appeared upon the wall behind Alan as he spoke to his friend on the tower. Peter's eyes widened as he pointed.

Alan turned to see what his comrade was gesturing towards. The figure had a long, curved sword held high above its head.

Suddenly, the warrior's chest burst open as the archer's sword pierced through from behind. Alan copped another squirt of blood in the face.

The archer retrieved his blade and pushed the warrior over the wall to join his other fallen companion.

"Thank you," Alan said to the archer.

"Don't thank me yet, my lord," the archer replied. "I don't think we're finished yet."

"More coming," Peter informed his friend.

Turning towards the west, Alan saw three hooded warriors approaching. He slapped the archer on the back and nodded towards the enemy. Both men ran at the Night Demons, swords held high.

Surprise took the first.

Both men plunged their blades into its torso and tipped it over the wall's edge in one swift move. It fell screaming all the way to the bottom, where sudden silence ensued.

The two remaining warriors came at each man simultaneously.

One for the archer.

One for Alan.

Swords rang as they clashed upon the wall. The enemy warrior hacked through the air towards Alan who, in turn, blocked each blow with his own blade.

Realising it would not defeat him with only its sword, it raised its foot and kicked Alan onto his back. The hooded Night Demon raised its blade and swiftly brought it down.

Rolling to his right, pressing himself tightly against the battlement, Alan heard the enemy's blade hit the walk, missing him by inches. He rolled back and stabbed towards the warrior, finding his mark in the crotch.

A terrible deafening cry bellowed from beneath the dark hood. Alan grabbed the Night Demon by the shoulder and shoved him off the wall. "Shut up."

Turning to see how the archer was holding up, he saw the young man blocking and parrying blows successfully, but not able to turn the fight in his favour.

Alan quickly made his way over to the skirmish and slid his blade into the enemy's side. The archer pushed his sword beneath the hood, finding some resistance there. So, he pushed his blade deeper.

There was no screaming; only a disgusting crunch as the blade pierced bone and muscle. The warrior just fell limply onto the wall-walk.

"Good job," Peter called. "Keep it up. More coming over the side."

***

Splinters from the deck hit his face hard. The curved blade stuck into the wood and the Night Demon struggled to free it from the platform's grasp. Hugh saw his opportunity and acted.

Lying on his back after being knocked down by the warrior, he swung his leg around, connecting with the back of the enemy's knees. The hooded figure fell backwards onto the tower's platform with a hard thud.

Hugh reached to retrieve his sword from the floor, near to his head. Tightening his grip around the hilt, he looked over to the fallen figure. It was rolling onto its side, attempting to get back to its feet.

As quickly as he could, Hugh moved onto his knees and sliced the air with his sword. The blade slid through the Night Demon's back, spilling dark blood across the floorboards of the platform.

Lifting himself to his feet, he plunged the sword deep into the warrior's chest. Vapour escaped from beneath the dark hood as the enemy fighter breathed out the last of his air.

Dropping back to his knees, Hugh took a moment to catch his breath. Behind him, one tower guard lay dead with his innards exposed from a great wound that split him open from the neck to the groin. The other guard continued to plunge his dagger into the chest of a dead Night Demon, over and over and over.

He looked to his left, along the western wall where many of the archers were engaged in similar combat to what he had just experienced.

There were simply too many to keep going at this rate. Eventually, he knew, the men would tire and exhibit delayed reactions. The enemy would use this to their advantage.

He surmised that the Night Demons had not exposed their entire forces yet. Some reserves were still waiting out of sight for the opportunity to come in to finish what was started by this first wave of attackers.

Hugh wondered if he would live long enough to see that.

Looking past the fighters on the wall, he saw the orange glow in the clouds above the orchards. He saw the giant beasts circling in the sky above the fields. Until that moment, he didn't know the plantations were on fire.

Several hooded figures dropped to the ground inside the wall. Hugh looked to where they had jumped.

Armed soldiers raced to meet the invaders on the streets. Sword met sword. Hilt met flesh. The fight had moved to within the village.

Upon the wall, several young men stared blankly, with dead eyes, into the night sky. Their throats or bellies sliced open by enemy blades.

Continuing their advance, more Night Demons climbed upon the wall. Finding the numbers of defenders had thinned, some invaders dropped to the village below while others moved to eliminate what resistance remained.

Using his sword to assist him, Hugh lifted himself to his feet and took a deep breath. A clawed hand scraped against the guardrail as a Night Demon pulled itself over the battlement.

Hugh swung his long sword up and over his head as he spun to face the warrior. Just as the enemy soldier placed one foot onto the platform, the blade hacked through its left shoulder, stopping when it had reached deep into the chest cavity.

The tower guard snapped back to reality and rushed to his commander's side. He pushed the Night Demon off the tower and watched it plummet to the ground.

"Come on," he bellowed into the darkness. "Is that the best you can do, you bastards?"

Hugh moved to the guardrail overlooking the village. Below the wall and the tower, many cloaked figures ran through the streets. Several soldiers were in combat with the invaders.

From his vantage, Hugh saw a few cloaked figures lying lifeless in the streets. Some armed soldiers pursued those who were running further into the village. Others continued to engage with the warriors near the wall.

"Bring more," the tower guard coaxed towards the grove. "Bring us your best."

The archers continued to hold as many of the encroaching enemy back as they could. With every ounce of strength they had, they fought and defended against the onslaught. It seemed, to Hugh, that it was in vain. Immense peril fell upon them as more and more hooded warriors advanced upon the wall and climbed into the village.

"I'll take you all on," shouted the tower guard. His voice was losing its strength. "I'll kill every single one of y-"

The sudden silence deafened Hugh.

He turned to see the tower guard stuck with a black arrow through the neck.

The shaft had penetrated the throat and stuck out at the base of his skull.

The guard turned slowly to face his commander. A slither of blood slid down the front of the guard's tunic as he hissed one word.

"Bastards."

He fell face-first to the floor, forcing the arrow further into the wound.

Now Hugh was alone on the tower.

He wondered again how long he had left to live.

***

"Get those bastards," shouted the stable master, pointing along a crooked street to three Night Demons running away from him, further towards the centre of town.

The horseman was dressed in old leather armour and brandished a dull sword. His men had mocked him for not keeping his blade sharpened, claiming that it wouldn't be able to cut butter. He threatened to prove its use by slicing their manhood, to which they fell silent and let him be.

Since then, his blade had met two of the cloaked warriors and left them to bleed out in the streets by the western wall. Other enemy soldiers slipped by during the scuffle, so now he and a few of the stable hands gave chase.

"This way, Francis," one of the armoured stable hands called. "They're heading for the Great Hall."

"Of course, they are," called the big man. "That's where everybody is."

"We should've saddled some horses," another hand puffed as he struggled to keep up.

The cloaked figures were too fast. They ran like men, but much faster. The stable master silently agreed with the stable hand.

We should have saddled some horses.

"We can't go back for them now," he replied. "If the Night Demons get inside the Great Hall, the women and children will die."

The group of men ran as fast as they could towards the centre of the village. They saw the steep roof of the Great Hall above the peaks of the surrounding buildings.

The men halted once they rounded the corner and saw the giant building completely. Three cloaked warriors stood at the base of the steps leading up to the Great Hall's doors.

"Stop," the stable master called. "You need to defeat us before you get to try for those doors."

The three Night Demons revealed long curved blades from beneath their cloaks. The six stable workers ran at their enemy, shouting as they closed the distance.

Standing their ground, the hooded warriors waited for their foes to come to them. Within moments, the clanging of swords rang through the empty street in front of the Great Hall.

***

"The battle has moved to just outside these doors," called an elderly lady near the grand fireplace.

Frederick, the elder, moved to her and placed a reassuring hand on her arm.

"It was bound to happen," he said. "But do not fear. These doors are strong and our soldiers are out there doing their best to defend us."

He helped her back to her bed, where she sat and looked to the others in the room with fear-filled eyes.

Catherine's thoughts turned to her son, who was out there alone. She hoped and prayed for his safety, but feared the worst.

If the combat had made it this far into the town, then surely it must be raging around him right now.

Sybil tightened her embracing arms about Catherine's shoulders. She too worried for the safety of all loved ones outside in the thick of battle.

The sound of swordplay filled the auditorium. Some children cried as mothers desperately attempted to calm them by rocking them in their arms. The mothers, however, had no one to help them overcome their fears.

Hearts raced as the clanging grew louder and louder in their heads. Their breathing became faster and faster as their anxieties gained control.

A chorus of screams ensued when a loud thud shook the doors.

***

A cloaked invader held the stable master firmly against the large timber entrance to the Great Hall. The horseman's sword crossed his body, preventing the Night Demon from slicing his neck open.

With all of its weight, the enemy soldier pushed against the burly man. The bulky horseman could smell the foul breath of the hooded figure and tried to hold his own.

"What do you eat?" he asked as he pushed back with all of his might. "Dragon dung?"

The hooded warrior fell backwards and tumbled down the steps. The stable master almost fell after it, except that he corrected his balance before he toppled over.

Immediately, he gave chase down the steps and slashed at the Night Demon while it attempted to lift itself from the ground.

The blade sank into the warrior's back with a loud crack, sending it to the ground where it lay unmoving.

The two other dark figures were still engaged with his men. One of the stable hands was sitting with his back against a wall to the side of the street with his entrails streaming across his lap.

"Francis," called one of the other hands. "Help, please."

Francis Lytton, the stable master, bolted across the street to the scuffle. Until now, the enemy had been fighting against two stable workers. He wasn't about to give it a chance to see how it would go against three. So, before it could protest, Francis slid his rusty sword into the enemy's back just below where its ribs, aiming upwards into the vital organs.

The Night Demon's arms dropped to its sides, and the curved sword hit the dirt with a dull clang.

Pulling the blade from the warrior's corpse, the stable master ran to the aid of the other men, still exchanging blows with a cloaked warrior.

The remaining Night Demon saw they outnumbered it, and that the five men had blocked any escape.

"Where are you going to go now?" a stable hand asked confidently.

The warrior lunged at him, causing him to jump back and squeal.

Francis used the opportunity to plunge his blade deep into the Night Demon's back. He wrenched his sword from the enemy, sending a spray of blood across the ground.

The figure turned to face its attacker, opening itself up to another attack from a stable hand behind it.

The blade hacked deep into its shoulder, separating the flesh in a great open wound.

Soon, another blade from another man found its mark. Then another, and another. Pretty soon all five men were chopping the body into pieces in the empty street outside the Great Hall.

***

A loud trumpet call sounded from the grove. The onslaught of climbers stopped on the northern wall. The Night Demons withdrew to the tree line of the grove and gathered in a line just in front of the woods. Those still battling upon the wall recoiled and leapt off the side of the wall, either into the village or back across to the open ground. All enemy soldiers outside the wall ran to the gathering multitude, while those inside continued to fight.

It was a curious and unexpected manoeuvre from Peter's perspective. The enemy had the advantage and was, in his mind, winning.

Why retreat when victory was so close?

"They're leaving," Peter called to his friend on the wall.

"To go where?"

"How should I know?" he barked back. "To the royal ball."

"I'm coming up," Alan announced.

"Hoorah!" Peter called sarcastically.

Within moments, Alan was standing back upon the platform. Before him, across the open ground and in front of the trees, was a long line of hooded figures stretching from directly before the north-eastern tower, all the way as far as his eyes saw to the west.

There were still so many of them.

So, what were they waiting for?

As if to answer, a great roar erupted in the sky above.

"By the gods," Peter breathed as he peered skywards.

A great dragon beat its giant wings as it lowered itself outside the northern wall, about halfway between the two towers. Many of the remaining men upon the wall nearby leapt to the ground inside the walls and fled towards the village centre.

Alan couldn't blame them. The beast was enormous.

Its neck and head craned over the battlements as it peered along the wall one way before turning its colossal head to look along the expanse of the structure in the other direction.

"What do we do now, Alan?" Peter asked with a tremble in his voice.

Alan simply shook his head and shrugged his shoulders.

The dragon moved its head towards the sky. The men hoped this meant it was about to take to the air once again.

Another roar from the sky announced the second dragon. Bursting through the clouds from the west, it soared over Woodmyst and over the pasturelands in the east.

Reaching the space above the eastern hill, it turned sharply and floated back towards the village again. Spreading its wings wide, it caught the air like sails and slowed its descent, pulling up just outside the eastern gate.

It looked over to the first dragon and called to it with a short, deep, guttural noise. The other replied in kind.

Suddenly, the trumpet cried again.

Fire spewed from the mouths of the beast, engulfing the wall-walk above the east gate and middle of the northern wall.

The beasts turned their heads to aim their jets at any man remaining upon the walls near them.

Alan felt the sting of bile rising in his throat as the screams of men burning alive filled the night air.

Twenty-One

Chief Shelley fell to his knees, mouth agape. Michael couldn't tell if he was screaming or not. The deafening noise of the fire spewing from the dragons overwhelmed all other sounds.

Burning bodies fell, writhing in agony, from the wall to the streets below. A few of them tried to move away, only to fall after a few paces, losing their fight with the flames.

Giant tongues of fire above the eastern gate lapped the air near the great beast. It swung its head through the flames, unscathed by the heat, and spat a jet of fire towards the fleeing men upon the ground.

The flames consumed many instantly. The sound of screams could be heard as their skin and flesh peeled from their bones.

"We are lost," the chief blubbered. "We are all lost."

"Shut it, Barnard," Michael barked. He called to the men on the eastern wall, "Find cover. Get off the wall and find cover." Spinning on his heels, he addressed those upon the southern wall within earshot. "You too. Get off the wall and find cover."

The men didn't hesitate. They relayed the call along the walls as Michael placed an arm under the chief's elbow, hoisting the man to his feet.

"Move it, you fat bastard," he said to his friend. "It's only a matter of time before that thing turns its attention upon us."

They descended the ladder and returned to the ground.

"Where do we go?" Chief Shelley asked the other.

"Back to the Great Hall," Michael replied. "Where else?"

As he spoke, he heard a tremendous crash coming from the direction of the eastern gate.

"What was that?" called an archer.

***

A monstrous cloud of dust billowed into the sky. The eastern gate was gone.

The beast cried a thunderous roar as it spread its wings, clearing some of the dust clouds to reveal its majesty. It stood tall above the debris, as if proud of its handiwork.

Suddenly, the burning section of the northern wall collapsed as the other dragon pushed itself through the barrier. It was as if the wall was made of nothing but parchment. First, it was there, and now it was gone.

The trumpet blew a long call from the grove.

A thunderous roar of many voices boomed across the open ground towards the tower where both Alan and Peter stood. As they watched, many hooded warriors upon steeds emerged from the tree line.

Too many to count.

Beating their wings and sending great gusts of air in all directions, the two dragons took to the sky again.

Peering along the wall in both directions, Alan didn't see many men upon the wall. There wasn't enough to defend against what was coming.

"Get to ground," he bellowed. "Get to ground."

"What are you doing?" Peter grabbed him by the arm.

Alan stared at him blankly. "What do you mean?"

"We can't abandon our post."

"Wake up, Peter," Alan replied. "We have no post. We have lost. All we can do now is defend our families until we have no breath left." He pointed to the riders outside. "This is their second wave and we have no fortitude to defend with. We fight them head-on. Down there on the ground."

He stood upon the platform as Alan started down the ladder. His friend had a point. There were two enormous gaps in the wall for the enemy to enter the village through. Their numbers vastly surpassed those of the remaining soldiers of Woodmyst. There was none left to defend the wall, or what remained of it.

The fight was going to be on the ground.

He moved towards the ladder as the trumpet call was given again.

Hundreds of hoof falls rumbled through the earth as the mounted warriors advanced upon the village.

***

Hugh was on the street, running for the section of the northern wall that the giant beasts circling in the air above Woodmyst had decimated. He assumed they were waiting for their next command.

In the meantime, a throng of hooded riders charged towards the tumbled section of the wall, intent upon entering the village. Leading a large band of men, archers from the wall and soldiers upon the ground, Hugh sprinted towards the dust cloud that rose above the rooftops of nearby structures.

He had ordered all men near the tower to climb off the wall with him, believing that holding the defensive structure was pointless. With the destruction that the fire-breathing monsters had produced upon two sections of the wall, the enemy would concentrate their attention on those positions.

Making a rash decision, Hugh quickly gathered as many men as he could before racing to his house to release his dogs from their kennels. Knowing the animals to be loyal, he knew they would join him in battle, but freeing them gave them the opportunity to flee to safety.

Presently, his six hounds ran alongside him. Their faces fixed forward as they bolted along the street with the twenty swordsmen and archers in tow.

An incredible thunderous roar of many voices resonated along the street towards them as they ran. Hugh ignored it, pushing fear away and choosing anger as his driving force.

They rounded a bend in the road, and the scene before them looked like a nightmare. Not only was the wall here fallen and destroyed, several houses and buildings nearby had turned into rubble as well.

Dust and smoke rose from the debris in many places. Flames still lapped at what tinder they could feast upon. Partly covered bodies, scorched and burnt beyond recognition, were laced amongst the stone and timber.

Beyond all of this came the terrible sound of a deafening war cry. The voices sounded nothing like men.

Pausing near the pile of rubble, Hugh gripped his sword in both hands. He quickly looked at those around him.

His dogs bared their teeth, growling and hackles standing on end. The men were a mixed bunch. Some shared his emotion, scowling and ready for a fight. Others appeared whiter than usual and ready to run.

"Don't fear them," Hugh shouted as he turned his face towards the darkness beyond the dust and flames.

"They're just the Night Demons. If you want to fear something, fear the gods and what honour they will bestow upon you for cowardice. Especially Grolle. That bastard is having his fun tonight. Let's not disappoint him."

The first of the riders burst through the dust, charging directly for Hugh. The dogman held his ground as the steed rapidly closed the ground between them. He tightened his grip on his sword as the hooded warrior raised his curved sword high.

The mount drew to arms' reach.

The warrior swung his blade towards Hugh.

The man ducked and chopped at the steed's legs with his sword as if it were an axe to a tree.

Blood sprayed as the forelegs of the charger separated from the animal's body. The beast fell headfirst into the ground, sending the rider flying from the saddle and into the streets.

With a quick glance at the hounds, Hugh silently instructed his pets to complete the task.

Instantly, the six dogs charged the hooded warrior as it lay sprawled upon the street. Growls and snapping could be heard as the sickening sound of flesh tearing apart caused the anxious soldiers nearby to feel knots grow in their stomachs.

Their nausea would need to wait as several riders suddenly appeared upon the heap, speeding towards the men of Woodmyst.

Hugh gave a great shout and ran towards the invaders. He slashed and hacked with his heavy blade, not caring if he hit rider or steed.

"Kill them all," he cried.

The archers rapidly loaded their bows and fired at the approaching horde beyond the wall as the swordsmen dealt with those who had got through.

The dogs packed together and spooked several horses as they entered through the gap in the wall. The horses rose upon the back legs, kicking wildly with their forelimbs. A few of their riders fell to the ground where the hounds met them with snapping teeth and a painful death.

Seeing the sheer number of approaching enemy soldiers, Hugh knew he and the twenty fighters with him would not hold the ground for long. The enemy was simply too many.

The riders crowded at the passageway created by the dragon, so many that Hugh couldn't keep count.

"Grolle has come," he called to his men.

Gripping his blade tightly in both hands, he ran into the throng.

***

Alan cautiously weaved his way through the streets, moving from the eastern tower towards the break in the northern wall. Behind was a line of almost thirty men. They had encountered several hooded warriors that had entered the village earlier in the night by climbing the wall.

Now the enemy was being hunted.

Shooting his hand up, a signal to halt, Alan observed two Night Demons slinking in the shadows. They were using the cover of darkness as they made their way towards the Great Hall.

The men pressed themselves against the walls of nearby buildings to conceal themselves in the darkness.

He extended two fingers upon his hand, signalling to the soldiers behind him he saw two enemy warriors. He then made a fist.

Two archers silently sidled up to him. He gestured to a section of shadow by a small cottage. The archers peered to the darkness, barely able to make out the two shapes.

Then the shadows moved.

The archers instantly and quietly loaded their bows, and pulled back on the stings, which creaked softly as the tension increased.

The Night Demons must have heard it. Both hoods turned towards the direction of the men.

Worried the dark warriors would flee, Alan pointed to the enemy soldiers, signalling the archers to fire.

Both bowmen let the shafts loose. Both found their targets, deep in the throats of the cloaked figures.

Falling to the ground with a thud, the hooded warriors writhed in pain. There were no screams or cries. The two archers' impeccable aim had seen to that.

Alan signalled a swordsman to finish the job. As one soldier pierced the fallen Night Demons with his blade, Alan continued along the winding street towards the noise of battle.

He considered whether the hunt should continue, or if he and his men should assist at the breach. It wasn't a tough decision to make.

"Let's go," he ordered.

Running towards the sound of swords clashing, Alan pulled his blade from its sheath. He heard horses screaming, men calling, and dogs barking.

Upon arriving at the scene, he saw riders bursting through the rupture in the wall, only to be met by a ragtag group of men. At their forefront stood Hugh Clarke, swinging his sword wildly at Night Demon and steed alike.

Running between the chargers' legs, snapping at their hooves, were six savage hounds. Alan moved his eyes across the debris where he saw charred bodies of his village men. Amongst them lay the freshly killed bodies of cloaked figures.

It would appear that Hugh and his men were having some small successes. But the numbers of enemy chargers entering through the ruptured wall also informed him they were vastly outnumbered.

"Coming in," Alan shouted over the din of battle.

The men behind him repeated the call-in chorus, assuring that their allies heard them.

"Hurry up and get in here, then," shouted one swordsman near Hugh.

Charging hard, Alan and his men lifted their blades and engaged the enemy.

"Some got through, Alan," Hugh called as he plunged his blade into the ribs of an enemy warrior. "There were just too many."

"How many?" he asked as he slashed his blade across a steed's chest. The horse fell hard, and the rider fell upon one of the charred remains of a man. Two of Hugh's dogs were instantly upon the fallen figure, burying their muzzles into its fleshy torso.

Alan turned from the scene only to be confronted with another mounted steed heading straight for him.

"I'm not sure," Hugh answered as he slid his blade across the chest of a Night Demon. "Perhaps five on horseback."

An arrow shot through the air and hit the charging rider in the side of the head before it reached Alan.

"There will be more before the night is over," he called back. The rider fell at his feet. He stabbed his blade into its chest, just to be sure.

"I know," Hugh replied.

***

The southern fields continued to burn, sending plumes of smoke and ash into the sky. Richard could only assume that the intense heat from the dragon fire had scorched the earth in that area so deep that life would cease to exist in the plantations for some time to come.

Turning his back upon the orchards, he observed the mayhem unfolding inside the village walls. Dust and smoke still sat thickly above the two breached areas of the defensive barrier.

The sound of combat rang across the rooftops towards him. The battle was now inside Woodmyst.

The surrounding men had given up on watching the forest to the west and the region to the south.

The plantations were lost.

The enemy was entering the town.

There was no need for any attack to occur in their sector. Such an act would be overkill and unnecessary.

Panning across the faces of the men about him, Richard saw mixed reactions upon all of them.

Some wanted to stay, and secretly, a part of him did too.

Here, upon the southern section of the wall, they had been left alone. There had been no attacks and sight of the Night Demons. The dragons' attack was distant from them. The noise of battle was on the far side of the village and not posing a threat to the southern defence.

They were safe here, for the time being.

Eventually, however, the enemy would make its way towards them and they would be discovered. Their options would be to either flee or fight.

The fear on several men's faces displayed the desire to flee. But having an enemy with dragons that could fly and breathe fire, fleeing would prove fruitless.

Standing to fight would cause imminent death. But it would be a brave death and he didn't want to be known for cowardice.

The faces of the other men surrounding him upon the wall informed him of a desire to climb down from the wall and enter the fray.

Some of them had family in the Great Hall and the giant structure was the endgame for the Night Demons. He didn't have a family of his own, but he understood their yearning to be with their loved ones.

Again, facing the enemy in the streets of Woodmyst would certainly result in death. Cowardice, however, would not enter the equation. Surely, the gods would look favourably upon them if they confronted their fears head-on.

So, Richard made a decision.

"Men," he called, "there is no need for us to defend this wall any longer. The enemy has breached our defences in the north and east. They have now entered our village. I believe they intend to harm your families who are safe within the Great Hall. I intend to stop as many of them as I can. Join me, or not. You decide."

He descended the tower ladder and hurried towards the centre of town.

Before long, there was a throng of men following him.

The night had revealed a powerful enemy that outnumbered them immensely.

One by one, they brandished their blades as they marched.

They were afraid.

They were brave.

Twenty-Two

Michael pulled the men upon the southern side of the East Bridge. He peered across the river to the enormous cloud of dust above the rubble of the eastern gate. A flickering orange glow projected against it, caused by the fires that burned beneath.

"What are you doing?" Chief Shelley called.

"I think we should split up," Michael replied.

The chief looked puzzled. He turned to the faces of the men nearby to see if they could make sense of his friend's words. Each of them shared his expression of confusion.

"Are you mad?"

"The enemy is at the breach." He pointed across the gables between their position and the rupture in the wall.

"Yes," Chief Shelley agreed. "So, let's kill some of them."

"The Great Hall remains practically unprotected," Michael continued.

The chief moved his eyes towards the town centre and then back to the glowing dust cloud.

"Right," he nodded.

"I think you should take some men and protect the Great Hall," suggested Michael.

"What?" Chief Shelley quickly turned his head left and right, glancing in the directions of both the breach and the giant building in the centre of the village. "Why don't you go to the Great Hall and I go to the wall?"

Michael looked directly into his friend's eyes and placed his hands on the chief's shoulders.

"I don't have a wife and children, Barnard," he replied. "You take the men who do, and I'll take those who don't. Go to the Great Hall where your families are. Protect them with everything you have. We'll try to hold them off for as long as we can."

Chief Shelley touched his forehead against Michael's brow. "You're a good friend, Michael."

The men separated, the chief taking the married men while the single warriors remained with the other. Michael quickly counted the two parties. It appeared there were more with families than without.

As a result, some forty men left with the chief, leaving Michael with a little fewer than twenty.

It would have to do.

"To battle, I guess." He smiled at the men in his charge.

They crossed the bridge at full pace and wound their way towards the eastern gate.

***

The Night Demons raced their steeds around the north-eastern corner of the wall, passing beneath the tower and heading towards the breach where the eastern gate once stood. Awaiting them were thirteen men with Peter at the helm.

They had already slain fifteen of the enemy riders, but knew there was more to come for them. The men at the eastern gate, as with those at the northern breach, prevented the enemy from a full assault within the walls. Peter, however, knew they wouldn't be able to hold them off for long.

Over twenty men were lying dead around him, victims of dark arrows and curved blades. He needed more men to help him hold the breach.

The horses suddenly appeared in the glow of the fire that still burnt upon the fallen debris.

Swinging his sword, Peter connected with the lead charger. The beast screamed, and the rider fell. As quickly as he could, Peter jumped to the side, pressing himself against the inside surface of the wall next to the breach.

Other riders flooded through the gap, riding over their fallen comrade, trampling the cloaked figure into the rubble.

The other men attacked ferociously.

"We hold them here," Peter called as he joined the fight.

His men hacked and slashed wildly. They were untrained and not particularly skilled. But they were focused. They were intent on killing as many of the invaders as they could.

Thirteen became twelve, then eleven, as the conflict persisted.

Several enemy riders broke through the blockade and disappeared into the village. Peter looked after them and counted five, but knew he could not pursue. He turned back to the onslaught of riders and slashed wildly.

Some Night Demons fell from their horses where they met the Woodmyst blades. Upon seeing this, some riders dismounted and engaged the men on the ground.

Occupied with hand-to-hand combat, the men could not focus their attention upon the encroaching chargers who slipped through the breach and into the village without resistance.

Peter cried out in frustration as he blocked and parried blows from a hooded warrior. His family was in the Great Hall and something inside of him knew the riders were intent on getting there.

He fought with every ounce of strength he had. There was no way he would simply allow his family to fall victim to the Night Demons.

The riders needed to be stopped. But now they simply rode through the gap, as if invited.

His heart sank as the sensation of defeat filled his spirit.

He pictured his family falling prey to the curved blade of the enemy. Anger and rage suddenly filled his senses, and he pushed the warrior back with his sword.

The Night Demon stumbled slightly before swinging the blade overhead towards Peter. In one swift motion, Peter blocked with his sword and pulled his dagger from his belt, plunging it deep into the chest of his foe.

Twisting the blade, Peter retracted his knife and let the warrior fall to the ground. He replaced the dagger back upon his belt as he bolted onto the mound, swinging his sword from right to left in order to connect with the neck of a passing steed.

With a quick spin, he withdrew the blade and swung from left to right. The horse continued to fall, lowering its rider to just the right height for Peter to sink his blade into the warrior's back.

"We number eight," a swordsman announced as he took his place by Peter's side.

"Coming in," a familiar voice called from behind them.

Twenty men suddenly emerged from the shadows of the street, Michael in the lead.

"Not anymore," Peter replied to the swordsman beside him.

More riders appeared in the breach as the soldiers arrived on the mound.

"Some made it through," Peter announced. "I think they're heading for the Great Hall."

"Barnard has taken forty men to defend the Great Hall," Michael replied as he slashed at a passing steed. The rider was flung to the ground, hard. Before it could rise back to its feet, a swordsman plunged his blade into the fallen warrior's head.

"Do you think we can win?" Peter asked.

"No," Michael replied, "but we can make them second guess the reason why they tried to take us down.

Perhaps we can scare them away."

Peter chuckled as he swung his blade again.

***

The Night Demon riders raced through the streets of Woodmyst. Their current course would lead them directly to the steps outside of the Great Hall. Holding their curved swords high, they called with loud hoots and shouts through the streets to any of their comrades who had infiltrated the walls and make their way towards the village centre.

Several answered from the shadows and continued to make their way towards the enormous building in the middle of town.

The riders found more warriors upon steeds as they wound their way through the thin back streets of Woodmyst. Gradually, their numbers grew with eleven upon steeds and twenty on foot.

Before long, the Great Hall was within view. The riders pulled their horses to a halt a little way down the street from the steps leading up the giant doors.

Standing upon the steps were Francis Lytton and his three remaining workers brandishing swords stained with the blood of Night Demons.

The stable master scrutinised the invaders carefully.

The cloaked figures, both upon steed and foot, peered back at the men from beneath their dark hoods.

"Quite a few of them," said one of the hands softly to the hefty horseman. "Aren't there, Francis?"

"Is that all you got?" Francis called.

One rider charged forward, directing his steed straight for the stable master. Raising his sword over his head, the horseman flung his weapon towards the oncoming warrior.

The blade turned in the air and buried itself deep into the steed's forehead, right between the eyes.

The horse fell, and the rider tumbled across the street, landing in a heap at the base of the stairs. One of the stable hands quickly slid his blade into the cloaked figure as the stable master ripped his sword from the animal's head.

"Good shot, Francis," said another hand.

"I was aiming for the rider," Francis informed the man. "Poor horse didn't need that."

Suddenly, the other Night Demons bolted towards the men on the stairs.

"Here we go," a hand announced.

Twenty-Three

The noise of clanging steel urged Chief Shelley to increase his pace. He led the men across the Centre Bridge and onto the street that led directly to the steps of the Great Hall.

As they ran along the road towards the building, he saw a small group of men fighting many enemy warriors. He increased his pace as much as he could. His men kept pace behind him.

He witnessed a curved blade take the head from one of the brave men near the steps. Suddenly afraid his band of men wouldn't get to the fight before the remaining soldiers in the fray were taken, he hollered to the ones behind him.

"Go, go. Don't wait for me. Take those bastards down."

Men bolted past him and towards the conflict. By the time he joined them, they had already engaged and taken out three of the Night Demons.

Chief Shelley, still running, swung his sword towards a hooded figure dismounting a steed. The blade cut through the enemy soldier's shoulder and dropped him to the ground.

Blood oozed from the wound, pooling onto the ground near the body. He hadn't seen blood during battle since the days of the Realm War. His stomach tightened and his knees felt weak.

"Wake up, Chief," called Francis Lytton from his side.

Chief Shelley turned just in time to see another hooded warrior running at him from his left.

The chief pointed the tip of his blade towards the advancing soldier and used his legs to help him run the blade deep into the chest of the enemy.

The curved blade dropped onto the street moments before its owner fell next to it.

Chief Shelley turned to face the thick of the battle.

Before him were forty of his village men overpowering the band of enemy warriors.

"Save the horses if you can," called the stable master as he pulled a rider from his charge, stabbing his sword into the invader's chest with one hand.

The chief jogged into the fight and hacked his way through two of the Night Demons to sidle up to the large man.

"Been at this long?" he asked.

"Long enough," Francis answered. "How are you holding up?"

"It's coming back to me," the chief grunted.

"Good," replied the brawny horse keeper as he watched two swordsmen hack the life out of the last standing Night Demon. "Because this is only just starting."

Chief Shelley moved his gaze slowly over the carnage that filled the street in front of the Great Hall.

Twisted bodies of village men, enemy soldiers and horses lay strewn from the base of the steps, crossing from one side of the street to the other.

"The serves will have a grand old-time cleaning this mess up," said one of the stable hands. "Won't they, Francis?"

"I suspect they will," Francis chuckled.

***

They had crossed the West Bridge and made their way along the wide street that led from the western gate to the Great Hall. In the distance, near the steps of the Great Hall, those at the forefront of the mass saw several men moving about.

"Who goes there?" someone called from the group ahead.

"It's Richard Dering," called a man amongst the approaching mob.

"Richard." Chief Shelley stepped forward. "Thank the gods."

The chief ran forward and embraced his friend. Richard embraced the chief's broad shoulders.

"Good to see you too, Barnard," he retorted. "It looks as if you've had some trouble.

"No trouble," Chief Shelley objected playfully.

"Well," Richard said as he looked towards the north, "I expect we will have some sooner or later."

The chief moved his eyes across the men, following his friend. He quickly calculated the numbers of men combined that now stood near the Great Hall.

"I think we pose a formidable force," Chief Shelley proposed. "We number near to one hundred strong."

"They number at least twice that," Richard replied. "We couldn't clearly see the enemy from our position on the south wall, but it looked like a lot more than we have here."

"You're full of optimism, Richard," the chief replied sarcastically.

"Do your wife and children know you're out here?" Richard asked.

"No," he replied as he turned to walk towards the steps. Richard joined him as he continued to speak. "I don't see the point of reuniting until we have won the battle."

Richard mulled that thought over for some time. The possibility of winning was a very distant possibility. They had lost so much already.

Glancing towards the sky, he saw the two giant beasts still circling high above. Their wing tips dipped in and out of the cloud cover as they soared in magnificent spirals.

Winning?

His optimism definitely needed improving.

"What's your strategy?" Richard asked.

"To hold the Great Hall," Francis answered before Chief Shelley could say a word.

The chief shot a smile to his friend as he sidled up to the burly man standing on the stairs.

"Richard Dering," Chief Shelley said, "meet Francis Lytton. Woodmyst's stable master."

The two men clasped arms and said their greetings.

"I was really asking for specifics." Richard returned to the chief. "Where would you like the men?"

The chief considered this for a moment. He scanned the surrounding area with his eyes carefully and finally lowered his eyes to the bodies in the street.

"Right," he finally said. "Let's get what archers we can spare on the rooftops. We can put twenty men here on the steps and, let's say, ten around the back near the rear entrance. The passage narrows there and we could set a trap for any of the Night Demons who try for the serves' door."

"Sounds fair," Richard replied. "Archers to me," he called to the men standing in the street.

He instructed the men to climb certain buildings surrounding the Great Hall that offered the best vantage points. Before long, they positioned nearly twenty men upon the gables of nearby structures.

***

The stable master took his three remaining stable hands and six more men to the rear of the building. They placed an overturned cart upon its end to block the eastern end of the passageway, stacking barrels of flour and wheat with sacks of oats into the gaps between the cart and walls.

This would, with luck, be enough deterrence for any invaders attempting to penetrate the rear entrance at that end of the back alley. It would force the enemy to enter by the western end of the passage, causing them to pass by the three doors to the kitchens before they reached the tiny door that was used by the serves.

Francis placed his men inside the three doors. The enemy could enter from the west, be attacked by the hidden men, and either perish or run back the way they came from.

The hefty man placed a barrel near the tiny door and plopped himself upon it before laying his rusty sword across his lap. He held a freshly baked loaf of bread in his hand and tore off a steaming piece before shoving it into his mouth.

"Where did you get that then, Francis?" asked one of the stable hands hungrily.

"From the kitchen," he muffled through the mouthful of bread.

"Was there any more?"

"There was an entire tray in the oven," Francis answered. "Check on the table. The second door, right at the back."

The stable hand ran back down the alley towards the kitchen doors, disappearing inside where he was directed to go.

"Oy," he called out after some time. "There's warm cider in here too."

Jumping up from his perch upon the barrel, sword in one hand and bread in the other, Francis ran back towards the kitchens.

"Cider?" he called as he disappeared through the door to join the hand.

***

Seventeen men, along with three dogs, had been slaughtered during the conflict. Alan and Hugh continued to hold the breach with what force they had remaining. The men were tiring, and the dogs were slowing their attack.

Fatigue was setting in.

Still, the fifteen men and three hounds continued to fight as the riders pushed through the gap in an attempt to enter the village. Swords clashed and blood drained upon the mound.

Several men hacked the body of a fallen warrior as it fell from its steed. It was a pattern that was repeated consistently. The men would take a rider from the charger and introduce their blades to the enemy.

As they returned their attention to the riders appearing in the breach, Alan saw the way they let their swords hang from their grip; loosely and carelessly.

Suddenly aware that he was doing the same, he composed himself as he swiped his blade towards an approaching steed. It fell hard and sent the rider toppling. Two of the hounds were there to meet the warrior on the ground.

Alan wondered how much more of this he and the surrounding men could take. He couldn't imagine the situation becoming much worse.

Then the trumpet blew a long whining note.

***

Peter looked over at Michael, who was buckled over, trying to catch his breath.

"What was that?" he asked as the last of the trumpet note died away.

The riders in the breach suddenly disappeared back into the darkness beyond the wall.

"I don't know," Michael replied. He glanced at the remaining men and counted nine.

"Do you think they're sending the dragons back?" a worried swordsman quizzed.

"Let's hope not," Peter replied. He stared into the void. His eyes could barely distinguish the forms of the farmhouses in the meadow.

A thick white mist had rolled across the ground, like a soft blanket covering the grass. The sight made him feel cold inside.

"Listen," Michael started. "I don't know how to say it, so I'll just say it. Lawrence is dead."

Peter turned his head to lock eyes with his friend.

"Elara too," continued Michael. "One of the flying beasts dropped them both and their cart outside the south wall. I don't know what else to say."

"Did you see the children?"

"No," Michael admitted. "From where I was standing, I could only see Lawrence and Elara. But the cart's a mess and it's dark. There's no way to know if they..."

He stopped talking as he thought of his friend still lying on the wreckage with his wife. The prospect of the children being amongst the clutter never occurred to him until now.

"He must have been trying to escape." Peter turned to face the pastureland again. "Damn fool. We warned him, Michael. We all did. Damn stubborn fool."

A terrible thought crossed Michael's mind.

"What if the Night Demons took the children?"

"You think they were eaten?" Peter asked. "Like the missing meat from the scouts' legs?"

Michael nodded, ashamed that he could think of such a thing. "Yes."

"That is a possibility." Peter gripped the hilt of his sword. His thoughts flashed images of children being tossed upon a fire to prepare for a feast.

Suddenly, his mind flipped through images of mud huts and crude wooden tables deep within a marshland.

Images of blood and fire followed immediately.

He shook the thoughts away, forcing them out of his mind as he focused on his current situation.

"They'll return soon," Peter announced. "Let's be ready for them."

The men climbed to the top of the mound, brandishing their blood-stained blades as they waited for the next wave of attack.

***

A sudden yelp from one dog caused all the men to snap their heads towards the animal. It fell onto its side, a dark arrow sticking from its ribs.

"Oh no," Hugh gasped. He ran towards his pet but fell short as another arrow shot towards him from the blackness beyond the wall, striking him in the ribs just below his armpit.

He breathed hard, a loud wheeze hissing from his lips as he rolled upon his back.

"Hugh," Alan called. He started towards his fallen friend, but never made it more than two paces.

A sudden throng of shafts shot through the air towards the men upon the rubble, piercing their flesh in many places at once.

The pain was immense as Alan felt countless tiny bites all over his body. He dropped to his knees and screamed a terrible cry into the night.

His men fell, some dead instantly, others still writhing in pain.

Arrows continued the stick into them again and again until they moved no more.

Alan, still screaming, turned towards the dark expanse of the breach.

There, in the gap, stood lone Night Demon glaring at him.

***

Michael crawled across the rubble, trailing blood behind him as he drew near to his fallen friend. Lying awkwardly on his back, Peter stared into the night sky with fourteen arrows sticking from his chest.

Gripping his friend's hand, Michael rested his head on Peter's shoulder and wept.

The crunching sound of footfalls in the rubble caused him to tremble. He heard the breath of the approaching warrior and the creak of the tightening bowstring.

The loud thwack of the arrow piercing his skull rang in his ears as darkness filled his vision.

Then he couldn't hear or see a thing.

***

The lone hooded figure approached. It carried a bow laden with a dark arrow, tiny sharp barbs upon its pointy iron head. Fastened to the warrior's belt was a curved horn taken from the skull of some poor beast. Alan surmised this was the trumpet they had heard throughout the night. He realised this was the commander of the Night Demons.

"Come to pay me tribute, have we?" Alan smiled as blood oozed from his mouth.

The warrior removed his hood, revealing himself to the man on his knees.

Alan's eyes grew wide with reverence and terror.

A tear fell from his eye and trailed over his cheek as he recognised the face of his enemy.

He understood what this was all about.

It was his fault.

"By the gods," he gasped.

The last arrow passed through his throat and out the back of his neck, sticking there.

Alan fell, slumped to his side.

***

The riders and foot soldiers poured into the breach like flowing water. They shot through the streets, drawing closer and closer towards the centre of town. All the Night Demons bellowed a loud call as they approached.

The sound was like something from a nightmare.

Chief Shelley shuddered, an icy shiver crawling along his spine as he listened and waited.

"From the north and east," shouted an archer on a nearby roof.

"How many?" called Richard.

"Can't say," the archer called back. "Too bloody many to count."

The noise grew increasingly louder and louder as the enemy drew closer and closer.

Richard tightened his grip on his sword.

The enemy was coming.

He was about to get into the fight.

Twenty-Four

Twenty men stood upon the steps of the Great Hall awaiting the onslaught of enemy riders and soldiers that ran towards their positions. The thunderous sound of shouting and hooting from the Night Demons was deafening.

"They're here," an archer called from a nearby rooftop.

"Let loose," Richard hollered above the din.

Arrows flew through the air, hitting targets hidden from the view of the men in front of the Great Hall. Screams and wails of pain could be heard amongst the roaring call of the approaching enemy. They saw several arrows flying in the opposite direction, answering the archers' greeting.

Richard watched as a few archers upon the rooftops were hit and slid uncontrollably, lifelessly over the sides of the buildings.

The enduring archers continued to send shaft after shaft into the invaders, thinning the assault as much as they could before it reached the men waiting upon the ground.

The sound of a hundred footfalls increased as the roaring voices grew nearer. Chief Barnard knew the attack was imminent. The enemy would be upon them at any moment.

He raised his sword high. "Ready men," he called. "The enemy is upon us. We will fight and we will win. We must." He lowered his sword and swept his sword across all of them, pointing to the men around him. "For our wives. For our children and for our people."

He lifted his sword high again. "For Woodmyst."

A dark arrow streaked through the air with a loud whistle, burying deep into Chief Barnard's chest.

"For Woodmyst," he breathed as he stared wide-eyed into the sky.

Falling upon his back, he lay sprawled upon the steps watching the dragons float high above the village.

Arrows continued to fly into the enemy that was still out of view as a great number of them, some upon steeds and others on foot, rounded a corner and bolted for the Great Hall.

"Hold your ground," Richard commanded. Some archers aimed for the chargers, hitting the horses and sending them into a tumble. The warriors toppled slightly before lifting themselves to their feet, continuing towards the men on the steps.

"Attack," Richard called as he ran to meet the enemy. The other swordsmen obeyed and started slashing and hacking at the enemy with vicious energy.

The men were impeccably accurate with their strikes. Enemy intestines were spilt, limbs separated, and lives destroyed.

In a matter of what seemed no time at all, they left sixteen Night Demons lying in the street. The only losses to the men of Woodmyst were the few fallen archers upon the rooftops and Chief Barnard Shelley, who lay dead upon the steps of the Great Hall.

Before time allowed the men to reorganise, a multitude of enemy warriors appeared from several side streets. Richard realised they had moved some distance away from the steps. The doors were now vulnerable.

The Night Demons raced towards the men on the ground and they met in a flurry of sword exchanges. The swordsmen blocked, parried and slashed as well as any man could, taking several of the hooded warriors down as possible.

The enemy, however, was overbearing and pushed the swordsmen back along the street. Before Richard realised, they were almost halfway towards the Centre Bridge and nowhere near enough to the Great Hall to be of any use to it.

Several Night Demons climbed the steps with their steeds. They attached ropes to the saddles and then the foot soldiers extended and applied them to the large timber doors. Other cloaked figures lifted Chief Shelley's body and carried it out of view towards the east.

Richard couldn't believe his eyes.

Why would they want the chief's body but leave the others lying in the street?

The horses with ropes attached to their saddles started pulling, pulling.

The doors creaked under the pressure.

"Come on," Richard cried. Frustration filled his heart.

He swung his blade wildly, connecting with his foe and sending the warrior to the ground. But where that one fell; another took its place. The enemy intended to keep them at bay until the attack on the Great Hall was complete.

***

A small band of seven Night Demons moved into the alley behind the Great Hall, creeping towards the kitchen doors. Their bodies hunched and their footsteps silent, they edged closer and closer to the tiny door that led into the giant structure.

The lead warrior paused near the first kitchen door. It gripped the handle with its long fingers, scraping its claws against the timber frame. A slow twist to the left, then the right informed it that the door was locked.

Slowly, it moved to the next door and repeated the process. Upon realising the door was also sealed, it moved on.

The last door was open. It stopped dead in its tracks, directly in front of the open doorway, and turned to the others behind it.

Unexpectedly, it disappeared, ripped from where it was, and dragged into the darkness of the kitchen. It screamed hysterically before it fell suddenly silent.

The other kitchen doors flung open and outburst three stable hands and six swordsmen.

The Night Demons pulled their curved blades from beneath their cloaks, but it was too late.

The hands and swordsmen cut them down before any chance of a fight began. The six hooded warriors fell lifeless onto the ground, leaving a pool of blood where they rested.

"Now what?" asked one swordsman.

"Pile them up near the wagon," Francis ordered. "Could be more coming and I don't want to trip on anything."

"You want help with that one, Francis?" asked a hand.

"Yeah," he replied, disappearing back into the kitchen. "You take the leg and I'll take the rest."

The stable master re-emerged, dragging the body by the arms, while the stable hand carried a severed leg over his shoulder by the ankle like a knapsack. They threw both onto the pile of corpses near the overturned wagon.

"How's about some of that cider?" asked Francis.

The other men simply nodded and smiled.

***

The doors shook violently. Brief outbursts of wails and screams filled the auditorium as mothers covered their children's ears and eyes. The noise of hooves upon stone just outside the entrance, along with deep hooting calls and grunts, filled each man, woman and child with terror.

Catherine held Linet. Both were crying uncontrollably. Soothing words escaped Catherine's lips as she attempted to comfort her tiny daughter, but her own ears paid no homage to them.

She rocked back and forth as the doors were given another tremendous tug from outside. Dust exploded from the joints and fell from the beams above as the vibration from the sudden jolt reverberated throughout the building.

Frederick and Edmond approached the large wooden accesses. They had lowered two thick beams in place across the entrance, resting upon iron brackets positioned upon the two side jambs and near the centre of the doors themselves.

Carefully, and as quietly as they could, they inspected the barricades, ensuring that the beams were still secure and not weakening.

The doors shook again, sending a rumble through the expanse of the room. Puffs of dust sprinkled from the beams high above the nervous people gathered on the floor.

Turning towards the villagers, Frederick patted the air with an open hand, signalling that it was all right; telling them to stay calm.

Continuing to rock back and forth, holding her little girl tightly, Catherine whispered calming words as tears welled in her eyes. She glanced towards Martha Fysher, who sat on the edge of her bed with her arms around her two daughters, leaning against either side of her. The girls were blubbering as Martha made gently shushing sounds.

Sybil had wrapped a blanket around herself and her two daughters and snuggled with them upon her cot. They lay upon their sides, mother facing the two girls in an embrace.

They had heard Barnard outside the doors sometime earlier, shouting and calling. Some of his words made it inside and filled their ears with hope. Sybil believed in her heart that she would see her husband again soon. Perhaps victory was on their side.

Then they heard him no longer.

Some time had passed since his voice filled their ears, and hope dwindled soon after. The sound of swords clashing had returned and grew distant just before the noise at the door began.

The doors rattled loudly. The lower beam across the door jiggled slightly but continued to hold.

Several quick screams ensued, and more children cried. Some asked for their fathers, while others wanted to go home. The novelty of sleeping out in the Great Hall had worn off.

Their mothers tried to tell them they needed to stay, but they were too young to understand the dangers that waited for them outside the doors. War and conflict were incomprehensible to them, as they had never known of it until now.

Peering around the room, Catherine saw several young female serves had taken to the arms of several older women. Still children themselves, they cried, fearing for their safety.

The mature serves comforted them in a motherly way, assuring them that the men outside would not let the Night Demons harm them. They embraced the young girls, rubbing their backs and rocking gently as they attempted to ease their concerns.

Believing the words spoken to the young serves as much as she believed her own, she had whispered to her daughter, Catherine wept. Her hopes had been dashed when she first heard the doors rumbling.

In her mind, it was just a matter of time before the enemy was inside the auditorium and upon them. With no weapons to defend themselves, she knew their young daughters and sons would become victims to the curved swords of the Night Demons. She believed the elderly, and the crippled would be slain before the young serve girls and women of the village would be treated as toys for the enemy.

Her hopes had been dashed.

She awaited imminent doom.

The doors rumbled again.

The lower beam cracked.

***

In the back alley behind the Great Hall, the men had taken up their positions in the kitchens once again. A clatter from around the corner of the giant structure signalled the approach of enemy soldiers.

The Night Demons approached casually, possibly not expecting resistance. They were noisy and made loud vocal sounds, communicating with one another.

They rounded the corner and stopped at the end of the alley. From his position, just inside the open door where the dark shadows concealed him, the stable master saw them holding a discussion. One gestured towards the little door across the thin lane from the horse master's position.

The group of hooded figures numbered at least twelve from what he saw. They peered towards the pile of corpses near the overturned cart and pulled their curved swords from beneath their cloaks.

Francis almost swore. He wished he had more men hidden in the alley with him. The enemy now outnumbered them.

The cloaked warriors strode into the alley, heading directly towards their fallen allies. They passed by the two closed doors to the kitchens and paused between the open door where the horseman waited and the second, which concealed a number of his men.

One of the hooded figures continued past the bulky horseman's position and crouched near the slain bodies. Twisting its head, it barked something deep and raucous to the other Night Demons.

Two of them instantly turned towards the closed doors and kicked at them with the heels of their boots.

The doors smashed in with a loud crack.

Swords flashed from the darkness and caught the intruders in the guts.

The other hooded warriors recoiled as ten men burst from the tiny rooms, weapons ready.

Rising from beside the remains near the wagon, the cloaked figure lifted his sword, ready to run into the fray.

The stable master caught him by surprise and brought his own dull blade down upon the warrior's head.

Blood spewed from beneath the hood as the figure fell lifelessly onto the ground.

Francis turned towards the fight. One of his stable hands and a swordsman were positioned awkwardly upon the ground, great wounds in each of their chests.

He moved upon them, slashing and hacking with his rusty sword, putting another two down as he fought his way towards his men. The small troop fought just as wildly.

The sound of clashing swords echoed along the tiny passageway as the men of Woodmyst deflected and circumvented the enemy's blows.

The scuffle grew tiresome, and the men turned from defending themselves to attacking their foes. Soon, it was the Night Demons who blocked and parried as the stable workers and the swordsmen hacked and chopped into the flesh of their enemy.

Eventually, when all rival warriors were defeated, and blood had splashed upon all of them, they met in the middle.

"We showed them," said a stable hand. "Didn't we, Francis?"

The burly man just stared at the slain bodies of his worker and the swordsman.

"We should move the bodies," suggested a soldier, breathing hard.

Francis Lytton, the stable master, nodded. "Our people get moved inside," he said, pointing to the first kitchen. "Theirs get thrown upon the heap."

They hurried. Others nearby would no doubt have heard the sound of swordplay.

As they cleared the bodies in the alleyway, they heard the noise of guttural speech calls could from beyond the western edge of the Great Hall.

There was no time for refreshments. Not even for a swig of warm cider.

More Night Demons were coming.

Twenty-Five

Standing by the mare, Tomas continued to whisper to her and rub her muzzle. She nickered softly, as if speaking to him as he comforted her. She appeared to be calmer now.

Staring through the darkness of the stables, he saw many other horses had settled as well. Some of the timider steeds had made their way from the back of their stalls to the food troughs, where they munched on grain noisily.

The sound of battle had moved away from them.

Tomas hoped it was all over.

He felt tempted to venture outside to see exactly what was going on, but stayed where he was. Surely, adults would eventually come to check the stables. When they did, he would return to the Great Hall where he intended to find his father, mother, and sister.

The mare lowered her head to allow the boy to give her a scratch behind her ear. This was something she had done a few times before. He guessed it was something she enjoyed having done, so he complied and moved his fingers behind the pointy appendage.

Suddenly, all the steeds lifted their heads.

Their ears twitched around nervously.

The mare snorted and stepped away from Tomas.

"What's the matter?" he asked calmly.

Several other horses disappeared into their stalls, spooked by something the boy could not see.

The stable door rattled and creaked.

A revelation that the enemy was here made Tomas look for a place to hide. A ladder hallway between the stable doors and the back wall appeared to be his only chance. It led to a loft above the horses where the stable master kept supplies of straw and oats.

He ascended quickly as the doors rattled again.

Squeaking open slowly, the doors let a little more light into the stables as Tomas quietly buried himself in the straw.

He couldn't tell how well he had been covered. Hoping it was enough, he lay as still as he could as four shadows entered the building.

Several horses snorted and stamped their hooves in protest.

Listening intently, Tomas heard two of the invaders conversing in deep grunts and sounds unfamiliar to him.

The noise of two stalls being opened alarmed him a little. He hoped his mare would be spared any misdeed these shadows had planned.

The horses grunted and jerked their bodies about in the stalls as the cloaked intruders approached them.

Soft clicks and low rumbling noises emitted from the shadowy figures seemed to calm the beasts. Before long, the two horses were being led out of the barn quietly.

Tomas couldn't believe his ears.

He wondered what they planned for the steeds.

Soon, they had returned for more horses.

They repeated the process and took two more horses from the stables. Then led two more away, and another two.

Realising that soon they would reach his beloved mare, Tomas struggled internally with two choices. Should he stay where he was, possibly safe from the enemy, or should he defend his horse?

The shadows opened another two stalls, and the horses were more than willing to be taken. It would seem they no longer feared the cloaked ones.

Wrestling in his mind, Tomas felt a small slither of sweat trickle over his brow.

He couldn't let them take the mare.

He couldn't let them near her.

He jumped from his hiding place, ran for the ladder and descended.

The horses reared and snorted at the sudden appearance of the boy. The hooded heads of the Night Demons turned to watch the lad bolt across the floor of the stable to stand defiantly in front of the mare's stall.

"No," he said. He balled his hands into fists, ready to fight. "You can't have her."

One of the hooded warriors, wearing a curved horn upon its belt, stepped towards him. Tomas pointed to the mare and then to himself.

"She's mine," he said boldly.

The shadowy figure stopped. It turned its hooded face towards the mare at the rear of the pen and back to the boy. Stepping forward, it reached with a clawed hand towards Tomas.

Swinging madly with his fists, the boy connected with the warrior's forearm. Ignoring the boy's efforts, the figure spun the boy in a half-circle and held his fists against the youth's chest.

Tomas couldn't move. He was pinned.

The cloaked warrior called to one of the others behind him. Within moments, they gagged Tomas' mouth and bound his hands in twine. Holding him by the scruff of the neck, they moved him to the side of the stables.

Another cloaked figure opened the mare's stall and approached her with a bridle. It made soft clicks towards her as it gently placed the restraint over her head. After fastening the harness in place, it called another warrior over. The new figure carried a saddle.

Tomas was confused.

Until now, the Night Demons had merely led the captive steeds from the stables by the reins. They hadn't bothered with saddles.

They directed the mare from the pen and brought Tomas to his feet.

The warrior, holding the boy, placed his hands under Tomas' arms and hoisted him up on the saddle.

More confused, the boy furrowed his brow as he looked at the hooded figure.

The Night Demon pointed to the horse and then to Tomas.

The mare is yours.

Riding upon the horse, a warrior led Tomas out of the stable.

He was dumbfounded and didn't understand what was happening.

The cloaked warrior handed the reins to a mounted shadow. A small vocal exchange between the two hooded figures ensued before the rider brought his horse to a steady walk, leading the mare away from the stables and towards the eastern wall.

Around him, many mounted figures led the other captive horses in the same direction. They moved steadily through the streets and towards the breach where the eastern gate once stood.

Upon the ground, propped up against the wall of a nearby cottage, Tomas saw the lifeless bodies of Peter Fysher and Michael Forde, riddled with arrows. Next to them were the remains of Chief Shelley and the twisted corpse of Lawrence Verney.

As he continued to watch, they placed the bodies of Hugh Clarke and his own father beside the other council members. The shafts sticking from his body were countless.

Tomas imagined a painful death and wanted to know why his village, why his father had to suffer like this.

They slowly led the horses over the rubble and into the mist-covered lands beyond the wall. The six council members stared after him motionlessly, lifelessly.

He cried as they ushered him away into the darkness.

***

Viciously and ferociously, the men upon the centre road leading towards the Great Hall continued to fight. They had neither made nor lost any ground but had slain several of the enemy soldiers and lost many of their own.

Archers upon the rooftops shot bolt after bolt towards the warriors at the doors of the giant building. Enemy archers returned fire and were thinning the numbers of bowmen down to a mere few.

The riders continued to pull their horses, trying to tear the doors from their hinges. The steeds objected, kicking their forelimbs in the air and squealing.

With arrows bouncing off the steps and clanging swords along the road, the riders did their best to calm their animals. For a moment or two, the beasts would comply, allowing another great heave to be completed. But then a bowman would fall from a rooftop, or an arrow would hit a Night Demon, spooking the steeds once again.

"Push forward," Richard hollered. He had done so many times before, and experienced minor victories in doing so. Soon, their triumphs diminished as more enemy foot soldiers arrived in the fray, pushing them back to where they started.

Pushing his blade deep into the hidden face of a foe, Richard's sword stuck true. He pulled and twisted in a desperate attempt to free the blade, but it didn't budge.

A dark figure leapt towards Richard from his right, sword arching down towards him. He needed his blade, and he needed it now.

He twisted with all of his might, hearing a horrible crunch and feeling the resistance of bone-breaking and tissue snapping. The warrior's blade was almost upon him when his own sword was suddenly free.

Swinging the blood-soaked steel across his body with one hand he blocked the enemy's curved sword, preventing his own demise. He lifted his dagger from his belt and buried it into the warrior's chest.

Two Night Demon fell, allowing Richard to return to the fight.

The ringing of clanging swords was tremendous, and the smell of blood and spilt intestines was wearing. But the men continued to press in.

"Push forward," Richard called again.

The men stepped into the battle, slashing and hewing the enemy soldiers one by one.

They released limbs from torsos, allowing curved swords to clang upon the street's surface.

The swordsmen were steadily making ground. The Great Hall was still a fair distance from them, but they were drawing nearer.

The horses upon the steps heaved the doors again.

Even from his current distance from the building, Richard heard a very loud crack from the entrance as something gave way.

***

The women screamed frantically at the sudden sound. The four elders stared disbelievingly towards the doors. Frederick moved towards the entrance gingerly, peering at the source of the noise.

The lower beam across the door had snapped right in the centre. The upper plank was still holding and with luck would continue to do so.

But two would have been better.

Frederick turned towards the other elders.

"Is there a spare?"

"Of course not," Eowyn replied as he moved forward to inspect the damage. "It's beyond repair."

"We should move the people away from the doors and upon the platform," suggested Nicolas as he scanned the room. "Perhaps we can move the children upstairs?"

"Some are too young to be away from their mothers," Edmond replied. "No. We will all remain here." He beckoned to the other three elders to step closer. "If we meet with Grolle tonight, better we do so in unity. Families should be together, not separated."

"Agreed," said Eowyn as he moved his gaze towards the platform. "Still, we should move as many as we can to the rear of the auditorium and away from here."

The men moved about the room quietly, helping families to move their gathered belongings and bedding to the platform. All the while, the horses continued to pull upon the doors.

The rumbles from the entrance continued to vibrate throughout the room, sending dust trickling down from high above.

Eowyn returned from assisting one group up to the platform and made his way to help another.

The doors were tugged upon again and a soft creak was heard throughout the room.

Several gasps followed as all eyes turned towards the doors.

Eowyn crept towards the large wooden structure. The doors rattled again.

He watched the upper beam hold in place. To him, it seemed fine.

Turning back to the frightened people huddled inside the Great Hall, he held his hands up reassuringly and smiled.

"It's all right," he said as he nodded his grey head. "It's holding fast."

Violently, the doors shook again.

An enormous, deafening crack filled the expanse of the room as the great panels vanished into the street.

The confident elder turned towards the opening and dropped to his knees as a tall, hooded figure entered the Great Hall. It sliced its curved sword through the air and took Eowyn's head clean from his shoulders.

Screams erupted as the elder's body fell to the floor.

Many Night Demons dashed into the auditorium.

Three of them made their way to the remaining elders who stood defiantly with heads held high.

The cloaked figures sank curved blades into their bellies and retracted quickly. The elders fell to their knees in pain and iron slid across their throats.

The other cloaked figures moved about the room, lifting children away from their protesting mothers and carrying them into the night.

Catherine stared, mouth agape as the warriors made their way towards her. She gripped Linet tightly and shook her head at the hooded figure.

"No, no," she cried. "Please, no!"

The clawed hands reached out and tore the little girl away from her mother. Linet screamed frantically, tears streaking down her face.

Catherine stood to pursue, but the enemy warrior pushed her to the floor.

Sybil grabbed both of her daughters by the arms and bolted up the stairs to the living quarters above the auditorium. A warrior followed her, disappearing from the view of those in the main room.

A warrior lifted Agnes from Martha's arms next and tucked her under its arm. Its claw-like hand then took Jane by the arm and pulled her from her mother. Martha screamed and crawled after them, but was kicked by another cloaked figure.

Both women lay on the ground, bawling uncontrollably. There was nothing they could do as the enemy took their children from them.

The Night Demons lifted young suckling babies gently as their mothers were bound and led outside as well.

They also took away the youngest of the female serves in such a manner.

The sound of something bouncing down the stairs to the living quarters caused Catherine and Martha to turn their heads. As they watched, Sybil's head rolled across the floor as the pursuing Night Demon re-emerged gripping Isabel and Alanna by the arms with each hand.

The warrior made a deep coughing noise, and two others hastily made their way over. Each of them took one of the young girls and jostled them through the auditorium and out the broken door.

Eventually, they cleared the Great Hall of all youngsters and adolescent girls. All that remained were the ill, elderly and heartbroken mothers who wept loudly, calling after their children.

The Night Demons started filing out of the room one by one, leaving the grieving mothers to themselves. As the last of them retreated through the door, they heard a trumpet blast.

A thick silence followed and hung in the air for a very long time.

Some mothers continued to bawl while others lay wide-eyed and frightened, staring towards the open door.

Suddenly vulnerable to whatever was outside, they wondered what the Night Demons had in store for them.

Then the answer came.

A great whooshing sound and a sudden gust of wind announced the arrival of their doom.

It slowly stuck its head through the doorway of the Great Hall and roared thunder.

Hands clasped to ears, and screams of fear and terror ensued.

The beast let out a low guttural noise before taking a deep breath of air.

"Gods, please," Catherine whimpered as a great jet of fire filled her vision.

Twenty-Six

Richard dropped to his knees as the beast spewed fire into the Great Hall. Flames burst through the roof as the fire took hold of the building.

The dragon took another breath and spat another jet of fire through the door. Even from this distance, Richard felt the heat of the flames.

Several of the attackers had turned and fled while a large number remained to continue the fight. Rising to his feet, full of rage, Richard hacked through the warriors one by one.

Nine of his men still stood by his side as they fought the last three dark warriors. It wasn't long before the three hooded Night Demons were lying on the street.

Looking up from the bodies, Richard saw the great dragon still positioned before the Great Hall, disgorging flames into the auditorium.

He ran along the road, the sound of his footfalls dimmed by the eruptive noise of dragon breath.

The beast lay on the steps with its wings folded upon itself, exposing its side to the council member.

Not knowing what else to do, Richard plunged his long sword into the dragon's flesh just below the wing. He pushed with all of his might, feeling something break inside the beast. As he pushed, the blade vanished below the scaly surface until only the hilt remained bare.

The dragon roared and recoiled its head from the Great Hall's entry. Stepping back, Richard saw enormous flames engulfing everything inside the building.

As far as he knew, and apart from the nine men approaching from behind him, the enemy had killed all of his friends and fellow village men.

He no longer cared what happened to him.

The dragon turned its giant head towards its attacker and snarled, baring impressive and immense sharp teeth.

With no sword in his hand, Richard spread his arms and closed his eyes.

"Here I am, dragon," he yelled. "Take me."

The beast opened its mouth and recoiled its head.

The nine men standing behind their commander surmised that fire was about to engulf them all. They too closed their eyes and prepared for their journey with Grolle.

The beast swayed to the right before toppling over and smashing into a group of cottages.

The crash forced all eyes open. When it was apparent that they were not on fire and that the beast had fallen, they laughed.

A terrible roar bellowed from the clouds above.

They had briefly forgotten about the other monster in the sky.

It dived towards them from the west, its mouth agape as it drew nearer and nearer.

This time, there would be no escape from the beast's flames. Lifting his hands to the sky, Richard prepared for death.

The dragon's speed intensified as it drew air into its lungs.

"Here I come Grolle," Richard called.

A trumpet call sounded, long and loud.

The dragon abruptly swooped back towards the sky.

A powerful gust of wind hit the ten men on the ground and knocked them off their feet.

Richard turned to watch the great beast climb further into the western sky.

"Come back," Richard called as he rose to his feet, feeling cheated. "Bastard."

The dragon disappeared into the clouds with a thunderous roar.

Richard stared after it for a moment before turning towards the fallen beast. He walked towards the giant carcase with determination.

"Where are you going?" asked a soldier.

"To get my bloody sword," he answered.

***

Flames had burst through the rear door of the Great Hall and forced the nine surviving men in the alley to seek refuge inside the first kitchen. They couldn't comprehend what had happened.

After jousting with the twelve Night Demons, they prepared to face another onslaught from the enemy. Their hearts raced in anticipation and they all but ran down the alley to greet their foes.

Then the trumpet call bellowed through the air, and their enemy withdrew.

Left alone to wait and wonder what was going on, the men returned to drinking cider and eating bread. In some ways, they felt relieved to rest up, but they couldn't help sharing a curiosity about what was happening beyond their little passageway. The stable master was tempted to leave and lead the men from their post to see what was happening.

Then the trumpet sounded again.

Within moments of the call, the great flying beast passed low overhead. Not waiting to find out the beast's target, Francis ordered all of his men to take cover in the kitchens.

Considering that the outer walls of the building were made of stone, the horse master believed they were much safer from the dragon's breath inside than upon open ground.

He wasn't far from wrong.

Incredible intense heat wafted towards them from the back of the Great Hall. The men concluded that the building was being attacked from the front. Their thoughts were with Richard, the thirty swordsmen and bowmen upon the roofs as they cowered in the back room of the little kitchen.

They could hear crackling and splintering beams of timber as the jet of fire enveloped everything inside the building. The worst sounds of all were the screams and cries of the women and old men trapped inside.

The men huddled together for their own safety as they heard many poor souls perishing in the deadly blaze.

When at last the beast ceased its incessant barrage of fire, the men braved the chance to move back into the alleyway to inspect the damage. Carefully and precariously, they moved to the door, ash falling from their tunics as they moved.

The stable master ventured out first and peered towards the roof of the Great Hall, where he saw colossal plumes of smoke billowing into the sky.

Fire had broken through the walls of the giant structure in several places where they lapped at the thick wooden structure. He imagined the building would be ablaze for some time.

Turning to his men, he saw grey shells of ash covering each one of them. The burly man chuckled, causing some of the ash to fall from him like powder to the ground.

The men looked at him curiously, not quite understanding how he could laugh at such a time as this.

"Sorry," he said, regaining his composure. "I know it's bad, but you should see yourselves."

"If it's anything like you, Francis," said a stable worker, "then it isn't any laughing matter."

They heard a loud crack and a snap from high above them. Large chunks of the flaming wall came crashing down upon the overturned wagon, setting the stacks of barrels on fire.

"Come on," the burly man instructed. "It isn't safe here anymore."

"I don't think it's safe anywhere," said a swordsman as they moved towards the western edge of the Great Hall.

They moved in single file, backs against the wall of the adjacent building to the giant structure, shifting their eyes from what lay ahead and the inferno before them.

Gradually, they edged their way to the street that led to the front doors of the Great Hall. There, they saw nine swordsmen standing near the entrance, peering down the road past them.

"Coming out," Francis Lytton called as he stepped into the street for all to see.

The soldiers glanced towards him momentarily before returning their gaze past him to further along the road.

"Is it dead?" one of the nine men called.

"What do you mean is it...?" the brawny man began.

"Well, it didn't complain when I got this back from it," Richard called from behind him.

The stable master turned to see the council member holding his blood-streaked sword up for his men to see.

Behind him lay the lifeless body of a giant beast.

Ashes continued to fall from the horseman as he stared, mouth agape and curious as to how Richard had accomplished this.

"Looks like you need a bath, my friend." Richard smiled, giving the big man a hard pat on the back. A large puff of white, powdery dust exploded all around Francis' face, causing him to cough and sneeze.

A solemn presence overcame them as all men gathered at the base of the steps to watch the flames burning from within the Great Hall. The heat was still intense and the smell of burning flesh drifted through the doors towards them.

"How many were in there?" asked a swordsman.

"They left all the women and the frail to burn," Richard replied as three archers ran along the street to join them.

"The children?" asked Francis.

"They were taken," Richard replied.

A swordsman turned to the archers. "Did you see where they took them?"

"They headed east," answered one. "But we didn't see if they made it to the wall or not."

"How many of you are left?" Richard asked.

"We are all that remain," the archer answered.

The men watched the flames as they silently prayed for the souls inside and pondered what actions to take next.

"Do you think we are all there is?" a stable hand asked them all.

"Maybe there are some who are hiding," suggested a swordsman optimistically.

"They would be the wise ones if they are," said another.

"Not very brave though," put in a young archer.

Richard smiled wryly. "In my experience, bravery kept no one safe from harm. Neither did cowardice. Hiding probably was wise for some, but it didn't help anyone in there now, did it?" He nodded to the burning remains of the Great Hall.

The long beams creaked and weakened in the flames, eventually crashing to the floor as they gave in to the weight of the roof. Embers and sparks exploded through the open doorway and lifted into the sky as the men looked on.

A pink glow touched the ends of the clouds in the east as a rooster crowed in the distance.

A new day had come.

Twenty-Seven

Tomas felt exhausted, but knew he wouldn't fall asleep. The sounds of movement around him kept him alert. He listened intently to the unrecognisable language spoken between the Night Demons. Most of it comprised low throaty sounds with hard and sharp noises.

They clicked mostly when they moved behind him and made soft purring sounds. Gentle nickering informed the boy that the horses were close.

He hoped his mare was all right.

The hessian bag placed over his head prevented him from seeing very much. Odd shapes moved back and forth about him as the warriors busied themselves. With his mouth still gagged and his hands bound, he was removed from the saddle, and placed upon the ground where a cloaked figure tied his feet together.

The light and warmth from a nearby campfire were a welcome treat. He lowered himself to his side, facing the orange glow. Some blurry shadows moved about it, but he couldn't make out what they were. He assumed they belonged to the Night Demons who, by the looks of it, were sitting around the flames to keep warm.

The surrounding sound seemed unusual, as if it bounced around him. He wasn't able to discover why this strange phenomenon was taking place.

That was until he heard the menacing roar of a dragon.

The sound was distant, but not too far away. He realised the great beast was outside in the open and he rested inside a cave, a prisoner.

The cavern must have been huge for the Night Demons to bring horses within its shelter.

Tomas knew it was near impossible to lead a mount into a dark, enclosed space without some kind of objection from the animals. Yet, here they were.

They had led his mare all the way to where he now lay.

The sound of the roaring dragon dimmed. The steeds snorted their disapproval of the monster, stamping their feet and squealing in complaint.

A hand suddenly hoisted Tomas to a seated position. At first, he thought they were going to make him sit for the duration of his stay. Perhaps this was their idea of torturing children. Possibly, this was a game to see how long the boy could stay in one position before passing out.

The clawed fingers lifted the hessian bag to expose his gagged mouth. The bag was folded back so that it stayed lifted to the bridge of his nose.

The fingers untied the gag and took it from his mouth. Before he could protest, something circular and small pressed against his lips.

It was a canteen.

He pursed his lips tightly, determined to not drink their poison. Who knew what it was they were trying to force down his throat?

The Night Demon squeezed both of the boy's jaws with one hand, forcing the mouth wide open. Tomas did not know how the warrior had done that to him.

The cool liquid flowed over his tongue. He had no choice but to swallow in great gulps as they lifted the canteen high, forcing the flow of the liquid to gush quickly into his mouth.

Water.

Swallowing hard and fast, Tomas took in as much as he could. It had been hours since his last drink and he was terribly thirsty.

Suddenly, the flow stopped, and the gag was tied back in place. The hessian bag lowered to cover his entire face, and he was gently placed back on his side before the warrior stepped away.

Confusion was the next emotion the boy experienced. He couldn't figure out why the Night Demons behaved the way they did.

First, they skinned men and left them for others to find. Then, they used fear causing unease amongst the villagers of Woodmyst. After that, they attacked with arrows and eventually with swords.

They seemed ruthless and emotionless in the way they attacked. Their victims were a mix of men and women, and how they claimed their victims were bloody and immensely violent.

Yet, they were gentle and kind to the horses, clicking and purring when they were around the steeds. Their treatment towards the animals was not dissimilar to the handling offered by the stable master and his workers.

Most of all, Tomas felt puzzled by the way they treated him. Even now, he didn't trust them and was waiting for the time when they would come and slit his throat or peel his skin from his bones.

Instead of this, they had shown him kindness. At least as much kindness as any captor could show towards a prisoner.

They had lifted him upon the mare and led him to where he now sat without laying a harmful hand upon him. One had carried him from the mare and gently placed him on the ground near a fire to keep warm. And just now, they had given him water to quench his thirst.

How could it be that such kindness could come from such horrific and terrible beings?

His thoughts returned to his father sitting propped against the building wall near the eastern wall's breach. So many arrows had pierced him. They must have been hitting him forever.

Tomas sobbed as he considered what his father's last moments must have been like. He wondered if Alan's last thoughts were about his mother. Or perhaps they were of Linet and him.

His mind ventured to the other children of the council members, all without their fathers now. Agnes and Jane Fysher, and Isabel and Alanna Shelley were still alive in the Great Hall when he had seen them last.

He hoped they were still all right.

He hoped they were still alive.

If they were, they would now need to grow up without their fathers, just as his sister would. He wondered if he would get to grow up.

Two he had not seen in the Great Hall were Lor and Sevrina Verney. Were they still alive?

Tomas had seen Lawrence, their father, slumped against the wall as well. His limbs were twisted and his neck sat in an awkward position. Like the other council members, he had suffered a terrible fate.

The treatment that those men, as well as other men of Woodmyst, had suffered simply didn't line up with the way they had treated him. It made little sense.

The sound of approaching horses made him sit up. He listened intently as he heard the low grumbles and grunts of the Night Demons exchanging words.

Beneath the conversations, he heard the muffled voices of others. He surmised that more captives had arrived. Some sounded young, like him, still children. Others were older and distinctly female. He wondered if his mother and Linet were among them.

He tried to call, but only a small muffled groan made it past the gag. He spun on his rear to face towards the newcomers, hoping to catch a distinguishing noise he might recognise as either his sister or mother.

From his listening, he deduced I had gagged them with their heads covered, just as he had.

The Night Demons took some past him and deeper into the cave. As they stepped by, he had a sense that most of them were adults or near adulthood. All of them, judging by their footfalls, were female.

The dragon gave a loud growl from outside the cave. Murmurs of children and muffled screams from the women echoed throughout the cavern.

Suddenly, a newborn infant cried. Then another.

Tomas now had a picture of part of the puzzle presented to him. They had captured mothers and babies, along with the youths of Woodmyst.

It was his belief that not one of them had probably one hair on their heads hurt.

But that didn't mean they would remain unharmed.

Even with his theory about the fair treatment of horses and captives, he still couldn't help returning to the image of his dead father and the many soldiers lying around the wall. How could he sympathise with or trust such brutes?

How could they be so contradictory in their actions?

They were bloodthirsty animals that tore the skin from their victims.

They were compassionate custodians who talked to horses and gently cared for their prisoners.

Tomas was more confused now than he had ever been before.

He listened as they placed the other prisoners throughout the caverns. They positioned some children not too far from where he sat so they could benefit from the fire that kept him warm.

He gently lowered himself to his side again and watched the blurry flames dance through his hessian mask.

Slowly, he closed his eyes.

He felt exhausted, but knew he wouldn't fall asleep.

***

Twenty-two men trudged through the quiet streets of Woodmyst as a group. They methodically searched buildings and back alleys for survivors and supplies, only to discover more carnage and destruction.

They gathered a few useful items as they progressed towards the western wall. The three bowmen foraged for what ammunition they could find upon the fallen archers, increasing their arsenal where they could.

Using tarps and blankets, they covered the bodies of their fallen comrades. The living hoped this would deter the birds and other vermin from scavenging from the dead.

"We'll come back for them," Richard said when they first laid coverings over the dead. "We'll take them to the Great Hall for burning."

"Not the west gate?" asked a swordsman.

"Their families are in the Great Hall," replied Francis. "Seems fitting to reunite them as best we can."

"We should gather the other fallen also," suggested a bowman. "Perhaps we could get some carts and load them up."

"What?" another swordsman retorted. "Throw them on a wagon like they were sacks of barley or something?"

"I don't hear you coming up with any better ideas," the bowman snapped back.

"Quiet," Richard hollered. "Both of you."

The scenery he was confronted with as they made their way through his village deeply disheartened him. So many of his fellows had perished; in ways beyond his comprehension.

Bodies discarded in the streets and yards about him lay twisted and split open. With entrails exposed, limbs removed, and some being trampled beyond recognition by horse hooves, Richard marvelled at the carnage.

The Great Hall also held its share of village folk, turned to piles of ash from the terrible fiery breath of the dragon. Extreme heat and an immense supply of fuel from the timber structure would ensure the building would burn for a very long time.

The bowman was right.

All the fallen warriors of Woodmyst deserved to be returned to their kin.

There would be one last pyre for the village, but it would not one kept to their traditions.

"We'll get some wagons," Richard said, "and we gather all the fallen we can."

The other men looked to the ground in thought, and most nodded their understanding.

"First," said Francis Lytton, "we need to replenish our water supplies."

"Kitchens are back that way, Francis." A stable hand pointed towards the direction of the plumes of smoke rising from the Great Hall. "Plenty of water barrels there."

"Plenty of water barrels at the stables too," said another worker. "We should check the horses. See if they're all right."

Richard glanced back towards the inferno in the centre of the village. It made little sense to backtrack when they had come so far. He also considered the advantage of using horses to pull the wagons. The decision was an easy one to make.

"Agreed," he said. "We go to the stables, but we keep searching for survivors as we go."

"What about the children?" asked a swordsman. "Shouldn't we go after them? The longer we tarry here, the farther they get from away from us."

"The children are gone," Richard replied. "The enemy outnumbers us. All that would happen to us if we pursue is, we would end up dead. That's it. Any more suggestions?" he asked the other men around him angrily. "No? Then let's move on."

The band of men moved onwards, continuing to venture into houses and yards to find anyone living among the dead.

***

Upon arriving at the stables, the men found the doors flung wide open and the deafening sound of silence filling their ears. It was unusual for the area to be so quiet. Even considering the steeds were usually a peaceful group, the stables would still emit the noises of clopping hooves, happy nickers and whinnies and the occasional snort.

Now, however, there was nothing.

A gentle breeze blowing from the east caused the doors to rattle upon their hinges as the men stood paralysed in front of the open stables. The horsemen feared that the Night Demons stole their beloved steeds, or at worst, slaughtered them. The archers and the swordsmen were more concerned with the possibility of enemy warriors lingering inside the dark expanse of the stable house.

Taking a deep breath to steady his nerves, Richard pulled his sword and stepped towards the open doorway.

Gathering behind him and brandishing their weapons, the men followed their commander into the building.

The scent of straw and horse dung stung Richard's nose as he cautiously moved past the doors and into the cavernous room. His eyes slowly adjusted to the limited light as he ventured deeper and deeper into the darkness.

Peering left and right, he looked into the open stalls, only to find them empty. He continued to the back of the building as he continued to search each pen as he passed by them.

Nothing.

No one.

He relaxed and turned to face the band of men behind him and saw the ladder that led up to the loft above the stalls on his right. He tensed again as he looked to a swordsman and pointed to it.

The soldier sheathed his sword and pulled the dagger from his belt. He quietly ascended the ladder until only his eyes peered over the ledge and into the space that the loft occupied.

Turning his head, he saw straw spread across the floor of the loft and hessian sacks piled against the wall directly in front of him.

Confident that there were no hidden dangers, he continued to the platform and replaced his dagger on his belt. He then unsheathed his sword and stabbed and swirled it through the more heaped areas of straw, just in case.

"Clear," he called down to the men below.

The men breathed a sigh of relief in unison.

"They took all the bloody horses," announced a worker, stating the obvious.

"Are you sure?" a bowman quipped.

Richard shook his head.

"We're here to gather water and carts," he reminded the men. "Focus your attention upon that."

"But they took all the horses," the worker said again. "How are we going to move the carts?"

The stable master furrowed his brow and glared at the man.

"You've got arms and legs, haven't you?" asked the hefty horseman.

"Yes," the worker replied, not quite understanding his boss's question.

"Well then," Francis continued, "you'll pull the cart yourself. Won't you?"

The worker pursed his lips and looked away ashamedly.

"Find some canteens and fill them with water," the hefty horseman commanded the worker. "You help him," he said to another.

"What did I do, Francis?"

"Just get the bloody water," the burly man snapped.

The two workers walked back through the stable doors, grumbling as they went.

"Do you have wagons here?" Richard asked the stable master as he peered around the room, not seeing what he desired.

"We're a stable," replied the man. "What do you think?"

The horseman turned and strode back into the morning light. Richard followed him around the outside of the stable to a large fenced yard at its side. The yard had a circular track worn into the turf where the stable hands broke the young steeds in.

Stacked against the wall were several barrels of water. The two workers were tapping one barrel with a small iron implement and a hammer as Richard and Francis entered the yard.

Across the expanse of land, on the opposite side of the enclosed yard, were four carts. They had been built for one steed to pull. With no horses, however, it would be up to the men to drive the wagons through the streets of Woodmyst, operating them like handcarts.

"We'll need to get started soon," Richard informed the other as they stared at the wagons. "I want us to meet up at the Great Hall at least two hours before dusk."

"You think those bastards are coming back, don't you?"

"I know they are," he replied. "They haven't finished what they started yet."

The stable master turned to the man beside him. He understood Richard's words all too clearly.

The Night Demons would return to end them all.

***

Splitting into four groups, one wagon each, the men took to the streets of Woodmyst. Steering the carts by their shafts, two men directed them through the winding roads as the others explored surrounding buildings and alleys for fallen comrades.

They found most of the bodies by the walls and piled them onto the wagons to the point of overflow. Richard directed the men to make several trips to and from the Great Hall and the walls so they could ensure all the departed soldiers were reclaimed.

With groups of five men upon each cart, they worked a roster out amongst them to take turns pulling the carts through the streets. Both Richard and Francis Lytton, the stable master, were free to move between the groups so they could pass instructions and offer a spare hand when needed.

After what seemed like countless trips between the eastern wall and the Great Hall, Richard had still not found the other council members amongst the dead. He stood before the giant building in the centre of the village, still ablaze with dragon fire, and took a long swig of water.

One wagon, just recently emptied of its cargo, rested on its shafts near the group of men who tended it. They sat in the shade of a nearby building drinking from their canteens as they took a quick break before they would return to the eastern wall, where more fallen soldiers awaited them.

The sound of an approaching cart from the north grabbed their attention. Emerging from a narrow street came the stable master with a fully laden wagon in tow.

The men looked utterly exhausted as they pulled up at the base of the Great Hall's steps. The five men working the cart unloaded the bodies and placed them in neat rows along the street.

There were so many. Richard had given up counting as the numbers continued to rise.

The horse master strode over to him, pulling the cork from his canteen as he drew closer.

"Any sign of them?" Richard asked.

"I was just about to ask you the same," he answered, taking a long gulp from the vessel.

Richard shook his head. "They're not here."

"You think they were taken?" asked the horseman.

"Where else could they be?" he replied.

"Perhaps they're still alive then," Francis suggested.

"No." Richard wiped his mouth upon his sleeve. "The chief's dead. I saw that myself."

The burly man nodded as he took another gulp.

"The day's getting on," he said, changing the subject. "How are you holding up?"

"I think we've cleared most of the dead from the wall," Richard replied. "The other group is moving through the back streets as we speak."

"We're still stuck at the wall," the horseman put in. "We sent the other wagon to the western wall to gather who they could find over there. It must have been terrible."

"It always is," Richard said as he turned towards his men. The men lifted themselves from the ground, two of them gripping the shafts of the cart and rolling it away towards the east.

"We still have about three hours left," Richard said to the stable master. "If there are still bodies to collect after then, leave them and meet back here. We'll deal with them if we live another day."

The hefty man nodded his understanding before Richard turned and trudged away after his men.

Twenty-Eight

Time passed quickly as the men busied themselves with gathering their slain comrades. Gathering before the steps of the Great Hall, the men compared stories and information, concluding they had collected every fallen soldier and bowman from the streets surrounding them.

The men mastering one cart reported they had ventured through the southern gate to collect bodies from the crumpled wagon dropped by one of the flying beasts during the night. Discovering only one body, that of a woman, they showed her to Richard, who dropped to his knees beside her on the ground near the steps of the Great Hall.

He recognised the twisted face of Elara Verney immediately. He wondered where her husband and children were, but guessed the answer to that question lay with the Night Demons.

He moved his eyes over the rows of men lying on the street around him. There were so many.

Grief-stricken, he wept. The other men shed tears of their own as they too, surveyed the dead.

Each man considered a fallen warrior was perhaps once a friend or family member he may have encountered daily. These were people they did business with, shared meals with, and laughed with.

Now, the streets were silent and the people of Woodmyst were gone.

Only twenty-two remained, and the macabre task before them caused their hearts to sink.

Composing himself, Richard turned to his men and addressed them.

"Right," he breathed, "there is no easy way to do this. We don't have a pyre or stretchers that are befitting of the traditions of this community. We don't really even have a community anymore." Tears welled in his eyes again, and his voice cracked a little. "We need to send these brave souls into the lands beyond our own, where their families await them. We need to reunite these heroes of Woodmyst with their wives and children. We need to give them back to their mothers and fathers. We need to deliver them into Grolle's care." Richard looked deeply into the faces of each of the gathered men. Their eyes were heavy. All of them wore fatigue and enervation after battling all night, only to clean up the streets all day.

"We don't have time to be gentle," Richard continued. "I hope our friends would understand. Our task is to throw these warriors into the dragon's flames before the sun falls below the horizon.

"Two men for each body," Richard instructed. "Let's get this done."

The men paired up and started carrying bodies up the steps of the Great Hall. One lifted the fallen by their arms while the other carried them by their legs.

As they approached the open access to the auditorium, they could still feel intense heat escaping the entrance in waves. Inside, bright flames filled the room as the pillars with dragonheads burned brightly and cross beams high above near the roof continued to blaze.

Richard and Francis Lytton carried the first of the bodies to the door. They swung the body, one – two – three, and flung the soldier into the inferno. The flames engulfed the warrior before he hit the floor.

The men didn't stay to watch or pay their respects. They instantly returned to the street to gather another fallen soldier as the two men behind them mirrored their actions.

After three swings, they tossed the fallen warrior into the flames and also descended the steps to gather another. The next two men in line repeated the action, as did the next two and the next two.

It was arduous work and took a lot of energy to accomplish. Their muscles ached and their bodies grew more and more tired as the work continued.

Slowly, but surely, they reduced the number of fallen warriors lying on the street as the day wore on. By the time they were halfway through the task, their pace had slowed.

Richard allowed them time for a water break. The stable master took his workers with him to the kitchens, where they gathered the remaining cider and some bread to share with the others.

They sat for a few minutes together, enjoying the makeshift meal, before returning to work. The food felt good in their stomachs and a rejuvenated band of men busied themselves with their task.

Richard's thoughts often wandered as he worked. He contemplated the whereabouts of his fellow council members and their current state of being.

He assumed, and secretly hoped, that they were all dead. He hated the idea of the enemy torturing them. Skinning them alive. He wanted to believe that they fell in battle as heroes.

Then there were the stolen children.

They were all taken during the night, right before his eyes. He shuddered to think what horrors they were subject to. Inside, he quietly prayed to the gods for their protection over the little ones.

But after the past few nights, and with the gruesome chore he was currently engaged in, he wondered if the gods were there at all.

He tossed another body into the furnace before returning down the steps to the next fallen warrior. His men continued to steadily gather and heave the dead upon the flames.

He peered up at the sun. It slowly made its way towards the western wall.

Richard guessed they had an hour, at best, to finish the task.

After that, he feared, the Night Demons would return.

He bent down and, with the help of a bowman, hoisted another soldier from the ground. The two carried the warrior along the street towards the steps as Richard's mind continued to wander.

His thoughts turned to questions as he considered how to counteract the enemy attack if they were to return.

The Night Demons were still a formidable force, with a vast number of warriors at their disposal. Woodmyst consisted of a small band of men who were extremely tired and seriously unfit to do battle.

Knowing they were a lost cause, Richard considered running away.

He then remembered the wagon dropped outside the gates of the southern wall. The image of Elara lying in the street, twisted and battered, returned to his thoughts. This appeared to be the fate of those who tried to escape.

Another option of escape entered his thoughts. Perhaps entering the flames would be a better option than meeting the doom the Night Demons had in store for them.

He pushed the thought aside as he and the bowman flung another body through the doors of the Great Hall.

As he descended the steps, he decided once and for all. It was the only choice that made sense. The struggle in his mind was pointless and had no substance.

He would fight the Night Demons until he had no more breath.

***

A great commotion erupted nearby. Several horses snorted and squealed, arousing Tomas from his half-sleep state.

He peered around and tried to see what was going on, only to have his vision obstructed by the hessian sack over his head.

Blurry figures passed by back and forth, frantically moving items about and causing a ruckus as they did so.

Several excited grunts and indistinct sounds were given by several warriors nearby.

It sounded, to Tomas, as if the Night Demons were preparing to move. The boy hoped it was to leave the area entirely. Perhaps the warriors would leave him, and the others held captive, and simply return to where they had come from.

He was intelligent enough to know his hopes would, most probably, remain unfulfilled.

The sounds of the steeds stamping their feet echoed throughout the cavern. Tomas wondered how long they had been there. Several times, they had lifted his hood, never enough for him to see clearly, in order to give him water. At other times, they led him to a secluded place to discharge his bladder.

Perhaps it was the same warrior each time. His own personal guard for his duration with the Night Demons.

He could never be sure.

One warrior moved behind the steeds nearby and offered them soft clicking sounds and low rumbles. He imagined the hooded figure rubbing his clawed hand over his mare's muzzle.

A tiny flare of anger welled up inside of him. He didn't like the idea of these fiends touching her.

Continuing to bustle about him, other Night Demons collected items that clattered on the hard floor of the cave.

The light of the campfire allowed him to see shapes like men, crouching and rolling items into bundles. He watched as they carried the bundles to the horses.

It was as he had thought.

They were preparing to leave.

A hissing caused him to turn his head back towards the fire. Water was being drizzled over the flames, dousing the makeshift hearth and stealing its warmth away.

Tomas suddenly missed the light and heat of the campfire. The light enabled him to see some things about him, albeit blurry. The warmth provided comfort as he lay on the floor of the cavern.

Now, all he saw was darkness while feeling cold at the same time. He suddenly felt very alone and vulnerable.

More noise continued around him as the Night Demons prepared their chargers. Tomas imagined leather straps and metal buckles being tightened as the warriors fit saddles and bridles placed onto the horses.

The sound of snorts and stamping hooves signified objection or excitement amongst the steeds. Tomas couldn't be sure without seeing the horses for himself, and currently, he saw nothing but blackness.

Two clawed hands slid underneath his armpits and lifted him to his feet. He felt vibration and movement around his ankles as the ropes binding his legs were untied. One hand then rested upon his shoulder and directed him towards his left. He turned, complying with the directions, and walked.

The warrior led him to a secluded place within the cavern. The sounds of Night Demons conversing in their language and hurried activity still surrounded him, but he could tell he was facing the rock wall of the cave.

He had been here before.

The warrior gave him two pats on the back, right between the shoulder blades. Tomas understood and undid his trousers with his bound hands. Moments later, he let his bladder expunge its contents before tucking himself away and tying the cord on his trousers as best as he could.

The warrior then directed the young boy back towards the horses. He was so close to them he could smell the animals.

It was a welcoming scent.

The Night Demon put his hands under Tomas' armpits again and hoisted from the ground. They swung the boy gently into the air, his right foot hitting something softly. He lifted his legs high to allow the object to pass beneath him.

The warrior then lowered him slightly. Tomas felt his thighs slide over the side of something smooth.

The clawed hands recoiled from his torso, and one moved to his bound hands and directed them to a space just in front of his crotch. He felt with his fingers and touched leather. He reached forward and moved his fingers over the edge of the leather object he sat upon and touched thick, coarse hair.

He was sitting in a saddle on a horse.

The warrior released Tomas' hands from his own grasp and left him upon the steed alone.

His feet found the stirrups, and he pushed them into the straps securely. With his hands still bound, he gripped the edge of the saddle. He had no false hopes that they would hand him the reins so he could control the beast himself. They had led him here upon the mare, so they would lead him away as well.

The sound of many riders leaving through the cave's entrance echoed through the cavern, like thunder. The first of the Night Demons were leaving.

His charger moved nervously as the noise of hooves upon flint made its way through the cavern. Reaching with his hand, he patted the horse on the top of its neck. It gave a gentle nicker in reply.

Tomas wondered if he was upon the mare or not.

He hoped so.

The surrounding warriors started mounting their steeds. The sound of an infant crying suddenly echoed through the cave. Tomas assumed it had been aroused from a peaceful sleep, perhaps to be carried by someone on another horse.

Feeling sudden compassion overwhelm him, he thought about the safety of the children and the mothers who had come to the cavern. He hoped they were all fine and that perhaps they too were upon steeds about to be led away.

Tomas then wondered where they were being taken. He still didn't trust the Night Demons. After all, they had killed his father and scores of men in Woodmyst. What was there to stop them from slaughtering him and the captives with him?

Perhaps they were being kept alive as men kept cattle or sheep. If they weren't to be meals for the Night Demons, then perhaps they were to be fed to the dragons.

But what was he to do about it?

With his hands tied and face covered, he couldn't see or shout.

He would have to face bravely whatever fate was in store for him.

The horse lurched forward as they began their journey.

The sound of many hooves falling upon the cavern floor echoed around him.

The dim light at the cave's entrance grew larger.

It was dusk.

Twenty-Nine

A flock of sheep had gathered near the river's edge and some cattle scattered here and about throughout the meadow. Richard watched them for a while from the breach where the eastern gate once stood. The others rested inside the stables, waiting for his return.

The sun had just dipped below the treetops in the west. The dark clouds had returned and donned pink and purple patches as the sun sent the last of her light into the sky. They were laden with rain and resembled the heaviness Richard felt as he watched them approach.

Distant thunder and flashes of light broke through the dark vapours above. It was going to be a long night, if he lasted through it.

He turned away from the meadow and slowly made his way back towards the stables not too far away.

They had gathered food from some of the neighbouring houses and made a banquet of sorts for what might be their last night alive. Two chickens were killed and potatoes boiled over a fire they had built just outside the stable's doors.

Torches lit in the barn, sent orange light into the dark corners and lit the expanse of the room.

Some men had gone back to the kitchens behind the Great Hall and returned with a barrel of mead. Usually, Richard would refrain from the drink when he believed he was going to engage in battle. Tonight, however, he filled his mug and sat on a stool by the fire, waiting for the chickens and potatoes to finish cooking.

The men stared into the flames solemnly, their minds on what could come for them. Some pondered why they should even raise a sword to the enemy. It was obvious their lack of numbers was their weakness and would work against them.

Fighting simply seemed useless.

Surrender seemed a better option, except that they knew the enemy was likely to ignore any attempt to capitulate.

With their spirits torn and their hearts in dismay, they simply stared at the flames in silence.

"You know," said Francis Lytton, the stable master, "I hope I marry a fine woman. One with huge tits."

The men all looked towards him, confused.

"I don't really care much for what she looks like," he continued. "Just as long as she can... Well, you know." He smiled bashfully. "I'd like maybe two or three younglings. A boy amongst them would be nice, but girls would be fine."

The men listened intently, shifting their puzzlement of his words to wanting to hear him tell them of his dreams.

"We could live on a farm, grow some crops. Horses." He suddenly sat up straight and looked at one of his workers. "You can guarantee there'll be horses. And rolling hills for as far as you can see."

Richard felt a lump grow in his throat.

"The house would be modest." Francis peered into the flames. "You know, two storeys, four bedrooms and an oversized kitchen with a humongous table. We would eat roast chicken or rack of lamb every night until we got sick of it.

"And as they got older, young gentlemen with great wealth would come from miles around to steal my beautiful daughters away from me. I would chase them off with my rusty sword and shout, do you know who I am, you bastards. I'm Francis Lytton, the stable master, destroyer of Night Demons and keeper of horses. Get off my land.

"That's what I hope to do one day." He turned to Richard. "What about you?"

Richard looked up from the flames and locked eyes with the burly man.

"What?"

"Tell us what you hope for," the horseman said.

The council member looked around the fire to the ambitious faces of the men sitting in the firelight. They were waiting for him to speak.

How could he top the words of the stable master?

"Is the chicken ready, yet?" he asked.

"Oh, come on," whined a stable hand.

Richard returned his gaze to the fireplace.

"I don't know if I can ever get the things I hope for," Richard began. "I don't know if I deserve anything like that. There are so many things that I've done in my life that I regret and perhaps, because of those things, I shouldn't get the things I hope for.

"Do I desire a wife? Yes, of course. Children? What man wouldn't want sons, or daughters." He gave Francis a quick glance. The brawny man smiled.

"I think it's every man's wish to find himself a home where he feels he belongs. Somewhere he can feel wanted, respected, loved. I think that's what home is meant to be.

"Does it need to be upon rolling hills or maybe a farm? Those were the dreams of our fathers, passed on to us.

"We just don't have any dreams of our own. We haven't had a chance to sit and think about what it is we really want.

"I think what I really hope for is that our children, if we ever get the opportunity to sire any after tonight, have the opportunity to have hopes of their own and see them through. That's what I hope for," Richard finished.

"Now," he said. "Is the bloody chicken ready?"

***

They had placed the roast meat and boiled potatoes on a plate and positioned it onto a trestle table fashioned out of two sawhorses and a plank of timber. The men stood around the spread, picking at what they wanted as they stood around and discussed many things of triviality.

Conversations traversed through important subjects such as how to grow monstrous pumpkins and how to grow tasty pumpkins. No one, however, could tell anyone how to grow tasty, monstrous pumpkins.

"It's one or the other," said a stable hand. "Nevertheless, horse manure is the best fertiliser you could invest in."

The discussion moved on to places they had visited outside of their village. One of the bowmen told of how he had travelled to Oldcastle, at which the men scoffed.

"That's just on the other side of the forest," one swordsman said. "The riders have travelled farther than that and back within a day."

"Well, where have you been?" the archer asked, pointing at the other with a half-eaten chicken leg.

"I don't admit to having travelled far, but I have been to Winterspring and Selidien."

Selidien.

The name rang in Richard's head over and over like a clanging toll.

Why did that name set his nerves on edge?

"I've been to Dweagan," said a stable worker. "You would think they don't know what a push broom is, or they have millions of horses. I didn't see that many though. But, oh the mounds of horse turds piled up beside the road."

"You've got horse manure on your brain," announced Francis. "Something is wrong with you, boy."

"Wait," Richard instructed. "What was that you said?"

"What?" the soldier replied. "About me going to Winterspring?"

"No," Richard replied. "The other place."

"Selidien?"

"Yes, Selidien," he acknowledged. "Why does that place spark an ember in me?"

"It burnt down," said one of the stable hands. "Just the other day."

"That's right," a swordsman agreed. "We sent a rider to Winterspring, and he said he went out to Selidien with their riders. You remember, my lord?"

It was coming back to Richard, but that wasn't it.

There was something else about the name that itched at the back of his mind.

"Something troubles you," Francis said, placing a hand on Richard's shoulder.

"Yes," he replied, "but I'm not sure what it is. It has something to do with that village."

Well, I'm Travis from Selidien and this is Lewyn from Rhendalith.

The sudden return of this memory sent a shiver up his spine.

Thunder cracked in the sky to the east, signalling the approach of another storm.

"By the gods," he said. Finding a stool by the fire, he left the men and sat down.

The men watched him, befuddled and perplexed.

They followed him over to the fire, some choosing to sit nearby. Francis lowered himself onto the stool next to the council member.

"What is it?"

"Selidien and Rhendalith," he answered. "Selidien was destroyed. Quite possibly by these Night Demons."

"But why?" asked a swordsman. "Do you think it's something to do with the Realm War?"

"Does anyone know if Rhendalith was destroyed?"

The men exchanged glances. Some hadn't even heard of the place.

"What is this about, Richard?" Francis asked.

He shook his head. "It's probably just a coincidence," he answered. "I apologise, gentlemen."

Some men nearby gave him a pat on the shoulders before they all returned to the makeshift table with their meal upon it.

The rain started to fall.

Tiny hisses erupted from the fire that Richard sat by as tiny drops of water fell into the flames.

He rose from the stool and entered the stable to get out of the rain.

***

Just when the men were enjoying their meal again, and the conversation returned to trivial subjects, a trumpet called from the east.

All heads turned to the open doors of the barn.

The rain was falling steadily, and darkness had fallen upon everything in the street. No one wanted to venture into the rain, through the darkness and the void beyond. The stable was warm and much more inviting than anything that the Night Demons could have prepared for them.

Still, they prepared themselves to go.

The bowmen slung their quivers and bows over their shoulders as the swordsmen checked their blades. Alan tightened the straps of his armour and took a deep breath.

"What's the plan?" asked a bowman.

"You seriously think there's a plan?" quipped Francis.

"We hold the breach on the eastern wall," Richard informed them. "Archers on the wall and swordsmen in the gap."

"That's it?" asked a stable worker. "What about the northern breach? They'll sneak up behind us."

"I don't think so," Richard replied. "They won't need to. There's twenty-two of us and, the gods know how many more of them. They won't need to use such tactics upon us tonight."

"Simply put, lad," reaffirmed the burly horseman, "we will fight and hold the ground until we can't anymore. Understand?"

The man nodded.

"Let's go then." Richard led the band of men into the rain. Together, strengthened by their solidarity, they moved towards the breach to face their enemy one last time.

Behind them, the Great Hall continued to burn. The roof had collapsed and giant flames lapped the sky as an enormous pillar of smoke mingled with the clouds above.

The men moved forward with determination, drawing closer to the eastern wall. They saw the upper section of the breach over the rooftops of nearby cottages first.

Their hearts raced as anxiety and fear pumped through their veins. They rounded the corner past the nearby buildings so they saw the mound that was once part of the wall, heaped at the base of the breach.

What stood beyond the gap made them stop cold.

Their hearts froze, and their jaws dropped in shock and awe.

They had neatly positioned six large lampposts in a row just on the meadow side of the breach.

Large torches were aflame on top of the posts, casting light in a wide circle into the pastureland.

Bound to each lamppost was one body.

The bodies were those belonging to the missing council members of Woodmyst.

Michael Forde, Lawrence Verney, Alan Warde, Chief Shelley, Peter Fysher and Hugh Clarke.

Their heads rested loosely on their necks, chins upon their chests, their hands bound behind the lampposts and their feet tied together. The men hung upon the posts several feet above the ground and their tunics removed, exposing their bare torsos to the stormy night.

What was most shocking of all was the sight of their bellies sliced open and their intestines left to dangle from the open wounds, almost touching the ground below them.

Blood still spilt from their cuts, leaving Richard to believe that this spectacle had they had put only just in place.

The taste of bile burnt his throat.

He swallowed hard, but that just made the sensation feel worse.

What kind of beings would do this?

How could anyone destroy men and their families in such a horrifying manner?

The trumpet blew again, and a terrible, thunderous roar of many voices called from the darkness.

Thirty

"Quickly," Richard hollered to the bowmen, "climb upon the wall."

Two of the men ran northward along the inside of the wall to climb the nearest ladder, while the other archer ran towards the south to do the same. Within moments, the archers positioned themselves behind battlements, ready to fire.

The enemy remained hidden in the darkness beyond the light cast from the lampposts. Richard and the remaining men of Woodmyst could hear their hoots and calls, giving the gathered men the impression that the Night Demons were not too far away.

The remaining nineteen men upon the mount formed a line, swords brandished and eyes wide open. Fatigue and exhaustion had faded as fear and anger took control.

The men were ready for a fight.

A great roar from the sky signalled the arrival of the flying monster. The men saw its dark form exploding through the clouds above the hill as it spread its wings and dived straight for them.

Richard believed the battle would be over before it began as the giant beast drew closer and closer.

"Nice knowing you, boys," called Francis as he braced himself for the worst.

The dragon corrected its trajectory at the last moment and passed over the men, continuing towards the inferno at the centre of the village. The three men on the wall were nearly blown back to the ground from the force of wind caused by the passing beast.

One swordsman followed the dragon with his eyes, watching it soar over the rooftops as it moved away. It circled the plume of smoke rising from the Great Hall before lowering itself nearby.

It was a guess, but the swordsman believed it had grounded itself beside the fallen monster Richard had slain in the dark hours of the morning. The dragon lowered its head out of the soldier's view. All he saw were its wings and scaly back as it moved slightly.

The soldier turned his face back towards the sound of howls and hoots coming from the darkness. Lightning flashed, revealing countless hooded figures in the meadow.

"The dragon is on the ground," the swordsman reported. "It landed near the Great Hall."

"Good to know," replied a stable worker. "With luck, it will remain there while we deal with this lot. After that, we'll go and deal with it."

The men laughed loudly. Richard believed their wits had finally broken. His laughter was among the loudest.

The trumpet blew long and loud.

A group of warriors appeared in the lamplight. A quick calculation by the stable master and he suddenly shouted, "Only fifty."

They flung a few arrows at the oncoming group. The bowmen knocked eight of them to the dirt before they reached the men on the ground.

The swordsmen ran forward a short distance to meet the enemy. A few of the blades rang in the night air as they clashed near the onlooking corpses of the fallen councilmen.

Richard's blade came down heavily upon his chosen adversary, slicing through the shoulder and landing deep in the warrior's chest. The pouring rain rinsed the blood away to the mud on the ground.

The body fell with a slap as Richard swung his sword rapidly, connecting with another hooded figure in the belly. It crumpled on top of the other fallen Night Demon in the mud.

Richard looked around to see how his men were holding up.

Each of them had placed his share of enemy warriors on the field and was ready for the next charge.

They backed away from the lampposts without taking their eyes from the dark meadow. Together, they stood upon the mound again, waiting, listening and watching.

The horn blew again, two quick blasts.

The sound of warriors approaching rapidly from two directions alarmed one bowman.

"Let them come in," he called down to the men gathered near the breach. "Force them to climb through the rubble. Don't let them surround you."

Richard understood. They would need to bottleneck the invaders in the mess by the walls, forcing them to funnel through the gap in order to reach them.

"Back," Richard commanded. "Back to the base of the mound."

The stable master pointed to the lone archer on the right of the gap. "You shoot as many of the ones who make it through as you can." He then looked at the two archers positioned on the left. "You two, shoot every bastard before they get to the breach. Got it?"

The two bowmen nodded and turned their attention to what was coming beyond the wall.

Several hoods appeared in the lamplight and met a barrage of deadly arrows. They fell upon the mud in awkward heaps, causing a few of their comrades to trip over them and splash into the puddles at the base of the poles.

More arrows hit them as they struggled to rise out of the mire.

Additional hoods appeared and navigated past the fallen warriors. Arrows from above still hit a few of them before they reached the gap, but a vast number pushed through. The third archer, positioned on the southern side of the breach, picked off as many as he could, but there were too many for him to prevent them all from getting to the band of men.

Francis, the stable master, didn't need to count his opponents this time. He realised their numbers were substantially more than the previous group they had jostled with.

The nineteen swung and sliced their blades through the air, not caring what and where they hit as long as it wasn't one of their own. Careful to keep at a safe distance from one another, they cut and chopped into the hooded ones' flesh over and over as the bowman on the south side of the gap took potshots where he could.

One man of Woodmyst fell during the squabble, copping a curved blade through the guts. The young swordsman responded by lifting his dagger from his belt and sliding it into the Night Demon's throat.

Both warrior and soldier fell upon the ground in a pool of their own blood. The rain continued to streak over the slain corpses as the battle continued around them.

One of the stable hands had the privilege of putting the last enemy warrior on the ground. It was only then that they noticed the fallen swordsman.

"Move him to the side," Richard ordered. "Near the side of that cottage."

Two soldiers dragged their comrade to a patch of grass by a cottage's wall and laid him down. They returned to the band of men, now numbering eighteen.

Gathering upon the mound again, the stable master taunted the enemy.

"Got any more?" he shouted into the blackness.

The trumpet blew three consecutive notes.

"Guess that means they're sending three groups this time," remarked a stable hand.

"You'd want to hope they count the same way as me and you," a soldier replied.

"All right," Richard called. "Three groups. Teams of six." He counted the stable master and five others. "You lot go down there a little way." He pointed to the thin street heading towards the south. "You guys go along there," he said to six swordsmen as he directed them a short distance to the north. "You lot with me," he said to the remaining five men.

The groups moved hastily to their positions.

The two archers on the northern side of the breach started firing bolts to a large group of Night Demons.

Richard heard the screams and groans of the dark warriors as they fell into the slush forming outside the walls.

A few hooded figures burst through the gap where arrows met them from behind. One of them turned to seek the bowman responsible for putting two of the Night Demon's comrades down. Before the archer could be located, Richard and Francis started calling from their positions. The swordsmen around the corner in the northern lane saw what the other two were doing and joined in with calling the enemy over.

The Night Demons split into three groups to confront their antagonists. The bowman continued to pick them off one by one, alternating between the three groups to even the odds.

By the time the hooded warriors reached their opponents, the balance of fighters had become six men to eleven Night Demons.

Francis was the first of his team to plunge his sword into the neck of a warrior. One of the stable hands thrust his blade through the leg of his foe, removing the limb entirely.

The swordsmen to the north used their team skills proficiently. While one hacked, another parried, and another plunged. They didn't single out one warrior for one soldier. They simply looked for openings and took advantage of them.

As the numbers of their rivals dropped, the ratio between the two parties improved in their favour. In the end, one enemy warrior had six Woodmyst men to contend with.

Richard's team used a similar approach. Most of them were young. It was Richard who was the odd one out. His technique was rusty, and he felt age in his muscles.

Warfare was a young man's game.

Old men belonged in rocking chairs.

He laughed out loud at the thought of himself in a rocking chair.

His men didn't understand what was humorous, but the laughter was infectious.

Before long, his team was laughing boisterously in the street. The stable master found the idea of laughing in the middle of the street while the rain pelted down from above a laughable thing in itself. So, he joined in.

The sound resonated across the grass beyond the wall.

It must have caused offence amongst the Night Demons for the trumpet sounded again.

"More coming," called a bowman.

"The same tactic," Richard called to the men.

The men readied themselves for the onslaught. If the pattern so far was anything to judge by, they should expect more Night Demons this time. Richard had to admit they had been quite fortunate until now. He could only hope their luck would hold up.

The bowmen loaded their arrows and pulled back upon their strings tightly.

Many hooded figures crowded into the circle of light beneath them. There was so many this time that the horde expanded beyond the illuminated region and spilt over into the darkness beyond.

The two archers let their arrows fly, dropping one enemy warrior after another. But the small decrease in numbers making it into the breach barely made a dent in the onslaught.

The third archer started his attack, aiming for the back of each hood. He dropped several of the invaders to the ground, but not enough to slow the throng.

Richard believed the only chance they had was to find a thin alley to draw the enemy into. This way, they would face three or four across instead of ten or fifteen in the wide streets.

"Move into an alley or a thin access," he called over the massing crowd of enemy warriors.

The other teams heard his command and immediately looked for a suitable place to make their stand.

The stable master chose a tiny lane that passed tightly between a cottage and a tiny baker's store.

"Up there," he shouted to his men.

They bolted into the lane as several cloaked warriors turned in their direction.

One of the stable hands raced ahead to the far end of the lane. Within seconds, he was running back towards them.

"Dead end this way," he informed them.

"Dead end that way too," said a swordsman, referring to the crowd of hooded soldiers blocking their exit.

"Guess this will have to do then," said Francis as he turned to face the enemy.

Three Night Demons led the charge towards them, as it was all that could fit shoulder to shoulder in the narrow passage.

The middle warrior raised his curved sword above his head. A stable hand swung his sword in an upward curve and stabbed the invader just below the ribs. The swordsman and the stable master hacked the two on either side.

More hooded figures crowded into the alleyway and ran towards the six men standing about halfway along the channel. With a quick parry from the big burly man, one of the stable workers standing behind him slid his blade between two of the three men before him and buried it into the chest of the attacking warrior.

"We need to do more of that," shouted Francis excitedly.

The men fought hard and wore their enemy down. Thinking the fight was over, they relaxed and admired their handiwork.

Using the constricted space to their advantage, they created quite an enormous pile of dead enemy soldiers.

The fight wasn't over, however, as suddenly, more Night Demons discovered the team's hiding place and started piling into the narrow alley.

Thirty-One

The team of swordsmen had no such luck in finding a narrow access lane to draw the enemy into. They ran back along the lane, only to find that it opened into a wide street.

A crowd of Night Demons had surrounded them within moments, forcing the six men to stand in a small circle, back-to-back.

The enemy lunged at them one by one, perhaps testing their bravado, only to be cut down by the soldiers.

The swordsmen had put thirteen of the hooded warriors in the mud.

At once, the Night Demons lunged, and the swordsmen blocked and swung their swords wildly in defence. They took down quite a few more of the cloaked figures. Then one man fell, holding his hand to his belly.

Dark blood flooded over his fingers and onto the wet ground as he dropped to his side.

Now they were five.

The throng of warriors pressed hard against the men and hit another two with their curved swords. One fell instantly, his face sliced open, exposing bone and tissue. The other fought on until the loss of so much blood seeping from his side caused him to drop into the mud.

The two remaining soldiers stood back-to-back, encircled by at least twenty Night Demons. The dark warriors lowered their blades and waited for the men to make the final advance.

"What do you say, my friend?" asked one.

"Do you think we can still run away?"

Both men laughed as they lunged forward, swords raised above their heads.

***

Swinging his blade wildly at the invaders, Richard took three out in one sweep. His blade slashed across the chest of one to his right and in the middle. The one on the left tried to duck out of the way and received the edge of the long sword in the back of his head.

The lane they had piled into offered little help. Five warriors could stand side by side as they approached from the front. The same for the area behind them.

The lane opened onto a courtyard to which the Night Demons could access from an adjacent road. At any given time, the six men trapped in the little alley were battling ten cloaked warriors.

Richard didn't know if this was better or worse than standing in the middle of the street.

Still, they were not about to give up. Their lives depended upon it. Even with the practical probability that they would most likely perish during the night, they had no intention of letting the Night Demons beat them. Nor were there any desires to become human sacrifices for any cause.

This was about survival.

Or, at least surviving for as long as they could.

The soldiers with Richard blocked and attacked, using every chance advantage they could to put a hooded warrior on the ground. They heaped a pile of corpses around their feet as they continued to fight for their lives.

The enemy soldiers were not easily dismayed, however. Even with the numbers of their dead increasing upon the ground, they were intent upon reaching the six men.

Their fervour increased the desperation of the team, and they increased their efforts to kill the enemy.

With no reprieve in sight, no time for rest, Richard fought through the sudden fatigue that hit like a hammer. His body ached and his eyes grew heavy.

Every thrust and blow became increasingly slower and less effective. He sometimes needed to give two or three swings of his blade where earlier he could complete the same task with one.

I've been awake for almost two days, he suddenly thought.

His mind wandered to a place where his cot was waiting for him. He imagined lying down and pulling the covers over his ears, curling up and floating away where he could dream of Night Demons.

You'll sleep soon. A very long sleep.

A rush of the dark warriors exploded from around the corners in front of him and behind. He hacked and chopped with his blade, connecting with as many of the enemy soldiers as he could.

Blood sprayed upon his face and chest plate again and again.

He suddenly felt revitalised as a second wind knocked some sense into him.

Slicing and blocking curved blades with his sword, he wondered how much longer he could keep this up. He had almost lost it there for a moment.

This had to stop eventually.

One way or another.

***

Francis Lytton poked his sword into the throng of dark figures squeezing into the thin alley. His reach was surprisingly long and, with his sword just as long as his arm, he could meet his mark before his enemy attacked him directly. Their curved swords were not as long as his blade, and they required a slashing or swinging motion to be effective.

The men of Woodmyst could use the long swords for hacking, chopping, slicing and stabbing. The downside to their weapons was that they were heavy.

Forged from tempered steel and quite thick along its fuller, the blade wore its user down before the enemy did.

The enemy blades were much thinner and easier to operate, but the handler would need to get in close to their enemy.

Both blades had their positive and negative points.

For now, however, the Woodmyst blade proved to be the more advantageous.

The narrow confines of the passageway prevented the soldiers from being able to chop and hack their enemies. But stabbing and poking in their current environment was ideal.

The need to block and parry was still paramount, and they used these defensive manoeuvres to their advantage. As an enemy warrior charged with a sword held high, intending to lower it forcefully into one man, one of the team members would block the blow with his blade while another would stab his sword into the invader.

The strategy was proving a successful one as bodies continued to pile upon each other in the narrow alley. The Night Demons now had to clamber over their own kind to attack the small band of men.

This too, proved to be profitable to the men, for as the enemy navigated their way over the carcases, the men would race forward and cut them down.

The enemy must have passed the word to their comrades of the tactics being used by the men and, consequently, they must have forged plans of their own.

As the men fought in the passageway, several Night Demons climbed upon the roofs of the surrounding buildings, some lowering themselves into the rear of the alley silently.

Francis, at the front of the fray, continued to block and stab wildly with his blade, oblivious to the gathering invaders behind him and his men. Their attention was given entirely to the hooded warriors attacking them from the opening to the passage.

The stable master didn't feel the spatter and spray against his bare neck as the three men behind him had their throats slit. The rain was pelting too hard and his temperature too warm from fighting for him to distinguish the feel of water from blood.

It was only when he heard their swords clang upon the ground that his head spun around to see the dead swordsmen lying in a heap and the five Night Demons standing before him.

The curved blade sank deep into his belly and twisted as the warrior slid it across to his left side, where it exited his body above his hip. Slowly, his innards slid through the wound to dangle from the fresh opening.

Strangely, as the rain pelted his face, he felt little pain. It was more of a discomforting sensation.

He swayed upon his feet and plunged his sword deep into the belly of his attacker.

"If I go," Francis told the Night Demon, "you go with me."

The remaining two men, a stable worker and a swordsman, turned to see their commander standing defiantly as he pulled his sword up into the warrior's ribs. They heard a loud crunch as blood sprayed from beneath the dark hood and into Fancis' face.

Two cloaked figures ran their blades along the necks of both the stable hand and the swordsman. They stood motionless for a moment as blood flowed across their leather breastplates before falling to the ground.

The stable master and the Night Demon both fell on their knees together. Francis pushed his sword into the warrior up to the hilt so that the blade was sticking from its back.

As the other dark warriors watched, both man and Night Demon fell against each other in what almost appeared an embrace. There, both breathed their last breath and fell to the earth.

The gathering of Night Demons stood around, staring at the spectacle in the narrow alley, as the pouring rain welled in the lifeless eyes of Francis Lytton, the stable master

of Woodmyst.

***

Enclosed in by a multitude of dark warriors, Richard and the five swordsmen with him fought frantically for their lives. They worked together as a unit, using their swords to block swinging curved blades, allowing another of their allies to plunge his long sword into the form of their enemy.

Repeatedly, they used this strategy, fighting with their backs to each other in a tight circle. The enemy changed their stratagem and focused their attack on one soldier at a time.

Being in a circular formation, and with three to four blades being thrust towards a particular man in unison, it became difficult to determine where to focus on evasive manoeuvres. The other men in the team would occasionally lend a hand by helping to block the oncoming swords, but this opened them up to attack from another Night Demon, waiting for the opportunity.

Eventually, fatigue and exhaustion drained the swordsmen, and their reactions slowed. Defending each other and themselves became a toilsome task.

It was only a matter of time.

While defending his fellow swordsman, they struck another in the leg. He fell to his knees. There, another swipe from a curved blade sliced through his neck. The head lolled upon the ground as the body swayed, as if trying to decide whether or not to fall.

Richard bumped the headless man, sending him sprawling onto the ground, as he blocked an attack from two warriors.

The trumpet blew a long note.

It sounded close.

Richard surmised from the volume of the sudden noise the trumpeter was inside the village walls.

He raised his sword quickly and hacked the two hooded brutes open as the circle of men tightened.

It almost seemed pointless. For every Night Demon that they destroyed, another was there to take its place.

Is there perhaps an endless supply of dark warriors outside of the walls?

Perhaps the rain sent them down in droves from the sky.

He raised his sword to block another curved blade, heading for his face.

The cloaked soldier used his body weight to push his sword closer and closer towards Richard.

The council member required both of his hands to hold the edge of the blade away from his flesh. He searched his mind for a solution to his current setback as another dark figure swung their sword towards him from his right.

Balls, he thought.

He thrust his knee into the aggressor as hard as he could. The warrior relaxed his attack and dropped to his knees, holding his crotch. Instantly, Richard swung his sword around to his right and blocked the oncoming strike from the other Night Demon.

The two blades clashed loudly. The curved sword bounced off the tempered steel, giving Richard the opportunity to plunge his sword deep into the heart of his foe.

The warrior dropped his sword and stepped back from the circle of men as a spray of blood pumped from the wound again and again before he fell to the ground. Placing his attention upon the other hooded figure, still holding his crotch, he buried his blade into the injured warrior's belly.

There was no time to celebrate as another Night Demon was already there, swinging its sword towards him.

Again, he blocked the blow and retaliated with his own strike. The warrior parried with its own blade.

Finally, someone formidable, Richard thought as he swung his sword towards the hooded figure. His sword dug into the dark soldier's elbow, separating the forearm from the rest of the brute.

Perhaps not, Richard supposed.

The long sword slid across the enemy's middle, spilling blood across the wet ground and sending the dark soldier into the mud.

Behind him, another of his men fell victim to the curved blade, and the circle tightened again.

As they continued to fight in the lane, a loud voice from the courtyard behind him made itself known to the attacking warriors. Its deep and raucous sound was harsh upon the ears.

Several of the attacking warriors shouted back in their own tongue. Richard did not know what the exchange between the Night Demons was about. Nor did he care.

Thrusting his sword, he connected with another dark warrior and sent it falling into the mire.

Another of his men fell to his right and suddenly there were only three left.

He knew they wouldn't last.

Theirs and his doom were imminent.

But they weren't about to simply give up and die.

"Kill them all, lads," he hollered as he stepped into the horde.

The enemy stepped away from him, allowing him to move into them. They blocked and parried his blows and dodged his attack if he drew too near to them.

Perhaps his exhaustion had finally overtaken him.

Perhaps the Night Demons had decided to just toy with him until they saw it fit to end his life.

He swung wildly and peered back at his men.

Both of them fell to the ground, dead.

He stared at them for a long time.

The rain fell hard all around him. The sound of the downpour filled his ears, so that it was the only noise he heard.

He lowered his sword lazily by his side, expecting the Night Demons to slice him open.

Moments before, he had conjured up the will to fight until he could fight no more.

Now, as he looked at the five young men lying in the mud amongst the bodies of dark warriors, he had no more fight left in him.

He was spent.

"What are you waiting for?" he asked, muttering to them as he stared at the bodies.

The Night Demons moved to the sides of the lane, forming a channel for Richard to move along.

What choice did he have?

Keeping his sword by his side, Richard walked through the lane back towards the street he had entered by.

On both sides of him, lined up against the building's walls, cloaked warriors watching him pass by.

He walked into the street and turned to his right, towards the bulk of Woodmyst. Sitting further along the street before him sat the great dragon.

It roared a thunderous cry as Richard emerged from the lane.

"So this is it." Richard nodded. "You're going to feed me to your dragon."

The dragon watched him carefully as it made a gargling growl at the man.

One of the hooded warriors pointed towards the eastern wall. Following his direction, Richard turned about slowly to see the street lined with more warriors all the way to the breach.

He dragged his sword behind him, causing it to clink softly against the stones in the road as he staggered towards the mound.

Atop of the mound stood a solitary figure with a hood upon his head and a curved horn attached to his belt.

Richard approached the lone Night Demon slowly, sword tip bouncing upon the pebbles in the street as the rain and wind washed over his face. He glanced up to the wall where he saw the three bowmen lying upon the wall-walk, throats cut and bled out.

Two of the dark warriors stepped forward, swords drawn, as the man approached.

He stopped in his tracks, not more than five paces away from the base of the mound, as he looked towards the two Night Demons.

He breathed rapidly, waiting for them to take him down. They didn't. Richard felt as if he was in a standoff.

What are they waiting for?

Thirty-Two

The warrior on the mound pointed to him with a clawed hand, gesturing to the long sword in Richard's hand. A sudden flick of the invader's hand, and Richard understood.

Drop the sword.

He complied.

With no strength left in him, he fell to his knees uncontrollably.

I'm tired, he thought. *So very tired.*

The lone warrior raced to him and crouched by his side, placing an arm around Richard's shoulder.

The man furrowed his brow, confused.

Why wasn't he being hacked to pieces by all the curved blades around him?

Why wasn't this one ripping him apart?

Why wasn't he dead already?

Tears welled in his eyes as he looked into the dark cavern beneath the warrior's hood.

The Night Demon placed Richard's back against the inside of his thigh to give the man some support so that he could remain seated. It signalled for one of the hooded figures to step forward. The other complied, handing the commander a canteen.

The commander popped the cork from the vessel and tilted it for Richard to drink.

Poison or not, Richard was thirsty and gulped the liquid down gratefully.

"Who are you?" Richard asked in a raspy voice.

The commander placed the canteen into the man's hands and lifted his own claw-like fingers to his hood.

Slowly, he pushed the covering to the back of his head, where it fell to the nape of his neck.

The warrior wore a dark scarf over his mouth and nose, but Richard already recognised the face.

The eyes bored into the council member like ice daggers to his heart.

The large, yellow, glaring eyes he hadn't seen for so many years.

The commander removed the scarf to reveal the rest of his face.

He was pale-skinned and hairless.

The warrior pulled the sleeve of its cloak up and revealed an old scar upon its forearm. It grunted as it held the mark closer to Richard's face.

The man nodded.

"I remember you," he blubbered.

Richard remembered the swamp where he had witnessed his friends murder captive soldiers.

He remembered the clay huts of the small village they had discovered nearby.

He recalled those who dwelled in the city with their grey skin and yellow eyes.

***

Richard saw creatures of varying sizes. Some as large as men and others appearing as only children. Their yellow eyes shared the same sensation. Fear.

These were timid people who had hidden well from the eyes of men.

The tragedy of war had brought them into the light. He silently wished they had never chased the four enemy soldiers into the forest.

"We should leave," he suggested.

"I'm hungry," Lawrence replied. "All we have is a dog to eat and Hugh won't let me near this mutt."

"Well then," Richard began. "Let's take their fruit and go."

"I'm in no mood for fruit, Richard," Lawrence sneered.

Richard looked at the faces of his companions.

Something sinister had invaded each of them. Their intent had suddenly become clear to him and he could not understand how they could let themselves come to this.

"Lawrence is right," Barnard said. "The stores back at the base are empty. There's only so much porridge a man can take. And I can't take any more. We need meat."

Richard couldn't believe his ears. Only moments ago, he fought side by side with these men on the battlefield.

Now they were contemplating doing something unspeakable.

"But these creatures—" Richard began.

"That's just it," Peter interrupted. "They're creatures. Look at them. They're not men. They're animals."

Richard saw construction, houses, tables, and family units. Although seemingly primitive, this was a civilisation. A society.

"I can't be a part of this," he said.

"Then starve," Alan said as he raised his sword and entered the nearest hovel.

The other men jeered and entered some other huts nearby.

Richard stared dumbly as he heard guttural calls as the men slew creature after creature in their own homes.

Lawrence dragged one into the open. It clawed at the ground in desperation with its thin fingers as it shrieked.

"Oh, shut up," Lawrence blurted as he stuck his blade into the creature's head.

It went limp and fell silent instantly.

A smaller creature came tearing out of the mud hut that Lawrence had dragged the first one from. It fixed its wide yellow eyes on the fallen beast as it ran screaming.

Lawrence spun around and struck the small being in the chest with his sword. It turned its face up to the man, glaring at him with a confused expression. In response, Lawrence placed his foot against the creature's chest and pushed with his leg to repel it away from him as he pulled the blade from its body.

It fell to the ground and attempted to crawl away before its energy diminished entirely. There it lay, not too far from the other on the ground, motionless.

Lifeless.

Richard stared blankly at the two dead beings. He realised he was looking at mother and child.

Stinging bile rose in his throat. He raised his hands to his head as his friends started laughing.

"Did you see that?" Lawrence called to the others. "Came straight for me, this one did."

"Probably has never seen such a lovely red beard before," Alan called back as he retrieved a flaming stick from a nearby campfire and tossed it into the nearest mud hut.

Flames took almost immediately, forcing the three inhabitants out of the shelter and into the open. Michael and Alan introduced the two youngsters and one adult to their blades.

Richard turned away repulsed and walked into the forest leaving the sounds of screaming, hacking and death behind him.

He felt responsible for what was happening. If only he hadn't been so curious. If only he had allowed that little creature by the tree to run away.

But he needed to know what it was.

He fell to his knees and wept beside the trunk of a large willow.

How his friends came to this was beyond his comprehension. He too, was hungry. But to lower oneself to this level of depravity was something he just simply couldn't do. Nor should any man be able to do.

With his mind racing, his stomach churning, he couldn't understand his friends' behaviour.

Can they not understand how their actions are wrong?

Evil?

Footsteps to his side made him snap his head around.

Before him stood two tiny figures clad in tattered rags and hand in hand. Their pale grey faces stared at him with wide yellow eyes, petrified.

One carried a large round object wrapped in a hessian sack. The other had a deep wound upon the forearm, caused by a blade.

Inflicted by one of his friends, no doubt.

He beckoned to them. The little one with the sack turned to protect its treasure. The larger of the two snarled.

They had just seen what men were capable of, so he didn't blame them for not trusting him.

Digging into his pouch, he retrieved a length of cloth. He reached out and grabbed the injured infant by the arm and pulled it towards him.

It hissed and struggled.

Richard placed the cloth over the wound and wrapped it around the arm as best as he could. The creature seemed to understand and stopped struggling, eyeing the human with distrust.

Wrapping the arm with two hands was easier now he could let the creature loose. Richard tucked the cloth's ends under the wrapping and sat back against the tree.

The two creatures stared at him blankly.

Their heads suddenly looked back toward their home. Richard heard barking and footsteps approaching through the growth.

"Go," he said to the infants, waving them away with his hands. "Run. Go."

They took the hint and bolted into the forest, disappearing in the undergrowth with little sound.

The dog was first to arrive. It ran up to Richard and licked his face with its bloodied snout. He pushed it away from him. It stood facing him, panting and wagging its tail.

Hugh came next.

"There you are." He smiled. "We've started a fire. Come along."

"I think I'll camp here until you are finished," Richard replied. "Thank you all the same."

Hugh shrugged. "Have it your way," he said before turning away. "Come, dog."

The hound gave Richard one last confused look as it cocked its head before trailing off behind its master.

Richard took a long breath as they disappeared into the trees.

He started a small fire to keep warm and rested against the trunk of the willow tree as he watched the flames dance.

The smell of cooking meat gradually made its way towards him. He shook his head in disbelief and wept.

From somewhere in the growth, he felt their gaze upon him. Two sets of yellow eyes.

Frightened.

Alone.

***

Richard would always remember.

How could he not?

His eyes looked deeply into the commander of the Night Demons. The one he had bandaged in the swamp.

"What do you have planned for me?" he asked, expecting the worst.

The commander summoned two of his warriors over and grunted something to them. They hoisted Richard to his feet and allowed him to lean on them as they moved towards the breach.

The bodies of the other council members were still hanging from the lampposts.

"Is this my fate also?" he asked as they walked him over the mound.

The Night Demons filed out through the gap in the eastern wall after them as they continued past the lampposts and his dead friends into the darkness beyond.

They directed him towards a farmhouse near the river's edge about halfway between the wall and the hill in the east. There, under a large awning outside of the cottage, was a table with a burning lantern placed in the centre and a high-backed wooden chair.

The warriors lowered the man into the seat as the commander blew a long note on the trumpet again.

Thirty-Three

The great dragon unfurled its wings as the last of the Night Demons hurried out through the breach and into the meadow. Some remained behind to cut the bodies of the councilmen down from the lampposts and carry them back inside the village walls.

The dragon beat its wings and lifted into the night sky, sending swirling drifts of rain in all directions. It headed back towards the centre of the town, where a faint orange glow reflected from the clouds above the smouldering remains of the Great Hall.

A long jet of flame spewed from its mouth as it flew, igniting several buildings in the village.

The dark warriors returned from the breach, having discarded the bodies of Chief Shelley, Alan, Peter, Michael, Hugh and Lawrence.

Richard watched in awe and sadness as the magnificent beast swooped through the pouring rain, streaming its fiery breath over everything beneath it.

Flames rose like great blooming flowers, orange and red. The sight was humbling as the power that the dragon showed.

Richard thought back to the round object that the infant in the swamp carried all those years ago and wondered if it was an egg from which hatched a beast, such as the one he observed. Was it possible that this creature came from that egg?

The commander approached as the dragon passed by the eastern wall, sending a line of flames across the cottages just inside. Even from this distance, Richard felt the intense heat. The commander raised his arm over his face to shield himself from the sudden blast.

He pulled up a stool and sat across the table from Richard, watching the dragon circle back to send another barrage of fire down the centre of the town from north to south.

Richard looked across the table and caught the yellow eyes watching him. His stomach tightened as a sudden fear overwhelmed him.

The commander pointed to him, pressed his finger against his own head before pointing to the inferno.

Richard nodded. "Yes, I understand why you're doing this. You are destroying everything we have because my people destroyed everything you once had." He shook his head and wiped his eyes.

The commander moved his eyes back to the dragon as it swooped in an arch, throwing fire into the western region of the town.

"So many people died these past few nights," Richard whispered. He could tell from the expression on the commander's face that the Night Demon understood. "Yours and mine."

Taking a deep breath, the commander leant against the table as he watched the dragon burn the village to the ground.

"And what of the children?" Richard asked.

The commander glanced at the man sideways before standing to his feet. He walked a few paces into the rain and raised the trumpet to his mouth as he faced east. A long call ensued that echoed towards the mountains.

The dragon passed through the village again, igniting more buildings that were not yet ablaze. As it did so, a warrior ran to the commander's side, carrying Richard's sword. The commander took it from the dark soldier and inspected the blade.

He turned back towards the man, holding the hilt with one hand and nursing the blade in the other. He lifted it for Richard to see before placing its point into the soft ground in the middle of the meadow.

I guess I can get that later, Richard thought.

He returned his eyes to the devastation the dragon fashioned as it passed through the village again.

Some time passed.

Richard wasn't sure for how long he had been watching the dragon heap destruction upon his home, but the sky was changing its colour in the east as a deep mauve formed upon the dark rain clouds.

Dawn approached.

The commander blew his trumpet long and loud.

The dragon ceased spitting fire and took off towards the mountains in the north. Richard watched it intently as it grew smaller and smaller in the distance before disappearing behind the peaks of the nearby range.

It was gone.

But the damage it had caused was irreversible.

Woodmyst burned.

The sound of horses snorting and braying as they approached over the hill to the east drew Richard's attention away from the firestorm. There, he saw several dark riders leading other horses with women and children upon them.

The Night Demons were returning the youths of Woodmyst to their home.

They pulled the team of steeds to a halt on the grass near the farmhouse where Richard sat. The commander gave an order to his warriors, who pulled daggers from their belts to cut the bindings around the captives' wrists. Next, they lifted the hessian hoods from the prisoners' heads and moved their own chargers away.

The commander turned back to Richard and approached him again. He moved under the awning and leant upon the table, peering directly at the man. Richard faced him and gave his full attention to the warrior.

"We," the commander said in a deep, grating voice, "won't be back."

With that, he turned and walked back into the rain.

A rider, leading another steed, pulled up near the commander and handed him the reins. He mounted his charger and signalled his warriors with a wave of his hand.

The Night Demons climbed upon steeds of their own and awaited instructions.

With a last glare towards Richard, the commander blew his trumpet and tore off towards the hill with his warriors in tow.

As they disappeared, Richard stood up and peered after them.

"We need to run," a voice called.

Searching for the source of the voice, Richard found Tomas Warde sitting upon a brown mare.

"Tomas," Richard called. "Thank the gods."

"We need to go, Richard," he called again. "We need to go before they return."

"They won't be back," Richard replied as Tomas dismounted his ride and dropped to the ground.

"How do you know?"

"He told me so."

Richard looked towards the hill as the sky brightened above.

The clouds still loomed and rain fell heavily to earth.

The young women sitting upon the steeds wept as they stared towards their home, burning away in giant flames before them.

As the new day began, smoke and fire rose from Woodmyst.

Epilogue

Sitting by the bank of the river near the farmhouse, he sat watching the waterfowl play amongst the reeds and lily pads. The sound of insects buzzing and birds chattering was calming.

He turned to see the remains of Woodmyst still smouldering to the west and remembered what her streets were once like.

The markets with trinkets, the clanging hammers upon anvils in the blacksmith's stall, the shouting of bartering and haggling for the best bargain. He missed that almost as much as he missed the mead of the tavern and the wenches who served it.

He had gone back inside the village two days before; to see what they could scavenge and use as the young women and the mothers of newborns helped to care for the little ones left orphaned by the assault. They could salvage very little from the rubble. Almost everything had burnt, melted or turned to ash.

The dragon incinerated the three bridges and the only way to cross the river was by the fishing boats left near the farmhouses in the meadow. It mattered little, as most of the southern side of the town had been burnt to the ground.

The plantations far out were beyond repair. Dragon fire left the ground so scorched it had dried out completely.

The rain fell steadily afterwards, turning the area into a bog as the dry earth trapped the water, and had remained so.

Nothing of use would grow there for a long time.

The sounds of hammering nearby grabbed his attention.

He saw several young adolescent girls assisting some of the young lads with building a large pen for the horses. It was a crude design, made mostly of fallen logs and long limbs from trees in the grove, but it was a start.

The cattle had gathered upon the hill to eat the long grass growing upon its crest as the sheep favoured the company of people of late. Their memory of previous nights had not left them and sudden sounds that came from the line of trees to the north easily spooked them.

"Richard," called the boy. "Come and see."

He turned his face towards the crude enclosure. It appeared sturdy enough to serve its purpose.

Rising to his feet, he stretched and winced before heading in their direction. His muscles still ached, and he still needed more sleep.

"It looks good, Tomas," he called as he approached.

The task ahead was going to be an arduous one that would take a long time to accomplish.

The small group of survivors had all promised one another to see it fulfilled, no matter what.

They intended to rebuild Woodmyst.

Starting was the hardest part. They had no delusions of recreating the village they once knew. This was a chance at a new beginning.

This was a chance to make things better than before.

He stepped up to the boy's side and gave the frame a firm shake with his hand. It was sturdy and would hold.

"Good work," he said to the gathering.

"Have you slept yet?" the boy asked, noticing the dark lines under the man's eyes.

"I will," he promised, not knowing if he could keep his word.

Night after night he closed his eyes, only to open them again suddenly as the terrors in his mind met him there.

Tossing and turning, sweating profusely, he struggled to rest and had not had a good slumber since before the dragon fire.

He was so tired that keeping the nightmares at bay was impossible. The terror had visited him during his waking hours.

The gentle sounds of running water and life on the meadow soothed the beast within.

But from time to time, when his guard was down, they came and attacked him.

Even now, he saw them.

The bulging yellow eyes of the Night Demons.

ABOUT THE AUTHOR

Robert E Kreig was born in Newcastle, Australia and grew up in its outer suburbs. He has always had a love for books, particularly well-told stories involving action, adventure and fear.

Some of Robert's favourite authors as a young reader included J. R. R. Tolkien, Stephen King, Orson Scott Card, Ray Bradbury and Frank Herbert. As he grew into adulthood, the list continued to lengthen, adding more influential writers such as George R. R. Martin, Matthew Reilly, Nathan M. Farrugia, Dan Brown, James Patterson, Michael Connelly and Lee Child just to name a few.

Inspired by movies like Star Wars, King Kong, Jaws, Jason and the Argonauts and other great adventure pieces, Robert listened to the voices in his head and entertained the strange visions dancing through his mind to assist him with writing his fantasy series The Woodmyst Chronicles.

Robert has penned ten books for the series which follow the lives of many characters, particularly focussing upon a family who must face many trials before the epic conclusion. Clashing swords, strange creatures, flying dragons and sorcery inhabit the world surrounding Woodmyst.

Robert is always working on something new and has also written two standalone books, Long Valley and I Am Calm Voice. Both are dark action pieces set in a modern world.

OTHER BOOKS BY THIS AUTHOR

I AM CALM VOICE

No one in the remote town of Edwards Hill could have known that she was capable of such carnage.

Least of all her parents, the first to die.

Driven by the gentle words of the Calm Voice, she inflicts a barrage of carnage and death, leaving a trail of blood in her wake.

Her goal is to bring death to all who have hurt her.

All she needs to do is listen to the Calm Voice.

All she needs to do is just focus...

Just focus...

Focus...

I Am Calm Voice by Robert E. Kreig is a dark psychological novel surrounding the actions of one girl on a fateful morning in April 2017. Kristin Matthews is fed up with her life, her oppressive parents, and her bullying schoolmates. A soothing voice thrumming in her head compels her to seek revenge on those who have wronged her. At the top of her list is a trio of girls who have taunted her to breaking point. After careful planning, she embarks on a deadly rampage through Edwards Hill State High School, bent on destroying all her pain one last time. What follows is a haunting description of the day's events, culminating in an ending no one will expect.

THE WOODMYST CHRONICLES

From a faraway land...
...comes a new adventure.

The Woodmyst Chronicles is the story of a small community that faces the hardest of trials in a world filled with darkness, violence and magic.

Books In This Series...

THE WALLS OF WOODMYST
THE SONS OF WOODMYST
THE HEIR OF WOODMYST
THE WARLORDS OF WOODMYST
THE HUNTRESS OF WOODMYST
THE SHADOW OF WOODMYST
THE BRIDES OF WOODMYST
THE GODS OF WOODMYST
THE WEAPONS OF WOODMYST
A FAREWELL TO WOODMYST

LONG VALLEY

In the small community of Long Valley, nestled comfortably beneath snow-capped mountains, people quietly go about their business. Everybody knows everybody and there are no worries to give mind to.

But something has awakened.

A tragic accident near the valley's army base sparks a number of terrifying events, placing the local civilians in mortal danger.

A contagion is subsequently released into Long Valley, infecting pets, livestock, wildlife and people.

It's up to the local law enforcement and a small band of citizens to try to keep the town safe.

In the end, it becomes a struggle for survival as the people of Long Valley are overcome by the urge to feed.

www.robertekreig.com

Lightning Source UK Ltd.
Milton Keynes UK
UKHW010628060223
416537UK00001B/156